Sweet Bliss

Sweet Bliss

HELENA RAC

Tryst Books

Tryst Books
720 Bathurst Street, Suite 303
Toronto, Ontario M5S 2R4

This is a work of fiction. Names, places, and incidents are either the product of the author's imagination or used fictitiously. Any resemblance to actual people, living or dead, events, or locations is entirely coincidental.

Copyright @ Helena Rac

All rights reserved. No part of this publication may be reproduced, stored in a retrieval system or transmitted, in any form or by any means (except brief passages for purposes of review) without the prior permission of the author or publisher.

Cover design: Ellen Yu
Front cover photo: courtesy of Shutterstock.com
Interior design: Meghan Behse

Library and Archives Canada Cataloguing in Publication

Rac, Helena, author
         Sweet Bliss / Helena Rac

Issued in print and electronic formats.
ISBN 978-0-9940297-7-5 (pbk)
ISBN 978-0-9940297-8-2 (epub)
ISBN 978-0-9940297-9-9 (kindle)

         I. Title

PS8635.A238S84 2015   C813'.6   C2015-907122-4
                                          C2015-907123-2

This is an original print edition of *Sweet Bliss*.

To life's sweet indulgences

Chapter 1

Fourteen months ago

This is going to be so freaking good…

Rich, creamy strawberry icing. Decadent chocolate cake. My mouth salivates and my stomach rumbles as I go for a bite of what is probably the worst breakfast choice ever – a cupcake, plucked fresh from the display case of my bakery, Lovely Cakes.

I'm running late for a meeting with a potential client who wants to order a whole lot of cupcakes for a corporate gala. Of course that's great for business, but running late, not so much. And honestly, I am never late, but this morning has turned out to be one I'd rather start over. After stumbling out of bed way too late courtesy of a late-night crazy-hot romance read and an alarm that never went off, I've spent exactly three minutes in the shower, two minutes frantically putting on clothes and makeup, and zero minutes drying my hair. To top things off, the elevator in my building was conveniently out of service and I had to race down seventeen flights instead. Mentally I give myself a high-five, pleased that I have made it this far in one piece. Hence my breakfast choice. Just something to hold me over during the meeting, I reason.

I'm texting my client to let her know I'm running ever so slightly behind while I'm gobbling up the cupcake and power-walking in stilettos down the crowded streets of

Chicago's financial district. So of course it's no surprise when I run straight into something. Someone, that is. A head-on collision.

The cupcake ends up half in my mouth and half on my nose; the strawberry icing conveniently spreads in between. To add embarrassment to an already messy situation, my feet stumble back and I lose my footing, tripping backwards and landing on my ass. Awesome.

This morning keeps getting worse. I'm beyond annoyed.

"For the love of cupcakes, watch where you're–" *Going* is what I'm about to say, but that's before I lock eyes with the knee-wobbling, head-spinning, mischievous gaze of a man.

Delicious.

Sexy.

Stranger.

Honestly, the cupcake doesn't even compare.

I may be a closet romance junkie, but I've never been a believer in love at first sight. Until just now. Okay, fine – I know it can't actually be love, but god, I'd like a bite of that. Or a few. *Calm down, my rapidly beating heart; this must be an apparition.* It's not physically possible, but he is the most stunning man I have ever run into. Not that I'm in the habit of running into men, or people in general. Normally I am the epitome of grace. Except right now, it appears.

"I am so sorry," the sexy stranger says, and the sound of his husky voice does funny things to my body. "I shouldn't have been texting and walking. Let me help you up," he offers as he reaches down to me.

"Umm … ouch. I'm … okay," I stammer. So much for my usual suave self. Normally words come so easily to me, I swear. I must have a concussion from the fall; that's it. Except I didn't actually hit my head. Nope, I'm undone by his rugged face, his captivating eyes, and his apologetic smile.

I reach out and take hold of his hand, and the soft yet firm touch of his fingers jolts me. As he pulls me up, I lose my balance again, and my body collides with his. As if instinctively, his arm reaches around my waist to steady me.

Just as instinctively, my palm presses against his abdomen. Jesus, his abs are harder than the Rockies.

Our faces are mere inches apart, our lips nearly touching, his breath of air mine, my breath of air his. Right now I can't even spell the word "cupcake." But I can with certainty spell out this: mischievous eyes gaze at me; dark, short-at-the-sides, messy-on-top hair tempts my fingers to play with it; just enough stubble, like he could do something about it but chooses not to, frames his square jaw; and those lips ... that bottom lip, in fact, whispers "taste me."

I can't help it. My thoughts impulsively wander to what he would look like naked, without his black suit and crisp shirt. His fresh, just-showered scent is intoxicating.

He shifts awkwardly, and I realize a few things:

First, I'm still clinging to a stranger I fell into like an idiot.

Second, before he moved, I think I felt something hard. Down there. Maybe.

Third, I have cupcake all over my face.

"Are you sure you're okay?" the stranger asks with genuine concern.

"Umm ... hmm." This is getting ridiculous. I can speak. Perfectly fine. Just apparently not right now.

"Here." A grin lights up his face as he pulls a tissue from his pocket and gently wipes the icing from around my lips, clutching the back of my neck to steady me. Which apparently has the opposite effect, since it weakens my knees. I have to remind myself to keep my eyes from closing and to not lean into the comfort of his hand.

"There, much better," he acknowledges, after taking what seem like a couple of very drawn out minutes to get me cleaned up. And then it feels like time stands still. He's just smirking and staring. Blatantly. Like he's absorbing me. Inhaling. Exhaling.

"God, you smell like strawberries and chocolate. My favorite." He grazes my lower lip with his finger, and I nearly tremble from the shivers that travel all the way down to my toes. If I was unable to move a moment ago, I am now barely able to breathe. I feel as though I'm about to melt like icing on top of a just-baked cupcake.

Two things come to mind right then.

One: Who says that to a complete stranger?

And two: God, I want to hear him say things like that to me over and over again. Preferably while we're naked.

And so I don't move at all, I don't dare to blink. I just drink in this Prince Charming who appears to have become my whole world within a mere moment. He is absolutely stunning. No one in my fantasies has ever compared. No one has even come close. This moment – it is pure bliss.

Just when I think nothing can ruin it, a car horn brings me back to reality. *Client meeting!*

I pull from his hold and mumble, "Umm, thanks … gotta go … running late." *Really smooth.*

I turn swiftly, utterly embarrassed, and start to walk away, but all the while I have this strange feeling that his eyes are following me. Even his unseen stare is giving me goose bumps. I'm seriously contemplating sprinting so that I can get out of the bubble I suddenly feel trapped in.

I'm not some swooning girly-girl, I swear. I'm a responsible adult who owns her own business and makes decisions based on logic and research and… *Ugh!* It's just that no one has ever had this effect on me. Only this incredibly sexy, deliciously fuckable stranger. Clearly I need to get out more.

"Hey, wait!" I hear him yell, and I turn back hesitantly. What could he possibly want now?

"Don't forget this." He jogs toward me, holding my phone. "I guess I wasn't the only one walking and texting," he teases. His closeness, his scent, and that damn sexy smile overwhelm me once more.

"Right … umm … thanks," I mumble, *again*, and I feel my cheeks blush. By now they must be the color of ripe strawberries. I snatch my phone away less than gracefully and fumble with it between my fingers. No, this cannot possibly get any more embarrassing. "Later, stranger," I blurt out, but I realize almost instantly the chances of seeing him again are pretty slim.

"Later, cupcake," he replies, still smirking, as he takes a few steps backwards before finally turning around and making his way back through the crowd. And I just stand there, frozen.

Minutes pass before I finally manage to get a hold of myself. Well, probably not *minutes* exactly, but it sure seems like it. And then my phone buzzes, a meeting reminder confirming that I am now very, very late. I start jogging, a skill only black-belt stiletto-wearers like me have mastered, but as my steps take me farther away, I can't stop thinking about those smoldering eyes and the delicious bottom lip that I really, really want to bite. The stranger's face is embedded in my mind and I am ... *Smitten? Love-struck?*

Crazy.

I may be in danger of losing a client this morning, but at least my fantasy life has taken a turn for the better. This delicious stranger has just shot up to the top of my book-boyfriend roster. Maybe I am a bit of a swooning girly-girl after all.

Chapter 2

Ten months ago

It's been a hectic summer at lovely cakes, and even though the wedding season is finally winding down, given it's early September, we're still going full steam. I have been on the go the entire day, finishing orders for the weekend, overseeing the deliveries, and meeting with clients to discuss their cake visions and timelines. I'm exhausted and have to recharge so that I'm ready to do it all again tomorrow. I absolutely love my career of choice and running my own business, so taking a break is something I have to force myself to do. Otherwise, I'd probably never see the light of day. I'd be holed up in my bakery, pretending that life is always perfectly sweet – just like the creations we design.

There's only one person who knows how to help me loosen up: my sister Clara. I stop by her place to hang out and unwind. One thing I can always count on is Clara's relentless optimism and bright personality. She's a happy-go-lucky kind of girl and knows just how to help me relax. Tonight's no different.

Clara's loft is cozy and charming, except it's just slightly overcrowded with all her … stuff. It's not like she's a hoarder, but she does have a thing for all sorts of unique items that would never catch my eye. Like weird art and peculiar little things that fill in all the nooks and crannies. And she very rarely manages to keep it neat and tidy. A perfect reflection of

Clara. Fashionable, spontaneous, charismatic, and a bit scatter-brained. There are clothes hanging here and there, shoes everywhere, and magazines, makeup, hair accessories, and all things girly scattered around. Honestly, if a stranger were to walk in, they'd think she'd been robbed – it looks like someone's had trouble finding whatever they were after. It's not that she's a slob; she just manages to not worry about the little things in life. She just lives it.

Clara and I spend some time chatting and catching up on the week's events. I may also spend some time tidying up as we talk. I can't help it. The place looks a thousand times better by the time I'm done.

"So what are you and Marcus up to tonight?" I'm referring to Clara's boyfriend, who's coming over shortly. The mere mention of his name makes Clara's eyes light up.

"I'm not sure yet. I think we may head out for dinner and a movie."

"Oh. That sounds like fun." I'm glad to see her happy. She's been in some messed up relationships over the years, yet, unlike me, she's always been on the lookout for "The One." It amazes me to see how resilient she is, even after the heart-shattering consequences she's experienced in the past. When she met Marcus, however, something changed. I can't help but think that maybe she's finally found him.

"He's bringing a friend, you know." She slides that in there, as if I should be intrigued.

"Your point?"

"Nothing. Just sayin'."

Clara's always trying to set me up with random guys. I'm not really interested and haven't been for a while. "Well, I'd better head home." My to-do list for tonight includes trying out a new cake recipe, steeping a fresh blend of loose-leaf tea, and taste-testing the results during an orgy of soothing comfort, sugar, and Channing Tatum movies. Unlike Clara's, my love life has been less than stellar. Instead, I live vicariously through fictional romances and dream of delicious sexy strangers who can never be mine.

"Have fun tonight." I give Clara a hug and make my way to the front door.

"You know I will." She winks, radiating the biggest I'm-crazy-about-this-guy smile.

As I reach to open the door, Marcus beats me to it. He pops in, beaming from ear to ear, taking just enough time to say, "Hi, Tessa!" as he passes me. He proceeds to grab Clara like he hasn't seen her in weeks, locks his lips on hers, and twirls her around, oblivious to anyone around them. *Christ.* Their cuteness makes me nauseous.

"Hey Marcus," I say and shake my head. Is that what love looks like? I don't know if I've ever felt that way about a guy.

Since the lovebirds appear to be completely disinterested in me, I turn to leave … and run straight into a wall of a man. Into a pair of bright eyes that meet mine with a flash of surprise. Captivating eyes that I remember instantly, even though my encounter with them months ago was all too brief. This cannot possibly be…

Delicious.

Sexy.

Stranger.

"Cupcake Girl?" the stranger asks uncertainly. Oh god, it definitely is. My fantasy seems to have materialized in front of me. Apparently fate *can* be your friend sometimes.

My eyes widen; my mouth opens in shock, but nothing, absolutely nothing comes out. That's it. I may officially be in need of an interpreter when faced with this guy.

And did he just call me Cupcake Girl? Excuse me while I take a moment to collect myself. Because right now my brain is not quite sure what its intended purpose is, and my heart … my heart is busy swooning over the man who's standing in front of me.

My fantasies may have served me well, but they are nothing compared to seeing him in person again. Short, playful, messy hair that I have a sudden urge to run my fingers through. Just a hint of stubble. That same steady, mischievous gaze that weakened my knees the last time. And that bottom lip – the lip

I can't help but want to taste. God, he is too tempting to not touch, a picture-perfect blend of rugged and polished.

He smiles, then reaches for my chin. I realize that I have not moved. At all. Or remembered how to use my mouth, it appears. Because it's still open. He reaches for my lips and gently closes them. But his fingers linger on my bottom lip as if he's remembering the moment we shared during our last encounter. The familiar rush of electricity zips through me, and I fight to stay composed and cool, because suddenly I feel a tad bit hot. I look down to break the eye contact, to break the hold he has on me. But he pushes my chin up, forcing me to look at him again. *Oh boy.*

"Hi," he whispers with a delicious smirk.

"Um, hi," I manage to say with a shaky voice.

"You know each other?" Clara interrupts our little exchange, which is more than welcome. Otherwise, I'm not sure how long I would just stand here, staring at him.

"Yes," he says, still facing me.

"No," I say at the same time, and I take a step back, needing some space. I look toward Clara, hoping to clarify. "I mean, yes and no … um … not really." Jesus, can I really not put a simple sentence together in his presence?

"Okay, now I'm really confused," Clara replies. Both she and Marcus look at us expectantly.

"It's a long story. We might have run into each other once," I explain vaguely, with a tentative smile. I never cared to mention my sexy-stranger encounter to Clara. I just didn't see how it was relevant or of any importance, other than to make her laugh at my clumsiness and tease me about my subsequent sexy-stranger fantasies.

"So, does Cupcake Girl have a name?"

"Um, it's Tessa. Tessa Conte."

"Nice to meet you, Tessa." He extends his hand in an invitation to formally meet me.

To random onlookers, a.k.a. Clara and Marcus, our handshake probably appears nothing but formal. But when our palms connect, the feeling is anything but. It's like the sparks of electricity that jump between us have found their home as they tingle through me all the way to my toes and right back up to my heart, to my lungs.

Breathe, Tessa.

I swallow deep. "Nice to meet you too … um…"

"Luke. Luke Callaghan," he says with a lot more confidence than I had when I was trying to remember my name.

"Luke." I stare at him with a lost-in-the-moment smile, and my heart constricts like it's been punctured by an arrow. "Nice to meet you, Luke. Again." I smile, he smiles back, and something I can't quite put my fingers on passes between us.

"*This* is your Cupcake Girl?" Marcus interrupts. "You have got to be kidding me!"

Apparently Marcus has been informed of Luke's encounter with a clumsy, inarticulate, strawberry-icing-covered brunette. I'm intrigued and embarrassed. And did he just refer to me as Luke's Cupcake Girl? If hearts could melt, that's what mine would be doing right now.

"What are you doing here?" I ask, hoping to figure out how the stars have aligned so seamlessly.

"What are you doing here?" he answers with a question of his own. Seems he's a bit of a smart mouth.

"Well," I point toward Clara, "my sister and I were hanging out, and I was just leaving. And you, Luke Callaghan, have not answered *my* question."

"Well," he mimics my response again, "I'm in town on business, and my friend Marcus and I were just hanging out. He thought it would be nice to meet up with Clara since I don't get to see them very often. Happy?"

I nod.

"We were going to have dinner and catch a movie," Luke says casually. "Why don't you join us?" It's likely nothing more but a friendly question, yet in my head it gets all twisted and sounds more like a demand. An enticing demand, but one that it's probably best to decline, because,

One: I'm exhausted;

Two: I already have the aforementioned plans, which, I have to admit, are starting to lose the appeal they had only minutes ago, before a certain someone walked into my life again; and

Three: Hmm, there's gotta be another good reason. They normally come in threes. I'm sure I'll think of something else.

"Thanks, but I was just on my way out. I ... I have a busy night ahead. So yeah, um, you guys have fun!" *Very convincing.*

"Oh, come on Tessa!" Clara whines. "It's not like you were going to do anything overly exciting anyway." I beg to differ. Channing Tatum is plenty exciting. "Just come out with us and have some *real* fun tonight! I'm sure Luke will be great company."

Of course he'd be fun. He oozes it. And I'm pretty sure he knows it.

"I don't know. I'm beat, and some of us actually have to work tomorrow."

Lame. That's what the excuse sounds like. Though I can't help but think that maybe doing something unplanned could actually turn out to be fun, especially with Luke, my real-life fantasy guy, in on the invitation. The temptation is becoming too difficult to resist.

The stares are now threefold; eyes are on me everywhere I turn. I'm caving in under the pressure. To heck with my predictable Friday night plans! A bit of fun never hurt anyone, right?

"Fine, I'm in, I'm in!" I try to sound annoyed, but my response comes out slightly more eager than I anticipate. "But before we head out, can I freshen up, at least? I'm not even dressed to go out," I plead with Clara. After spending the day at Lovely Cakes, I could use a makeover, but a hairbrush and a shopping trip through Clara's closet will have to do.

"Sure, I could use a few minutes to finish getting ready," Clara adds, understanding my plea. "The boys can chill."

"SO, WHAT'S UP WITH YOU AND LUKE? WHAT'S THE story?" Clara begins her interrogation the second her bedroom door closes.

"Really, there's not much to say." I play it off coolly, scanning the vast display of amazing clothes Clara is pulling from her closet and spreading across her bed. It's like my own personal fashion show. My sister's a shopper.

"Tessa, come on, I know you're holding back. I can read you like a book. You looked like you were shell-shocked!"

Oh good god, she noticed. And it's not surprising – it's Clara, after all. Is there any chance Luke didn't?

"Fine." I let out an exasperated sigh. Clara's persistent; she'd wrench it out of me sooner or later, so I might as well cave in now and give her an abbreviated version of my encounter with Luke.

"Wow, that *was* embarrassing. And totally adorable," she laughs. I try to shush her. "He's pretty hot, huh?"

"Yeah, a little."

"A little?" she questions, unconvinced.

"Okay, maybe more than a little." Something about him just pulls me in his direction. It's happened twice now. I can't help but wonder if someone up there is bored and playing a game with me, throwing little bits of Luke my way on occasion, just for the pure entertainment of seeing me get all worked up and incoherent when I'm around him.

"I think somebody's a bit more smitten with Luke than she's willing to admit."

"Whatever, Clar." I try to sound nonchalant. "Can we just move on?"

"Fine. This one." Clara points to a brown tunic dress.

"Really?" I look at her like she's crazy, but she just shrugs. "You're kidding, right? This tiny piece of fabric is barely going to cover my ass."

"Just put it on. It matches your hair and your eyes. You'll look so hot! And from what I gather, you may want to give Mr. Gorgeous out there a run for his money."

I laugh. She isn't entirely wrong. I let my hair drop from a bun, chocolate-brown waves falling naturally past my shoulders. After reapplying makeup and putting on a matching pair of high-heel sandals, I'm transformed. Clara's right; I do look pretty hot. And I have to admit, I'm feeling intrigued, for the first time in a while. Ever since the last guy I thought I cared about left me feeling heartbroken...

No – I remind myself not to think about the past. I'm just going to take a deep breath and go into this evening with an open mind. I'm sure I can do that; it can't possibly be that hard. Dinner and a movie and my delicious sexy stranger. Unplanned? Yes. But let's face it, way more thrilling than what would have otherwise been a very predictable evening.

"We're ready," Clara announces when we step out of her bedroom.

"Babe, you look absolutely gorgeous!" Marcus's eyes pop when he sees us, but they're glued on Clara's red-and-white-stripe tube dress. He sets his beer down, then struts toward her like an animal on the prowl, squeezing her butt cheeks and planting his mouth on hers, not giving her a moment to breathe. Hello? There are other people around. These two really need to get a room.

As I look from them toward Luke, I find his smoldering eyes glued on me, scanning my body top to bottom, practically undressing me with his stare. Or at least it seems that way. Unless, of course, I'm imagining it, which is quite possible given he's been the main star of my sexual fantasies for a few months. But it's definitely there. That feeling of captivating tension between us. The one I've so often read about or seen on the big screen, but never quite experienced. It's as if the air stands still, charged only by the hasty electrons that are bouncing vigorously off of us.

Clara finally breaks our staring contest with a simple, "Let's go, lovebirds, I'm starving!" as she and Marcus head toward the front door.

"Looks like we're ready to go," Luke states, sounding calm. But a swift readjustment of his jeans makes me think he's feeling anything but.

We get into Marcus's sleek convertible. He's a car enthusiast, so he has a few toys in his collection. Clara sits next to Marcus in the front passenger seat, leaving Luke and

I conveniently seated in the back. More like conveniently *squeezed*. There's barely any leg room. Really, how is this even a four-seater? We're so close, in fact, that our elbows and knees are touching and our thighs are practically superglued together.

Even with the sounds of music blasting from the stereo and the traffic and city bustle around us, it feels eerily quiet. What is it about this guy that makes me speechless and jumbled? Normally I'm the one who can't shut up, but for some reason I can't find my voice. I am so worried about saying something stupid that I can't think of anything to say at all.

"You look nice." Luke finally breaks the silence, his gaze fixed on me. I think this may be his attempt at a compliment. Albeit a pretty bland one. Or maybe just a safe way to start the conversation?

I respond with a simple, "Thanks," and the silence creeps around us again. This is getting uncomfortable. *For your own sake, say something, Tessa!*

"Umm … so, how do you and Marcus know each other?" I ask, relieved to have finally found my voice.

"We went to college together and then did our MBAs. Then we started working with the same hotel chain shortly after. Actually, he was the one who recommended I apply when a position came up. But I haven't had a chance to see him in a while."

"How come?" I ask, hoping to learn a bit more about the sexy stranger who has piqued my interest.

"I moved to London a few months ago," Luke says matter-of-factly. "Actually, come to think of it, I moved within days of running into you the first time." A faraway smirk appears on his face, as if he's re-living that first time we met.

"My mom's from England."

"Oh yeah? Whereabouts?"

"Lymington, on the southern coast. Have you heard of it?"

"Sounds familiar, but I don't know much about it. Have you been?"

"We visited once. But I was really young, just around four or five, so I don't remember much. Other than it's in Hampshire and a sailing hub, from what I recall."

"How come you haven't visited since?"

"My mom doesn't really have any relatives left there. My grandparents died when she was in her late teens, and both she and her younger sister moved here to live with their aunt and uncle. I guess there was just never much to go back to. But I think she misses it sometimes, even though everything she's needed is here." I neglect to mention that she's lost the most important person, the one and only who kept her heart and soul here all these years.

"Well, maybe you'll get a chance to visit another time. And I'm sure you'd love London. You could visit both. I've been told I'm a great tour guide." Luke winks, and I wonder how serious he's being. I mean, we barely know each other. Yet I'm surprisingly intrigued.

"Maybe, someday."

After a moment of comfortable silence, Luke sighs. "God, I am still dumbfounded to be seeing you again, Tessa. Don't you think it's kind of crazy?"

If he only knew how many times I've hoped to see him again, even if in passing, so that I could replenish my fantasies with another image of him. And now he's here, squeezed right next to me. And looking just as delicious as that first time I saw him.

"Just a weird coincidence," I say, nonchalant, because I am by no means admitting any of that. He'll think *I'm* some sort of crazy.

"That first time we ran into each other, Tessa ... you were stunning," he breathes, and my heart stalls. Did I hear him right?

"What are you talking about?" I try to deflect how giddy his words make me feel. "It was probably one of the most embarrassing moments of my life. Never mind that I fell flat on my ass – I was covered in icing."

"It's a good thing I enjoy icing. Very much, in fact." Luke replies, holding my gaze and smiling charmingly. I think I need water, a gulp of something to cool me down, because

I'm no longer thinking of icing on a cupcake. The icing is all over me. And he's ... licking. "You looked adorable, with your flushed cheeks and your mumbling..." His lips form a-lost-in-the-moment-smile, and all I can think of is how much I want to bite that bottom lip of his, because ... delicious. But I remind myself I need to come back down to Planet Earth before I float off into space.

"Are you always this forward?" I ask, not sure whether I want to know the answer. I have a feeling Luke is very comfortable in his own skin. Women probably naturally flock to him. And I can't help but think I am just another one of those women.

"Maybe." He winks.

"Hmm, I bet you're a player."

"A player? Now why would you think that?" He puts his palm against his heart and makes a pouty face, as if hurt. So I'm left to draw my own conclusion. I'd better tread carefully.

"I don't know. Maybe because you say things that make me all swoony." Oh god, I didn't just say that out loud, did I? I scramble for what to say or do next. Not only am I embarrassed by my choice of words, but I'm petrified of what he may say in response.

He chuckles and has that I-think-you're-kind-of-cute look on his face again, so I nudge his elbow and blurt, "That's for walking and texting, and making me look like a clumsy idiot."

"Hey, now. Let's just be clear here – we both know you're just as guilty as me," he retorts. "You were texting too!"

Yes, I definitely was. But I'm not letting him win this argument. "Maybe," is all I say instead.

"What was with the cupcake first thing in the morning anyways?"

"What do you mean? What's wrong with having a cupcake first thing in the morning?"

"Come on, Tessa. It's a *cupcake*. Last I checked, it's not normally served for breakfast."

"Well, I beg to differ."

"I'm all ears," he says like he can't wait to hear what kind of ridiculous reasoning I'm about to come up with.

"A cupcake's basically a muffin with the added bonus of icing. As far as I know, muffins are in the breakfast category."

Yes, he's definitely looking at me as if that's one of the most ridiculous things he's ever heard. "Right, right. Whatever you say."

"Fine," I give in. "It was my breakfast."

"Is that what you normally have?"

"Probably more often than I care to admit. I *may* have a sweet tooth."

"Is Tessa trying to justify her love of sweets?" Clara chimes in. I wonder how much of our conversation she's overheard.

"No," I scoff.

"Yes," Luke shouts at the same time, and then we both laugh.

As he laughs, his fingers travel to my knee, and I still at his sudden touch. I look down to where his hand is touching my skin, then follow the path of his arm all the way up to his face. He's looking at me, *really* looking, and I can't break away from his gaze. The skin his hand is touching tingles, and I am both intrigued and confused by the feelings he's awakened in me.

"You have got the cutest laugh," he remarks, still gazing at me with a look that is… I can't seem to interpret that look, and I come to the realization that I can't because I've never seen it before. Then another thought enters my mind. Maybe I've never bothered to look back at anyone else the way I am at Luke in this moment. He inches closer. I feel his breath travel to my mouth and I bite on my bottom lip instinctively. His gaze follows the movement of my lips and he… *Oh. My. God.* Is he going to…?

"We're here," Clara announces, interrupting our exchange. I welcome the interruption, yet I'm disappointed at the same time. I have a feeling that if our exchange had lasted a second longer, it would have turned into way more than we intended.

Chapter 3

Clara and Marcus are snuggled next to each other on their side of the restaurant booth as if they're joined at the hip. They're too cute together – it's a little bit sickening. Despite their almost total absorption in each other, we're having a great time. The conversation flows naturally and we bounce through several topics. Luke is easy to talk to now that I've passed the barrier into the land of speech again, and he's just as easy to listen to.

"And so about a year after I started work, I got an opportunity to transfer to the acquisitions department in the London office, so I took the chance and moved," Luke explains. "I've always loved to travel, and so it seemed a natural fit to explore Europe while looking for acquisition opportunities. I mean, I love Chicago, but Europe just has such charm."

"That sounds like an interesting career," I comment.

"It is. Though it's been difficult to balance my busy schedule since I started, so it's been more business than pleasure for the most part. I've been able to get away for a few weekends so far, but I've got a whole lot more of Europe to explore."

"It's great that you can do all that traveling while working."

"It's definitely a bonus. People wait to retire and travel the world, but I say, who knows what old age will bring, you know? And so I figured, might as well live life now, get the most out of every moment. After all, life is about taking chances, taking risks. And since I had nothing that tied me down in Chicago, I figured why not take the leap and move?"

"Makes sense." I try to sound casual, but I am absolutely immersed in this conversation. I love his outlook on life. I just wish I was able to live life in the moment the way he seems to. The truth is, I love traveling. We've traveled a lot as a family over the years. My dad was a big believer in the old adage, "Family that travels together stays together." He wanted us to see the world, to live life, to have no regrets. But five years ago he died, and all the excitement that came along with travel for us died with him. It took a couple of years before my mom got her spark back, and I'm not sure it has ever been as bright as it was with him around. It took time before Mom, Clara, and I felt even remotely whole again without Dad.

So, for the past five years or so, we've been pretty much stationary. But hearing Luke's take on life, his get-the-most-out-of-every-moment philosophy, his love for travel – it's refreshing and reminds me of how much I love to travel too. And how much I miss it.

"More wine?" Luke offers, interrupting my reverie.

"Sure." I smile candidly.

As we both reach for my glass, our fingers touch for a moment, but the sparks of our connection linger. Before I am able to pull away, Luke covers my knuckles with the palm of his hand, then proceeds to pour more wine in my glass. The connection I felt in the car not only lingers, but ignites and travels to a very Luke-aware spot between my thighs.

Suddenly, I'm aware of every little thing about him. The way he takes deep, slow breaths as if to steady his heart. The way he softly kneads my knuckles as if my skin is the most delicate he's ever touched. The way he looks at me with piercing eyes as he sets the wine bottle on the table. The way my body's reacting to all that I'm absorbing. *Uh-oh.*

Clara clears her throat and reminds me that we are not alone. Luke's not-so-discrete hand gesture has obviously not gone unnoticed by her always curious eyes. I will likely have some explaining to do later.

"Luke's always been the adventurous one," Marcus chimes in. "He's very fond of exploring. Let's just put it that way."

I wonder what exactly he means, but I think I have a pretty good idea. I take that second to warn myself that I need to stay away. Though I have a feeling this warning may be futile, because I seem to be too smitten with my sexy stranger to really give any weight to reason right now.

"Hey now, enough about me. No need to scare off the lovely brunette to my left." He nudges my shoulder just as his hand lands unexpectedly and inconspicuously on my knee. His fingers linger and brush my skin softly. My skin tingles, my toes curl, and my heart feels like it may need a moment to collect itself from wherever it scattered the second his hand landed on my knee.

"Yeah, that's never gonna happen," Clara jumps in. "Tessa really doesn't get scared very easily. She's normally the one to scare off the boys."

Great. I really should remind Clara of the definition of over-sharing, since she's obviously incapable of suppressing personal facts about me.

"Should I be worried?" The way Luke's smirking, I'd say he seems to find this information amusing. Or a challenge, maybe?

"All I can say is, you better watch it, Mr. Callaghan!" I challenge back confidently. It may seem as though I'm playing along, but the truth is, I'm dead serious. He really has no idea how accurate Clara's comment is. In the past three years, I've dodged pretty much every advance that's come my way. It was the safest alternative. Heartbreak can taste bitter for a while, and I much prefer the taste of sugar.

"Duly noted, Ms. Conte." He winks, then squeezes my knee gently. He does not appear to be intimidated at all. Who is this guy? "So I'm wondering, what do you do for a living, Tessa?" And yes, his fingers are definitely still on my knee ... and moving upwards. *Double uh-oh.*

"I own a bakery just a few blocks away. You know, one with cakes, not bread," I clarify. "We bake custom cakes and desserts for all sorts of occasions. It's something I really love to do and it keeps me busy. And of course, it keeps the cupcakes handy in times of desperation, so it has its benefits." Luke laughs at my comment.

"Oh, she's being modest, Luke," Clara jumps in. "You should see the cakes she's made! Trust me, Tessa can work magic with her hands."

"I'd like to see that someday." Luke holds my gaze as he says this, and I can't help but wonder if he's referring to cakes or whether he has something else in mind. I wouldn't be completely opposed to finding out what kind of magic he's thinking about, so I lose myself in my fantasy world for a moment. I seem to do that a lot around Luke.

"How'd you get into that?" Luke's voice brings me back, his fingers now bordering on the hem of the dress I'm wearing. Oh god, he is really, really close. The rush I'm feeling is something I haven't felt in a long time. I know that before I'm able to respond, I have to get some focus, clear my mind of the dangerously dirty path it's starting to take. I can't possibly think of a coherent response with him touching me. I need to take control of this blood-tingling predicament.

I reach for his hand and move it off my knee, shifting so that there's a bit more separation between us, so that I can avoid any further attempts of his to get into my panties. *This guy ... really.*

"Just something I always loved to do, you know," I say after I've taken a second to collect my thoughts. "I think it runs in my blood. My nonna – my grandma – taught me. And I guess it just grew into something I wanted to do for a living. I love exploring and letting my creativity guide me. I love being my own boss – it's exhilarating. And I love that it's something I'm passionate about, you know?"

"I totally do," Luke says thoughtfully. "Cheers to exploring and being passionate."

I'd like it if he explored me passionately. I silently curse myself and the thought that has crawled into my head. *Ugh.* It's no use. I'm starting to think I may be in trouble.

AFTER DINNER, WE WALK TO A NEARBY THEATER. OUR collective decision to see the newest Marvel movie means the theater is pretty much packed when we arrive. After charmingly rearranging a few people around, Clara finds a spot for her and Marcus, while Luke and I end up in the worst seats possible: in the last row, in the corner. An unattended seat separates him from the next moviegoer.

The silence creeps around Luke and me in the moments before the movie starts. Unlike the silence in the car, this one is heavy with the intimacy of the darkened theater, heavy with the closeness that we've been subjected to over the last couple of hours, heavy with anticipation. I'm not sure if Luke feels it too, but I can sense the sexual tension between us, and I can see it in the way he looks at me almost timidly, yet purposefully. Or maybe I'm just imagining it? It certainly wouldn't be the first time. Maybe he really is just uncomfortable sitting next to me.

But that theory is quashed the moment Luke's hand reaches for mine, for the one that's resting awkwardly on my knee. His fingers intertwine with mine, and the connection is enough to make me lose composure momentarily. I let out a gasp at the unexpected touch and look over at him, only to find his gaze fixated on the hold he has on my fingers.

As if he registers my confusion, he looks up and shifts toward me so that his lips are nearly touching my ear. Then he whispers, "You look more than nice tonight. You look fucking sexy." His words stir up a sense of thrill in my tummy. I feel my cheeks blush and am grateful for the darkened room.

If I am being honest, I only vaguely follow the movie. It's action-packed, and you'd think I'd be immersed in the plot, but no. Not even close. I fail miserably at trying to concentrate on the screen. Instead, what I am definitely immersed in is Luke. I focus on the way he plays with my fingers, the way he traces tiny circles on my palm, the way I feel like he's going to melt me with his touch. I know that's not really possible, but the warmth that I feel radiating off his hand is spreading through my already flushed body. It's as though every nerve, every pore of my skin responds to his touch. All I can seem to think about is how his fingers could do some very naughty things to me. His touch is soft, warm, and beyond stimulating. I have to fight the urge to straddle him and let him explore to his heart's content. He is making my normally uneventful Friday night spin slightly out of control.

Luke leans in again and whispers, his voice deep and low. "God, Tessa, you smell so fucking good, like strawberries and chocolate. I can't help but want to taste you."

Wow. That really is blunt and so very, very arousing.

His fingers tease my composure as they reach higher and higher and find themselves under my dress. Is he really going to do what I think he might? Oh god.

I tense momentarily because – let's face it – I'm kind of freaking out. I'm freaking out because we're in a movie theater and are about to do something that is less than socially acceptable in public. I'm freaking out because I think I'm about to let him do one of the wildest things I have ever let anyone do. My immediate reaction is to grab his arm and stop him, just like I did during dinner.

But Luke appears to have an uncanny ability to read my mind. He whispers, "Don't worry, no one is watching."

He's right. The crowd around us is glued to the action on the big screen, oblivious to the action that is happening in the back corner of the theater. And I'm so, so torn! The thought of being worked up by one of the sexiest men I've ever met is too tempting to pass on. So my next reaction is to wrap my fingers around his arm and pull him forward, giving him the silent okay. This is *so* happening.

I gasp as he slides his fingers underneath my panties, because his fingers are right *there*. Right where I've wanted them all night long. He's purposefully touching that hyper-sensitive spot, the one that is nearly ready to combust. My heart is beating at an exhilarating speed; my body tingles with feverish frenzy.

Tessa, what do you think you're doing? Oh, look. There it is. My conscience. But what Luke is doing right now makes it really, really hard to consider any kind of logic, to differentiate right from wrong, good from bad. Because right now, bad feels really, really good. So instead of pulling back, like the Tessa I know would normally have done at even the slightest possibility of something spontaneous, I slouch lower, spread my legs wider, and let Luke explore to his heart's content. He teases me with feather-light touches at first, and when I'm nearly mad with want, he rewards me with two fingers. Inside.

"You are so wet." He leans in and I can almost feel his lips touch my cheek. I can sense he's staring at me. I can sense he's wearing a cocky grin; I can see it from the corner of my eye. And he definitely knows what kind of effect he's having on me. Because right now, in this moment, I am lost in him, in his touch, in his closeness. My throat feels dry as my breathing becomes more rapid. I'm finding it extremely difficult to keep quiet. I may have magic hands, but I'm starting to think Luke has magic fingers.

I should make him stop, Rational Tessa reminds me as she sneaks back into my mind. *This is getting dangerous.* But being Spontaneous Tessa has its advantages. *I could get used to this.*

I take a mental scan of the theater and realize that even if anyone were to look over, they would never guess Luke's fingers are working their magic between my thighs. Then I steal a glance at Luke and notice two things: he appears to be concentrating on the big screen, but the corner of his mouth is tight, like he's smiling. It makes me wonder whether he's enjoying our private show more than the movie itself. Sensing my stare, he looks at me and our eyes connect. That same steady, mischievous look that nearly had me undone the first time we met is enough to make me forget about the crowd and the movie. Instead, it's as if I'm mesmerized, almost in a state of trance. I'm aware of only Luke and the way his fingers are exploring. In and out, massaging, circling my clit, taunting me – it's like a game, one that has me going wild. He's evoking a raw need within me, a need that builds and builds and is becoming more intense and difficult to control. I don't want him to stop, yet I'm not sure how much longer I can last before

I completely break apart, before the silent, barely controllable moans become heady, full-on screams. The movie patrons would not likely appreciate those. And then it happens. My body tenses in anticipation of the orgasm. My fingers dive deep into his bicep, and a lusty moan escapes me as my body gives in.

Well, *that* was not at all planned. Thankfully my not-so-quiet moan happens just as major action takes place on the screen. Perfect timing. My limbs feel numb. My body's limp in the seat. God, that felt *so* good, and it only involved Luke's fingers. I can't help but wonder what he could do with his cock. Also his mouth. Both equally enticing.

I'm overwhelmed and lost in the pleasure I just experienced, and shocked at my inability to exert control over what just happened. Then again, I've never experienced something as arousing and daring as I have with Luke tonight.

But as soon as my heartbeat returns to normal, I start to, well, think. *What was that all about?* I can't help myself – I kind of need to know, otherwise I imagine I'll end up being a total mess of emotions. I turn toward Luke, my expression pleading, needing answers. But he's staring at the screen, not registering – or at least pretending not to register – the demanding look on my face. Apparently I will not be getting my answers right now.

When the ending credits start to roll and the darkness that has filled the space lifts, Luke and I make our way out of the theater. His hand reaches for mine and brushes against it like he's about to hold it, but then he doesn't. I sense it's because we're about to meet up with Clara and Marcus and obviously he doesn't want to give them any hint about *us*. That leaves me a little bit confused.

Clara's grinning excitedly. "So, how did you guys like the movie?" she asks.

"Um, it was good. Yeah, I liked it," I mumble, because my head is still trying to figure out why his hand is not holding mine. She gives me the look, totally not buying it. "No really, it was great." I try to sound more convincing. I'm not sure I succeed. Clara knows me too well, knows that I normally go into much more detail and point out specifics of what I like or dislike.

"It was exciting," Luke says, then smiles as he steals a glance at me. My heart suddenly feels giddy – perhaps there's hand-holding in the near future after all. I've never been known to get so worked up over a guy in the span of a few hours. Then again, I *may* have already imagined Luke doing a variation of what I experienced with him tonight.

Clara gives him a questioning look. "Oh yeah? What did you find the most exciting?" She's onto something.

"The climax," Luke says with a smirk. But he quickly covers up by saying something movie-specific that's believable enough for Clara's appraising mind.

On our ride back to my apartment, I can't shake this eerie feeling. Something isn't right. In fact, something has definitely shifted. Luke is quiet, distant. He looks the other way, and not even a word is said between us. *What is going on?* The silence is bearable only because of the music coming from Marcus's stereo. I can't help but wonder if I'll ever figure out the reason for this sudden change in Luke's demeanor.

Feelings of unease and doubt start to creep up my spine. What felt so liberating a little while ago is now starting to feel like a chaotic rumble in my orderly world. And it messes with my head. I remember Marcus's words at dinner and very quickly realize that I'm probably nothing more than another woman Luke was just being adventurous with. And it's eating away at me. The last thing I want him to think is that I'm *that* easy. I mean, I have never, ever been so reckless and unguarded with a guy, especially one I just met.

What bothers me even more is that I'm normally the one in control of my interactions with the opposite sex. Well, at least I have been since I got burned by said opposite sex. I hate to admit it, but that's been a sore spot for close to three years. So when we pull up in front of my apartment building, I feel anything but in control. I am an emotionally charged mess. *Ugh!* Stupid, stupid Tessa. I should have known better.

"So ... I guess I'll see you later?" I'm going for indifferent, but instead come off hesitant. It may appear as though I'm asking the three of them, but my question is directed only at Luke. Of course it's Clara who replies excitedly, "See ya!" but she's not the person I'm hoping to hear from. All I get from Luke is a confusing ghost of a smile paired with a short, "Later, cupcake," and that's it. The same thing he said to me when we parted ways four months ago. That's all I get from the guy who so unexpectedly turned my Friday night upside down.

I put on a brave face and smile as I wave good-bye, as if nothing out of the ordinary happened. Meanwhile, I'm just short of fuming. Is he really just a pretentious prick, or am I dumb enough to think there would be more to it than a wild flirt of an evening? For some reason, I let my guard down with Luke tonight, and I'm not sure why. I'm angry and disappointed with myself, and so so so infatuated. Damn Luke and his– *ugh*, his stupid magic fingers!

I would be lying if I said I didn't at least anticipate a call from Luke, a text, anything the next day. But instead, there's a big, blank nothing. No calls, no sign of the person who made me feel so uninhibited and pleasured less than twenty-four hours ago. And the worst thing is I'm not even sure why I care. It's not like I've been craving any kind of relationship. At least not since Jason the Jerk.

Chapter 4

The present

"Come on Tessa, just give me a hint," Clara begs for the umpteenth time. "Please!" She bats her eyelashes innocently, as if that will somehow melt my resolve.

"Uh-uh. No way!" I shake my head while continuing to frost an elegant three-tiered wedding cake I'm working on for one of my clients.

It's lunchtime on Friday, and Clara has stopped by Lovely Cakes hoping to get a peek at her cake. Marcus did turn out to be The One. They're so sure that they're meant to be, in fact, that they're getting married next Saturday, after only a six-month engagement. Clara's been pestering me about the wedding cake the whole time, but there's no way I'm letting her see anything until the day of the wedding. It's a surprise, my gift to the happy couple.

"Ugh, you're no fun!" she scoffs, yet grins adorably at the same time. I know it's all just pretense. She *loves* surprises. I kind of hate them. "The one you're working on sure looks amazing." She motions to the cake.

I smile appreciatively. The cake I'm working on is elegant and intricate, but Clara's is going to be incredible. It's my sister we're talking about, after all, and she loves all things grand and glamorous.

"I really hope a day comes when you'll get to make one of these for you and your Prince Charming." *Here we go.* Since

I'm not giving in on the cake, she's going to start harassing me about my relationship status.

"Yeah, that's not likely to happen. I live in a world of romance, weddings, and cupcakes – a world that is dreamy and deliciously sweet and too good to be true, if you ask me. Hard to live up to those standards." I'm being sarcastic, but only because I know it's the sad and sour reality of my existence. I may *slightly* despise the opposite sex.

"Life is too short to live it through everyone else's happiness," Clara criticizes. "Not every guy is like…"

"Just say it." I know she knows I don't like to be reminded, but I also know what's coming.

"Like Jason."

Right, *that* guy. The guy I met when I was starting my senior year of college, shortly after my dad died. Looking back, I may have misinterpreted my emotional state at that time and attributed it to something more. After all, what Jason and I had was comfortable, safe. He fit the this-is-how-your-life's-supposed-to-turn-out plan. Finish school. Meet a guy. Fall in love. Get married. And on and on.

Sure, I was young and naïve and completely infatuated with him. I guess I thought that's what being in love felt like. On some level, I probably was in love. But then again, I thought and felt a lot of things when I was in my early twenties.

He was the guy I thought I would marry. He was smart and educated, and he liked to plan things out, just like me. But while I planned our happily-ever-after, he had obviously planned his own, without me in it. I was completely blindsided when he decided to move overseas, and yet we'd dated for almost three years. *That's* how well I knew the real Jason. Perhaps he wanted more from life than what he thought I was able to give him.

When he left, of course I was emotional. I felt heartbroken and confused, yet angry and betrayed; I despised him. I'd got burned by a person I trusted, by a person who was supposed to be my "One." And that left me overly cautious when it came to the opposite sex.

But I reasoned it all out. If he had planned to move and I had never considered anything but staying and opening my bakery, then it made sense that we'd have to part ways. So emotions very quickly gave way to logic. If I am really being honest with myself, I don't know if I have ever actually been *in love*. And Jason was probably never quite in love with me either.

"You just never know," Clara continues, "your Prince Charming could come along when you least expect it and sweep you off your feet!"

A less than likely possibility. Especially after how the guy who literally knocked me off my feet treated me, it's not like I would ever open myself up to the possibility of that happening again.

"I *don't* live my life through everyone else's happiness," I scoff. She gives me a look as if to say, *Yeah, right*. "It's just that between work and, um, stuff," I struggle to come up with another good reason that would make me seem like less of a workaholic, "I don't often find the time to go out and play the game." As soon as the words leave my mouth, I realize that sounds so pathetic.

"You and your work excuse. Pu-lease! If you don't make time and room in your heart for love, it will never happen."

I sigh, knowing she's probably right, even though I won't ever admit it outright.

"And then you'll die gray-haired and alone, with only a mob of cats attending your funeral."

I really want her to think I'm exasperated by her rant, but I can't help but laugh. She always knows how to make things light.

"Well, now that you've so pleasantly painted that picture, can we please talk about something else?" This is not the first time we've had this discussion. My love life sucks. I know.

A defeated look crosses her face. "Fine, I won't say another word." She pretends to zip her mouth with an invisible key and throws it away. "So everything's under control for next Saturday?"

"You bet. I've got a few more things to finalize, but I promise, it will be just like you've always imagined. I know you're going to love it." Of course, I'm referring to her wedding cake – I have the details nearly memorized by now. I've reviewed my coveted cake planning list a gazillion times to make sure everything goes smoothly and as planned. "I've got it under control, as always," I reassure her.

"I know you do. You always do. That's the one thing I can count on. I just... *Ugh*, it's just, the wedding is a week away, and I think it's getting to me," she sighs.

This is so not typical of Clara. She's been a bit more on edge with the wedding around the corner. Not her usual carefree self, whom I'm used to and admire. I figure the pressure of all that comes with planning a picture-perfect wedding must have gotten under her skin a bit. I have a feeling she secretly wants to run off to Vegas to get hitched without having to do much more than book a plane ticket. But then again, that wedding wouldn't come with the glory of it all, and she's definitely one for show.

"Don't worry, Clar. I'm sure everything will work out perfectly peachy." I smile and try to comfort her, even though she's normally the one to comfort me.

"Yeah. You're right. I don't know what's gotten into me. Oh wait, I do – the wedding." She laughs, and just like that she's back to normal. It's like's she's got an on and off switch. I wish I could borrow it sometimes. "I am so looking forward to our night out tonight!"

"Me too." I play along, not wanting to ruin her excitement.

Marcus and Clara have planned a night out for just their closest friends, those who will be part of their wedding party. They want to make sure everyone has a chance to get to know each other, since friends from all walks of their lives are merging to celebrate their special day. We're having dinner at a high-end restaurant that's owned by one of Marcus's groomsmen, and then we're heading to a nightclub.

Clara loves to party; she makes it a point to always have a good time. It's like her motto or something. Partying definitely isn't one of my favorite things to do on a Friday night.

She gives me yet another one of those I-don't-believe-you-for-a-second looks.

"What?" I plead innocently.

"I know how much you enjoy stuff like that, but please, just have fun tonight. For me?"

"I promise, I'll try." I sound as convincing as I can. "I know it's important to you, and I'm your big sister, your maid of honor, so it's important for me to see you happy."

"Thanks. That means a lot," Clara says as she walks over to give me a hug goodbye. "So I'll see you later on tonight, then. Can't wait!" she squeaks cheerfully once again, and then heads out. But before stepping outside onto the busy street, she pauses at the door and says, "And please don't just *try* to have fun, but *do*, okay?"

I nod reassuringly. "I'm pretty sure I can manage that, Clar. It can't be that hard." I smile, then wave her off so that I can get back to work. She may not be convinced, but tonight I'm determined to have fun.

AFTER WORK, I RUSH HOME TO MAKE SURE I HAVE enough time to get myself ready for the evening. I know I have time to spare, but I don't like being late. I think I've established that already. Run-ins with delicious, sexy, *manipulative* strangers happen when you're late.

I shower, pull my hair into a loose, low bun with a few tousles hanging freely on each side, and work on applying makeup as I contemplate what dress to wear for tonight's occasion. I could go for a sexy red or a summery pink, but I settle for a little black dress. Simple yet flirtatious, the dress is sleeveless with a deep v-cut at the front. It's tight fitting in all the right places, showing just the right amount of my ample cleavage. I top it off with crimson earrings and matching stilettos.

When I'm all done, I glance in the mirror one last time. Big, deep brown eyes stare excitedly back at me. Plump lips, high cheekbones, and chocolate-brown waves of hair frame my face. I'm attractive, but not what I would consider gorgeous – just a nice balance of curves and simple beauty.

"This should more than do the trick," I say out loud, grinning happily. "It's time to kick some ass!"

But as the words roll off my lips, a feeling of nervousness washes over me. My mind starts to wander from the control it exerts most of the time. It could be the fact that I am dreading being at a dinner table surrounded by appraising eyes reminding me that yes, I'm twenty-six and still single. Or the fact that my sister is getting ready to commit to a life of being somebody's significant other. Though deep down I know the unease I feel in my stomach has nothing to do with either. No, the nerves start to wreck me just a bit at the thought of seeing *him* again.

Since the movie incident, as I like to refer to it (because it was just that – a temporary lapse in judgment, I've convinced myself), I've struggled to keep Luke out of my head. I've teetered between anger and desire, resentment and infatuation, all mixed together in a perfect blend of messed-up emotions. I despise him, yet my imagination seems to think he's the only person able to fuel my sexual fantasies. It's downright frustrating and sad – pathetic, even – that I have not been able to break this weird infatuation I have with him.

But after months of what have bordered on obsessive thoughts of Luke and endless fantasies of his magic fingers traveling up and down my body, I have finally decided that I can't live like this anymore. It's not healthy having a relationship with a memory. It's actually kind of concerning. I've thought about it and come to the conclusion that I have no other option but to break this spell he has over me. If I can get back at him, if I somehow manage to return the "favor," I hope that I will finally get some closure. That I can get back to being Rational Tessa, who's in control of her feelings, of her life.

So I've done what I know best: I've crafted a plan. A perfect comeback. I grin villainously at the thought of how liberating it will feel when I bring Luke to a high and then leave him stranded, leave him wanting more. *Two can play at this game, Mr. Callaghan.* Tonight's the perfect night, and by the end of it, I'm going to be free from Luke and this damn infatuation. I have somehow convinced myself that I'm not entirely crazy for thinking this is possible. I mean, how hard can it be?

"TESSA!" I HEAR MY SISTER'S SQUEAL AS I ENTER THE private dining room of the restaurant. The room is rustic and elegant, with a long wooden table, brown leather chairs, and dim lighting. Clara makes her way toward me and gives me a tight squeeze, Marcus following close behind her.

"Hey there, easy! I just saw you a few hours ago," I gasp, almost breathless.

"I know. I'm just so glad you're here. You look amazing, Tessa!"

"Thanks. So do you!"

Clara's wearing a tight, pale yellow dress that accentuates her curves, plus a pair of matching pumps. She's inherited Mom's straight, dirty-blonde hair, which falls down her shoulders to her chest. She's also inherited my dad's ocean blue eyes that pierce right through you. She's gorgeous.

Marcus is standing right beside her, his hand resting lightly on the small of her back. His eyes always seem to be focused on her, in a sweet kind of way. I'm quite used to their PDA by now, unlike in the early stages of their relationship.

"Hi, Marcus." I give him a hug, even though I'm not normally the hugging type.

"Hey, Tessa. I'm so glad you made it." Marcus is one of the most genuine people I have ever met. He's polite and friendly, always a gentleman, and he's quite attractive. Light brown hair, blue eyes, tall, masculine, sculpted. Beyond his looks, he's absolutely crazy about Clara.

"Thanks. I'm glad to be here tonight." The week leading up to a wedding is always full of excitement. I'm thrilled that I can share in these moments with my sister and her soon-to-be husband.

"So I see mostly everyone's here?" I ask, but a little bit of intel I was able to obtain from Clara a few weeks ago means I know Luke will be arriving late. This has been of utmost importance as I've schemed and meticulously put together my plan. So as I quickly scan the table, I'm glad to see everyone is seated except for me and Luke. *Perfect.*

"Almost everyone. Luke's on his way in," Marcus confirms.

Ever since that night at the movies, Clara and Marcus have tried to get the scoop on whether anything happened between Luke and me. I decided it was best to keep things under wraps. I mean, obviously it's not something I would ever discuss with Marcus, because ... embarrassing and so not appropriate for discussion with your future brother-in-law. Even with Clara, who's clearly starved for signs of romance in my life, I chose to give only a few hints, rather than the full X-rated version. Not necessarily because it happened, but because I, Tessa Maria Conte, a self-professed emotional control freak, let my control slip so easily that night.

And after the way Luke left things between us, I sure as hell am not going to let that happen again. I'm not going to let him get to me this time around. I have an Evil, Kick-Ass Plan.

"Oh, I see," I reply. "Well, I'm glad that everyone else has made it in. This is such an exciting time for you guys!" I hope to change the subject and act as if I'm unaffected by the mere mention of Luke's name, but underneath, my stupid heart begins a dreadful yet exhilarating race, anticipating how it will likely stop beating at the first sight of him. This does not bode well for my plan.

Before we all get seated, I make sure to say hello to the rest of the wedding party. First, there are the three bridesmaids, Liz, Paige, and Lila. Liz is my cousin on my mom's side and a close friend. I don't know Paige and Lila well, though I've gotten to know them better over the last few months, since Clara's engagement.

As far as the groomsmen go, in addition to Luke, there's Levi and Theo, neither of whom I've met before. Levi is the owner and executive chef at the restaurant we're at, conveniently enough, and Theo is a lawyer. And then there's Ian, Marcus's childhood friend and his best man. I had the "pleasure" of meeting him a few weeks ago, when the four of us had dinner together to go over the wedding plans. He's an investment banker and isn't at all shy about sharing stories of his accomplishments.

Since I timed my arrival ever so perfectly, there are only two empty chairs left. I take a seat next to Ian and wait for the blank space next to me to be filled. What I mean by "wait" is alternate between looking nervously at the empty chair and looking at the door, anticipating the inevitable. I try not to fidget too much, but I feel like biting my manicured crimson nails. I hate to admit it, but I'm craving a glimpse of the man who made my heart flutter months ago. But I'm resolute – there is no way I'm going to let him take advantage of me this time around. Nope, I have a plan. Did I mention it was an Evil, Kick-Ass Plan? Because it is.

Ian tries making small talk with me. I hear the jumble of his words and nod, but I have difficulty focusing. At least I manage to provide brief responses when prompted. After all, I'm the maid of honor, and I have to behave.

As I take a sip of my wine, I hear Marcus call out, "Luke! You made it!"

And there he is. Popping up in my life yet again. I steal one glance, and his smoldering eyes capture mine. *Jesus. He is just so fucking hot.* That is the only thing I can process at the moment. I swear it feels as though I've forgotten how to breathe.

Luke's impeccably put together in black pants and a dark green button-up shirt with rolled-up sleeves that accentuate his sculpted arms. His hair is just as I remember it: short at the sides, messy at the top, ready to be played with. He's sporting day-old stubble that makes his lips pop. And not surprisingly at all, I have an urge to bite them.

"Everyone, last but not least, Luke," Marcus exclaims, patting Luke on the shoulder and then giving him a crazy-man bear-hug.

"Sorry I'm late," Luke replies cheerfully, waving a quick hello. "We were delayed out of Heathrow, and the traffic on a Friday night … well, I don't have to tell you."

Marcus introduces Luke as they make their way around the table, and when they finally come to me, he says matter-of-factly, "And of course, you've met Tessa."

"That I have," Luke replies, and his bright smile nearly knocks me off my chair. I gather myself rather quickly and smile back – a flirty smile, one that tells him I know exactly what kind of "meeting" we had last time. A hot, impromptu meeting of his fingers and my panties.

I extend my hand confidently, as if not at all affected by him. Because I'm not. Not by the way his gaze travels to my lips like he may want to taste them; not by the way he takes hold of my hand, brings it to his mouth, and plants a soft kiss; not by the way my body reacts to his scent, like he's freshly showered after a day of traveling. Warmth spreads through me, and it's not from the sip of wine I just took. I suddenly feel very, very hot. *Get yourself together, Tessa!*

"Nice to see you again, cupcake."

"Nice to see you again, too, stranger," I say confidently.

Luke smiles as he sits down next to me. The chair that was empty only minutes ago is no longer. And so here it goes – Evil, Kick-Ass Plan, Part A: The Flirting.

Step One: I don't want to seem too obvious, so I start things off slowly. As Luke sits down, I pretend not to pay attention to him, and chat instead with Ian. I sip my wine and act as if I'm having the most interesting discussion. While Ian is talking my ear off, out of the corner of my eye I notice Luke glancing at me in between exchanges with Lila. *Great start!*

Step Two: Luckily, as the main course arrives, Ian finally takes a break from boring me and decides instead to brag to Paige. Since I'm just about done my glass of wine, it's a perfect time for a refill. And also to drive Luke crazy. He's still talking with Lila, so he doesn't immediately notice when I reach for the bottle of wine that's in front of him. But of course, as I lean in, my breasts brush against his arm, and that's just enough of a connection for him to turn toward me.

His eyes travel to my breasts instantly, as if to confirm they were the source of the interruption (yes they were!), but he regains his focus and offers to help. As he grabs for the bottle, I reach for it too. Our hands connect again and ... *damn it!* I hate that simple skin-on-skin with Luke affects me so much. I thought that by now I would be better able to control my reaction to him.

I mentally count to five, gather my wits, and reply coolly, "Thanks. Allow me to return the favor," then smile as I fill his glass. Except as I do, my other hand travels ever so inconspicuously to his thigh. Familiar? It should be.

Step Three: "So how was your flight?" I ask, hoping to engage in some innocent conversation now that I have his attention. All the while my palm is less than innocently massaging the muscles that are hiding beneath the fabric of his pants. My touch is sensual and purposeful. The heat of his skin radiates through and creates a bubbly feeling in my stomach. God, he seems so fit – it's tight muscle all along his thigh. I wonder if he's a runner.

He looks down at my hand, takes a deep breath, and closes his eyes, like he's struggling with whatever feeling my touch may be evoking. When it's apparent his composure is back, he answers, "My flight was long. Too long. And high ... with anticipation."

Oh. Dare I ask? The question is out of my mouth before I can stop myself.

"And what is it that you were anticipating so highly?"

He mouths silently, "You."

His answer stalls the motion of my hand for a moment. I think I need more wine. In my fantasies I must have had Luke say he wants me in one form or another more than I'd like to admit, but now that I've heard him actually say it, it seems surreal. I didn't quite expect to hear it from him so directly, but I have obviously forgotten how bold Luke can be.

"I see. What about me?" I ask innocently, our exchange isolated by the chatty voices around us.

"Seeing you. Getting a chance to talk to you again, you know, after last time."

"After last time?" I take another sip of wine, trying to sound casual, but from the way my hand is traveling up his thigh, I think he knows exactly how well I remember the last time.

He takes a moment to respond. "Let's talk about it when it's more private, okay?"

"We've got days to talk this time around. I'm sure the topic will come up." I flirt easily, knowing full well that if my plan works out, there will be very little talking. In fact, this will probably be the last I see of him before the rehearsal dinner on Thursday. And on that note, I inch my hand higher, and I'm *there*.

Luke's eyes widen, like he didn't think I would actually make it all the way, and he responds, "I sure hope so," with a tight grin.

"So, you're looking forward to the week, then?" I ask expectantly, while the palm of my hand gently rubs the zipper-tight area of his pants. *God, he's so hard.* I remind myself to not focus too much on what exactly I'm doing. Except thanks to the way his cock twitches ever so slightly every time I rub, I have trouble putting together a coherent thought. My thoughts are like a broken record, stuck on repeat. *Giant cock ... giant cock ... giant cock...*

"Very much so," he replies, the "so" stretching into a hissing sound. His eyes connect with mine, and I see the intensity that's behind them. It's like he's thinking of not only what I'm doing to him right now, but also what he did to me in the movie theater. And, perhaps, what he'd like to do to me again? *Yes please.* What? *No no no. Focus.*

His gaze is intimidating, nonetheless. It's as if he's undressing me with his stare. I suddenly feel exposed, flushed. I squeeze my thighs in response as warm tension builds deep in my belly. I'm reminded of the way his fingers made me feel, and I long for them to make me feel that way right now.

Stirred by the thoughts that are heightening my arousal, I up the intensity and massage the firmness in his pants. He grows harder as he pulsates beneath my palm. I'm rewarded with a low growl, one that is audible only to me, given the buzz of the voices around us. God, that sound is so sexy. I need more of it; I want more of it. I want it loud.

I can't even remember what I asked or where our conversation was, I'm so caught up in our game. I've forgotten what the point of Step Three was to begin with. But a sudden laugh from the table brings me back from the land of giant cock. I take a quick look around and am glad to see that everyone is immersed in their chatter and not focused on us. *Thank god.* That was too close, and I've got a plan to stick to.

"To things to look forward to, then!" I pull my hand away and take a sip of wine to hide the fact that my cheeks are blushing from the little preview that just played out so flawlessly. Luke stares at me with a stunned, almost pained expression on his face, like he's confused and not quite ready for our game to end. *Oh, the game has just begun, Mr. Callaghan.*

Chapter 5

The drinks are flowing at the club, but I'm drunk on something else. Luke's gaze keeps finding me through the crowd, making me buzz despite myself. It's retro night, so the place is packed, but Marcus knows the owner, of course, so we're glamming it up in the VIP lounge.

Luke's sipping his beer and swallowing me. I can make out a small smile at the corner of his mouth and can't help but smile back. I'm drawn to his eyes, to his lips, to his presence. Why does he have to be so damn gorgeous? This plan would be so much easier to execute if he was less appealing. *Eyes on the prize, Conte!* Right. I can pull this off. No problem.

"Party Rock Anthem" blasts through the speakers, bringing cheers from the crowd. Clara squeals in her signature excitement. "I haven't heard this song in forever! Let's go!" When Clara's on a mission, she's unstoppable. She pulls me by my hand and leads us to the dance floor, making her way through the crowd. The rest of the bridesmaids follow suit.

When we get to the dance floor, I lose myself in the beat of the music, putting on my dance persona, that of Confident Tessa who moves seductively, who flirts with the music.

I've been dancing since I was five. My mom had to force me to attend the first few dance lessons because I'm not a natural performer and I totally hated it at first. I was shy compared to most of the girls in our class, who had the confidence that I so often lacked in new situations. But the more I practiced, the more fun it became. When I danced, all the spontaneity that normally felt so foreign to me became a bit more natural. And I've learned to love it. It combines the control I crave with just a touch of impulsiveness.

It's not long before the guys join us on the floor. All except for Luke. Where the hell is he? Somewhat desperately, I have to admit, I search the crowd that has by now grown quite dense, but I can't place him. *Damn it!* If my plan is going to work, I absolutely need to find him again tonight.

Just as I'm about to go into bounty-hunter mode, the swish of a familiar scent stops me. The soft hairs on the back of my neck rise up and goose bumps scatter over my body. I still at the touch of what I know is Luke's palm on my lower back.

"Hey," he calls deep and low through the music, his mouth nearly touching my ear.

"Hi," I say as I turn to face him. Except the move is not nearly as smooth as I anticipated. Instead, I kind of less-than-gracefully smack my nose right against his chin.

"Oh my god, I'm so sorry," Luke chuckles, although obviously my clumsiness is not something he needs to apologize for. "Are you okay?" He cups my cheeks in his palms and rubs my nose with his thumb, gently soothing the spot. The familiarity of this moment is so not lost on me.

But I'm no longer the mumbling Tessa he ran into the first time we met. No, this Tessa is confident. This Tessa is focused. This Tessa is going for a shiny trophy.

"Yeah, yeah, I'm fine. Just, you know, obviously still clumsy."

The way he smiles, the way his eyes gleam with amusement, I know he gets exactly what I'm referring to. But as his thumb pauses in rubbing my nose, a strange thing happens. Our eyes lock and we stand there, unmoving, caught up in the moment. The intensity in his eyes is palpable, the look of want, need, and anticipation all tangled together. At least that's what I think I'm seeing. It's kind of dark on the dance floor, after all.

But I definitely see when his gaze shifts down, right to my lips. And even though I know I shouldn't, my gaze mirrors his. *Oh god!* I've thought of tasting his lips so many times. We are so close, in fact, that I feel his breath on me. Surprisingly, it's minty, like he's just chewed a Tic Tac or something. From the way his eyes are fixated on my mouth, it seems as though he's bracing himself, holding back from getting another inch closer. Right now I am so not even thinking about my Evil, Kick-Ass Plan. My mouth is dry and my body's tingling all over. Is he going to? I so want him to. I want a taste of him, of his mouth. No no – I don't. *Ugh!* I hate myself for even considering it.

Perhaps it's the hesitation he reads on my face, or perhaps it's his own feelings of uncertainty, but with a slight shift of his gaze, the moment is gone. Instead he asks, "Dance with me?"

I nod, and it's like I've given him the green light. Luke wraps his arms around my waist and pulls my body close, so that my breasts connect with his firm chest and the area just below my tummy connects with something else that feels pretty firm. I whimper at the sudden friction it creates, and I have the urge to feel him bare.

My arms wrap around his neck and my fingers make their way into his hair. I've imagined running my fingers through his hair since I first ran into him and wondered what kind of reaction it would bring out in him. And his reaction is divine. He closes his eyes and leans into the palms of my hands, groaning.

When he opens his eyes again, they're glazed with need. He runs his fingers down my arms, tantalizing every pore along the way. He leaves a fiery trail, making my skin feel feverish. His hands move down to my hips and rock me to the rhythm of the song. We're moving like we're one – there's a connection between us that is undeniable. I feel the vibrations not only from the beat of the music, but also from having his body so close to me.

His hands inch lower and lower, then grab my bottom. My back arches and my breasts push up as he drives his pelvis against me. I let out a moan and close my eyes as my head falls back. And then I feel his touch, right down the middle of my chest, down the deep v-cut of my dress. His fingers trace the skin from my collarbone, in between my breasts, to just above my belly button. And they make my skin sizzle. I'm a torch, ready to set fire. I imagine being naked and against him; I imagine his lips on my bare skin, on my nipples, tugging, sucking. The thrill of the image makes my head spin – I am so turned on by what Luke is doing right now. And I'm lost in the way he feels, in the way our bodies connect. The crowd around us disappears, and the music fades into the background.

I bring my head up and meet his eyes. He holds my gaze, the lust in his telling me he feels as crazed as I am. He leans in closer, as if he's about to kiss me, but instead of closing the gap, he brushes his lips against my cheek and growls in my ear, "You are so damn sexy."

His breath lingers on my earlobe, sending shivers down my neck and all the way to my toes. God, I am so worked up right now, all I can think about is what we'd be doing next if we were alone.

But we're not alone. I register the loud roar as the song changes, and I remember that dancing is not quite what I have planned for tonight. I break from Luke's gaze so that I can gather the courage to move forward with Evil, Kick-Ass Plan, Part B: Kicking It Up a Notch. This time, I am the one taking charge. I'm in this for one thing and one thing only: evening the score so that I can finally break free. I want to bring some closure to my obsession, to the fantasies that have filled my days and nights since we first met. And I almost have him where I want him.

"Come," barely escapes my dry mouth as I pull his hand and lead him across the room. The music and the noise of the crowd come back loud and clear. Once we're past the dance floor, I lead us to a door that I ventured through a few weeks ago when Marcus, Clara, and I toured the club. It helps to know people who know people.

We go up a few sets of stairs and then through another door, which opens to the rooftop. I duck around a corner to a secluded nook, Luke following behind me. But before I'm able to move to the next stage of my plan and finish what I started, Luke grabs me by my elbow and pulls me against him. So close, and so suddenly, in fact, that my body collides with his, leaving me nearly breathless.

His darkened gaze is on me, and I can't seem to look away. Even with the sounds of the city humming around us, the only two sounds I'm aware of are Luke's breath and my rapidly beating heart.

"I can't wait another minute, Tessa." Luke cups my face with one hand, while his other hand reaches for the nape of my neck. Our lips are nearly touching, waiting for that inch of space to close between us. I feel his erection push against my lower belly and I suck in a deep breath.

I can't even begin to describe how much I want him at this very moment, how much I want his lips on mine, how much I want to feel him bare. After all the teasing at the restaurant and on the dance floor, I'm ready to tear off his clothes, and from the look on his face, I'm pretty certain he has something similar in mind. Restraining myself from kissing him at this point is practically impossible. The thought of having him kiss me back is more than appealing. I'm in a bit of a predicament.

I know if we do in fact kiss, I'll break. And my plan, my perfectly planned-out plan, will become unusable trash. I have to resist, even if the temptation to devour his mouth is too sweet. I will be at his mercy, and I'll regret it later when he gives me the cold shoulder, when he decides that what we've done was nothing more than a game in which I was the pawn. I have no intention of re-living the last several months. It's completely out of the question.

Just as he moves to place his mouth on mine, I place my fingers on his lips, stopping him from giving me what I can't help but want. And then I whisper, "Tonight's my turn."

His look turns from desire to confusion.

While holding his gaze, I trace my fingers from his mouth and down his neck, teasing his Adam's apple. The definition of his square jaw is so sexy. He swallows deep, and the movement stirs a sort of frenzy in my belly. I'm eager to see what's hiding beneath his shirt. I'm trying to stay composed, but I'm restless to feel him, to touch him everywhere. Especially down there.

I begin to unbutton his shirt with laboring patience. When I pull it open, my eyes are greeted with his bare, muscular torso, which is simply magnificent. My fingers move voluntarily over the hard lines of his chest and trace the light covering of hair. He sucks in a sharp breath in response. His chest rises, then falls; I swear I can feel the pounding of his heart underneath my palm. I've imagined how his skin would feel to my touch, I've thought of his reaction, but it's the first time I've actually seen him this exposed, the first time I've touched him like this.

I fight to keep my fingers from trembling. I have a sudden urge to lick him. *That's not part of the plan.* Maybe I can take a bit of a detour, taste what's on display, even though I probably shouldn't. Going against the plan is never advisable. But maybe just a little peck – it's harmless, right? I lean in, and my lips connect with his skin. The reasonable part of my brain reminds me, *Not a good idea.* The other needy and somewhat desperate parts counter with, *Oh god. Best. Idea. Ever.* The peck turns into a kiss, then another, and I'm almost panting.

Luke hisses and whispers, "Tessa." No other word escapes him, like his mouth's gone dry, like he's fighting to stay composed. But the sound of my name is just enough to bring me back from wherever I was lost a moment ago. *Head in the game, Conte!*

I break the connection, and without looking up at him – because frankly, I'm hesitant to read his expression – my eyes follow the trail of my fingers. I move down his tight abdomen, past the soft hair that leads to the ultimate goal. I know exactly what I want to do. My plan is coming along quite nicely. *I've got this.*

As I drop to my knees, I struggle for a bit to undo his belt, but that doesn't stop me. No, once the unbuckling is out of the way, I go right to undoing his pants and pulling them down with his boxers. When I finally have his fullness right in my face, I am momentarily stunned.

Wow! He's big, thick, hard … and ready for me. God, I am so in love. *What?* No – not love. I mean I am so in lust. Lust. And so so so aroused. I feel the wetness in my panties in response and curse my stupid, stupid hormones.

But I remind myself of all the times I've felt betrayed, angry, and used over the last several months. I remind myself of the plan and keep going.

I touch the tip of his cock with my finger, then rub the wetness around. This must send shock waves through Luke's body, because he draws a sharp breath and groans, "Take me."

Oh, I will. Patience, Mr. Callaghan.

I wrap my fingers tightly around his length, gently pulling back and forth. He grows thicker in response like he's urging me to do just as he suggested. My tongue connects with the tip and teases the soft skin. Pure torture. When I finally pull him into my mouth, I'm surprised at how distinctively delicious he tastes – salty, and tangy, yet so very sweet, unlike any other guy. I hear him groan, "Fuck, Tessa. Your mouth feels so amazing."

He grasps my head, then pulls me forward, pressing deeper, and it only makes me more ambitious. That's right – let's see who can play this game better! I want to make him pay for the ache he caused me so that I can finally move past it. I want him to remember how my mouth felt on him so he'll want more when I'm done. *Except he won't get more, ever.* Cue the evil laugh.

I close my eyes and work up and down his length, sucking gently, then hard, twirling my tongue around. And I'm rewarded with more groans, ragged breaths, and pleading from Luke.

"Deeper, Tessa. Take me real deep." And I do just that. His hips rock forward, creating delicious friction. My teeth graze him ever so slightly, and every time they do, his breathing becomes more uneven and his cock throbs. It feels incredible to be the one making him feel this way, to make him react like this. So incredible, in fact, that I feel tension between my thighs. I'm so aroused right now. My breathing is just as ragged and I'm making these soft noises. God, I'm actually moaning. I may be in this solely to exact revenge, yet the revenge is beyond sweet. I'm taken aback by how much I'm enjoying this game I'm playing.

It appears Luke is really enjoying what I'm doing, because he can barely put together a coherent sentence as he says through staggered breaths, "God, Tessa, just don't ... fucking ... stop."

There is no way I'm stopping. In fact, his words urge me on.

I'm so focused on his cock, so focused on the motions, that I haven't taken a moment to look up. But I'm tempted. I want to see what his face looks like while he's in this state of bliss. I want to see if his eyes will tell me what he's feeling. It will make it that much more gratifying when I'm done. I lift my gaze and realize instantly it was a mistake. His eyes are fixed on the way my mouth takes him in, but they lock with mine the moment he sees me looking at him. And what I see nearly has me undone. His eyes are full of feverish heat, full of emotion and greed. And there's something else. A pull, a spark. Something too intimate.

I avert my gaze immediately and close my eyes – it's safer that way. It's easier to get lost in just the action and not the feelings that come with it: a need to have him and not just his cock; an urge to kiss his lips and have him kiss me back; a desire to know what else would make him smile the way he's smiling right now. And what I think I'm feeling scares me, because it was not part of the script. It wasn't at all what I thought I'd be feeling.

"Faster, cupcake," Luke urges. "So fucking good."

I focus on his words and respond with what he needs. I'm nearly victorious – the sounds his worked-up voice is making and the force with which he rocks back and forth tell me he's close. I can sense his body tense and I feel his cock swell in my mouth. It's the moment I've been waiting for. The moment that will set me free. I rocked it– um, him, that is.

"Tessa, that was... God, I can't move," Luke manages to say as he collapses against the wall. Before he can gather himself, I pull myself up, place my fingers on his lips again, and kiss him over my fingers. A crooked grin lights up his face, and I can't help but smile. It's a moment of weakness, I admit; that's how ridiculously captivating his smile is, and I almost give in to him, almost let him take away my control. But logic prevails. I remember what I need to do next.

I pull away, leaving him with his pants down, nearly naked. I giggle because the befuddled look on his face is kind of adorable. Then I zero in on the area down below. Big mistake. He's still half-hard, and calling to me. I scan the rest of his body. It's calling to me too. The hard lines of his abs, his defined chest, the shirt that screams, "Fucking tear me off!" No – I'm not listening. I'm not looking. But god, I'm feeling so flushed, so aroused.

I avert my gaze and walk hurriedly toward the door that will lead me back to the club. My stride may appear confident, but my knees are shaky, my hands are trembling from the feel of him under my fingers, my mouth's thirsty from the taste he left behind.

"Tessa?" I hear him in the distance, confusion evident in his voice. As I reach the door, I'm pretty sure I hear him chuckle, though I'm terrified to look back. There is now way I'll be able to stick to my plan if I turn around.

I pull off my stilettos and sprint down the stairs. As I open the door, the loud music hits me in the face like a boxing glove. When the door shuts behind me, I lean against it, the chill of the metal cooling down my worked-up body. I am a Hot Mess. I had a plan, I executed it, but suddenly I am seriously doubting it. I am no longer sure I've got this.

Okay. I fucked his cock with my mouth. *Check.* He seems to have thoroughly enjoyed it. *Check.* I left him at a loss for words. *Check.* Plan accomplished. Score even. That's exactly what I set out to do.

Then why doesn't it feel as gratifying as I expected it to? No magic spell's been broken. Instead, I find myself even more captivated by him, even more addicted. I am overwhelmed by how he felt in my mouth, how he broke apart because of me.

I know almost instantly that my plan is very much flawed. Whatever possessed me to think it would work, to think I could do something so out of my comfort zone and not fuss over it, I have no idea. I'm not sure how to deal with this sudden onset of anxiety – one emotion I haven't felt in a very long time. I need to get out of here, ASAP.

I take a calming breath and manage to get my shoes back on, then make my way through the crowd to find Clara. Thankfully she is still in her bubble with Marcus, oblivious to anyone or anything around them, it seems. The rest of the wedding party appears to be just as oblivious – our temporary abandonment of the dance floor probably went entirely unnoticed.

I pull at Clara's arm and yell, "I'm feeling sick. All that wine at dinner, and then the martinis… I think I'm going to head home." God, I am such a bad liar.

"What?" Clara yells back, clearly unable to comprehend, even though that was the loudest I can be.

"Feeling. Sick." I say it slowly, then make a gagging gesture. "Home. Going home."

"You gonna be okay on your own?" she yells louder than necessary. Clearly she's had a bit too much to drink.

"Yeah, yeah. Just don't worry about me. I'll be fine." Though I seriously start to doubt that little affirmation.

"Where's Luke?" she asks expectantly.

"Luke?" I question, like I haven't seen him in a while. "No clue." I shrug innocently. The thought of him recovering on the rooftop after what must have been one of the most amazing mouth fucks ever makes me want to smile, though.

"I'll call you tomorrow," I say while giving her a quick hug. Then I scurry through the crowd, hoping not to run into Luke on my way out. I can't face him right now. I make it outside faster than humanly possible, and after hailing a cab, I feel safe in the confines of the four doors.

What the fuck happened up there, Conte? I thought I had it all figured out, a well-thought-out plan. It's not that my plan didn't work; I'm sure I have Luke hooked. It's just that it also backfired. As I relive the evening, from teasing him at dinner, to flirting on the dance floor, to the moments on the roof, I realize I am nowhere near where I thought I would be. Instead of the freedom I anticipated, I'm even more addicted. Running away from Luke did not bring me the relief I needed. Instead, it brought on more obsessive thinking, and panic at the realization that my girlish infatuation is more real than I was willing to admit. The little spark that ignited that first time I ran into him, the spark that caught fire at the movie theater, only became blazing hot tonight. I'm walking in uncharted territory. One wrong move and I am going to fall deeper than I ever anticipated, and way deeper than I want.

I'm determined to stick to the promise I made to myself after the fiasco with Jason. After he left me without much advance notice, I promised myself I'd live for me and not get distracted by the opposite sex ever again. But Luke makes me wonder if that promise is impossible to uphold. After all, I'm a woman with needs. And right now my needs appear to be selfish. They want Luke, and only Luke.

God, Tessa, this – whatever this is – was definitely not part of the plan! I have to face it: my Evil, Kick-Ass Plan is seriously and completely fucked. I need another plan, and fast. But after running through a handful of possible scenarios, I realize my options are pretty slim. I can't think of anything else but sticking with what I initially contemplated.

I'll just have to try to avoid Luke, even though I have a sneaky suspicion avoiding him till the wedding will be all but impossible. But I'll deal with that as it comes. And whatever these feelings are that are creeping over me will have to be buried deep down. The last thing I need is to fall head over heels for this guy. Pulling away is critical. Keeping the wounds closed is a must. That I know how to do. Surely I can manage it again.

Chapter 6

My sleep was … well, it was rather interesting: interrupted with thoughts of Luke, with the remnants of the sweet taste of him in my mouth, my realization haunting me in my dreams. I'm so confused about what my feelings may be telling me.

I'm not a fan of early mornings, but I love running. It helps me clear my mind and lets my thought-filled brain relax and absorb all that's happening around me. I don't normally think of the to-do lists; I just listen to my favorite songs and focus on the run. I stick to a routine most weekday mornings, whenever I'm not the one working the early shift. I'm up at seven, run my typical half-hour route, shower, have a bowl of Cheerios, and make my way to Lovely Cakes for nine. Just like a lot of things in my life, it's predictable. Orderly. Simple. I'm hoping this morning's run will help me sort out the mess in my head. It's mildly successful.

Thankfully there's always baking. I'm hoping that will hold my focus for the day and make my meandering thoughts break free for a bit. I have a ton of work ahead of me, especially with Clara's wedding a week away, amongst all sorts of other orders we have to finish. Keeping busy won't be a problem.

The sweet fragrance of Lovely Cakes is deliciously overpowering. It is my sanctuary, my little slice of heaven. Baking is my outlet and my passion; it's the one place where everything bottled up normally releases itself in beautiful creations. I love to plan out my masterpieces and then make them come to life with the skill of my hands. As a child, I was inspired by all the sweet things my nonna used to make. I baked my first cake when I was only eight and learned the decorating basics by the time I was ten just by observing and helping her.

The bakery is elegant yet cozy. The big bay windows on each side of the entrance bring warmth and brightness inside. They hold displays of our custom-designed cakes and showcase the variety that Lovely Cakes is locally famous for. Inside, white wainscoting and chocolate-brown walls make a warm, modern combination. There are colorful pictures of sweet indulgences and a board covered in the thank-you cards and pictures that we receive on a weekly basis. Along each side, there are a couple of small white tables with chairs where customers can sit down and indulge. Jars of loose leaf teas line a side counter, where customers can choose their favorite flavor or blend to go along with their dessert of choice. The glass counter near the back of the store displays cupcakes, cookies, and cake-pops, and behind the counter there's a small window that allows us to see customers coming into the store.

"Hey, sleepy head." Rose, my assistant, greets me with a warm smile as she catches me yawning as I get in the door. Thank goodness she's got my tea ready like always. "So how was last night?" she asks excitedly, fully expecting to hear the details of my plan's success. *If only...*

"Ugh," is all I say.

"That good, huh?"

Rose's sarcasm is not quite what I need today. I roll my eyes. "Don't ask."

"Come on, just tell me. You know it'll make you feel better."

"You're right. It always does," I admit.

As I start working on one of the orders for the week, I give her a detailed synopsis of the evening, from the teasing at dinner, to the dance floor, to the wild time on the rooftop, to my sudden rush to get out of there, to figuring out that I'm basically in a less-than-stellar predicament. Rose listens attentively, nods at the right times, and digs deeper whenever I manage to neglect to mention a few minor details.

"I mean, even a person with no commitment issues would probably think twice before getting involved with someone who will be back across the Atlantic in a few days. And you and I both know that long-distance relationships rarely work out." I give her a meaningful look. Of course I'm referring to Jason and his more than temporary move overseas. "Add commitment issues to the mix, and it's a concoction more complicated than some of the cakes we've made." I can't help but laugh nervously.

"Seems to me you're in deeper than you think," Rose says candidly when I'm finished my rambling.

"I thought you were supposed to help. That's not really helping."

She just shrugs. "Have you thought about talking to him, getting some answers?"

"I don't know if I can do that. I mean, every time I see him, it's as if the rational me disappears, and this new Tessa, one I've never met before, comes out from under her shell. How I even managed to follow through with the plan last night is beyond me. I was nearly ready to tear his clothes off."

"Well, you did do what you planned – sort of. But if I can just reiterate what I said when you came up with this plan of yours, did you seriously think it would work in the first place?" She shakes her head. "And you're crazy to think you can just avoid him for the rest of the week. You may have just upped the ante."

She's right. There's no hope in pretending Luke doesn't exist. The reality is that he's here for the next few days and I will just have to manage.

"I'll just … I'll figure it out. But there's no way I'm letting him get into my panties again." I'm still convinced, although perhaps delusional, that I can say no to Luke.

"Sure, sure. Let me know how *that* works out for you."

"Ugh! Forget it. Anyways, enough about me. How was your night?" I ask, desperate to change the subject.

"Oh, you know, as fun as always." She says that with the hint of sarcasm that I by now fully expect from Rose.

"Hey, come on. I just spent the last twenty minutes pouring my heart out, and this is all I get?"

She smiles, then dives into the details. Unlike me, who's avoided the opposite sex over the last few years, Rose has tried really hard to find love. "True love," as she likes to refer to it. Perhaps sometimes she tries too hard. Other times, I think she may be too blind to see what's dead center in front of her. Last night was one more of her speed-dating disasters.

Rose, a good friend of my cousin Liz, stopped by the bakery just a couple of months after I opened Lovely Cakes and asked if I needed help. I'm not sure what it was about her, but we clicked immediately. I felt comfortable offering her a job, possibly because she was Liz's friend, even though I didn't know her very well. Of course I made sure she was able to adequately answer a list of questions I had thoughtfully put together for purposes of interviewing potential candidates. Days turned into weeks, weeks turned into months, and we worked so well together that I've never looked back. She is an amazing assistant and a great friend. Over the last year, however, she's become more involved with an event planning business that she's been running on the side. It seems that working at the bakery has been a great way to meet new clientele, so her business has kind of flourished. Coincidentally, it goes hand in hand with generating more business for Lovely Cakes as well, so it's a win-win. As a matter of fact, she's the wedding planner for Clara and Marcus's wedding. She's so talented, I have no doubt it will be spectacular.

ROSE'S SQUEAL STARTLES ME. AT LEAST I THINK IT'S Rose. Her face is hidden by a giant bouquet of gerbera daisies. They're so bright and colorful.

"Um, Rose, what's this?"

Her big, honey-colored eyes peer from behind the bouquet. "They're for you!"

"Me?" I'm confused. Who would be sending me flowers?

I take the bouquet from her and place it on the table right next to the cake I'm working on, and then notice a small envelope that says, "Open me."

Our clients normally send thank-you cards, not giant bouquets. Rose is hovering over me, practically jumping like a four-year-old waiting to open her Christmas gift.

"Come on, open it!"

I take a moment to pull the card from the bouquet and dismiss the fact that my fingers are trembling slightly as I pry open the envelope. I have no idea why. I mean, it's just a card and a beautiful bouquet. It's not like I've never received one before.

Actually, now that I think about it, not really. Not during my time at Lovely Cakes, at least. So as I open the envelope, it feels as though I'm at the climax of a mystery novel.

You're unpredictable, cupcake.
Will you please go out with me?
LC

"So?" Rose snatches the card from between my fingers and reads it out loud, then looks up at me, confused. "Oh my god, is this from Luke?"

I nod, and against my better judgment, I smile. But I convince myself that the smile is not because I'm flattered or intrigued; rather, it's a result of the confirmation that my plan worked. Luke is hooked. Now he can enjoy the consequences.

"I told you. His kind is persistent." I'm not sure what "kind" she's referring to, but I do know she's got categories for the opposite sex. Several, actually.

"I am not going out with that asshole." I sound determined, but my palms are sweating for some weird reason. I wipe them on my apron and dismiss the bubbly feeling in my stomach. Luke wants me to go out with him. *After* last night.

I take the card back from her and, in what is probably an over-the-top reaction, tear it into tiny little pieces for effect. They flutter like confetti to the floor. I grab the bouquet and walk toward the garbage can.

"Nooo!" Rose's shriek stuns me momentarily. I look over at her, my eyes shooting daggers. "They're so beautiful," she cries out, as if she hasn't just heard me call Luke an asshole. "You can't throw them out. They're living things!" She's looking at me with her puppy-dog eyes again.

"Fine," I sigh, and she relaxes. I guess they are kind of pretty. I don't actually have the heart to throw them out. Because they are living things. They are not to blame for Luke's assholery. They'll look lovely among the display cakes. Until they die. Which they will. Like all lovely things.

Did you get the flowers?

It's a text from … Luke? How in the hell did he get my number? I can think of only two people who could be responsible for this: Clara and Marcus. Come to think of it, one of them must have also told him where I work – how else would he have known where to send the flowers in the first place? Luke appears to be on a mission. Good luck with that, Mr. Callaghan.

I may have, I reply.

Did you like them?

Hmm. I liked the flowers. I'm not sure I liked the offer that came with them. At least that's what I've been telling myself the entire afternoon, since said flowers arrived.

They were fine, I text back. There. That sounds like, "I'm not interested. Now let me get back to work."

A couple of minutes pass before there's another text. *Ugh!* Did he not get the message?

Did you get the card?

Of course. The card.

What card? I'm being purposefully obtuse.

The date card, he replies, and I can almost sense the frustration that's attached to the text.

There may have been a card, though it's suffered an untimely death. But he doesn't need to know that.

Yes, I got the card.

And?

And what? I text back.

Will you? Go on a date with me?

I'm surprised you'd even ask. How very nice of you. But no.

No?

No.

I just about think he's done when another text comes in.

Anything I can do to convince you?

No.

Luke appears to get the message, because I receive no more texts from him. Though, I have to admit, the exchange was kind of fun.

"I'M GOING TO GET SOME LUNCH," I TELL ROSE. "DID YOU want me to grab something for you too?"

"Sure, just get me the usual."

I head out to one of our favorite lunch spots and grab two chicken wraps and two strawberry-banana milkshakes. When I'm almost back at the bakery, my phone buzzes. A text from Rose.

Make it an hour.

Huh? I text her, confused.

Extend your lunch break, she texts back.

What?

Abort the return!

Why? I text back.

Code red! Certain someone is on his way out of the bakery. NOW!

Oh shit. I am three doors away from Lovely Cakes. I realize I failed to make a contingency plan for a face-to-face run-in with Luke. How did I not think of that? I scan my surroundings and scramble to figure out what to do. If I move forward, I'll run into him. So much for avoidance. If I move fast enough the other way, I may be able to lose him in the crowd. Maybe if I cross the street there will be enough separation to give me an advantage in case he decides to follow. My thinking is interrupted by a familiar voice yelling out, "Tessa?"

My head turns in the direction of the voice and our eyes lock. For a moment we hold onto the connection, and that strange, undefined *something* passes between us. I'm at a loss momentarily, because even though my head is resolute, my body responds with a need that I can't seem to control. I'm sixteen all over again and finding myself worked up from a simple glimpse of Luke.

"Wait!" I make out the movement of his mouth and hear him yell the word at the same time.

The call's enough of a reminder of my current predicament. I am so not waiting. Instead, I avert my gaze and break our exchange.

Shit. Why did I take the time to analyze the options? Note to self: Some situations require acting on impulse. And this is definitely one of those situations requiring reaction, not analysis.

I start jogging in the opposite direction. I'm holding on to the tray of milkshakes for dear life – the last thing I need is another Clumsy Tessa moment. My mind is racing. My heart is pounding in my chest. I'm a runner, but the adrenaline involved with this run is at a totally different level. This run is thrilling, adventurous. Kind of fun, actually.

What? Snap out of it, Conte! Right. We're one-for-one. Deal with it, Callaghan!

I take the next left because I know there's a coffee shop just around the corner. When I get inside, I make my way straight to the washroom. Not leaving this to chance, I actually go as far as locking myself in a stall, just in case Luke is intuitive enough (I wouldn't be surprised) and decides to burst in through the door clearly marked WOMEN. And so I sit on the toilet, wait, and think. *Really, Tessa? Hiding in the washroom?* I burst out laughing. This is ridiculous. Still, I'm beyond thankful to have a great employee-slash-friend in Rose.

I take a moment to text her back.

Disaster averted. Thanks for saving my ass.

What are friends for?

She definitely earns cupcake points for the warning. And a day off too.

IT'S ALMOST EIGHT WHEN I GET HOME AFTER WHAT'S turned out to be a really busy Saturday, which is not surprising given that it's July, a prime time for all sorts of celebrations. As I make my way down the hallway that leads to my door, I notice a gift bag hanging off the door handle. Attached to the bag – which contains a box of chocolate truffles, incidentally – is a card that reads "Truce?"

Did he break into my building? Jesus! I'm beginning to think his persistence borders on stalking. Also, I need to talk to Clara and Marcus about sharing my personal information. This has got to stop.

For a moment, I actually consider what he's asking. Truce? Maybe. But that's all I'm willing to give him. Perhaps I should stop acting like a child and not be so apprehensive about facing him again. No running away, no hiding in washroom stalls. After all, I'm a strong, independent woman. I can take care of myself. I can make rational decisions. Going out on a date with Luke is not rational. That's that.

I decide I'm not going to dwell on this anymore tonight. I'm tired and ready for bed. Not even a romance novel will keep me up right now. Except maybe I'll just take a moment to taste one of the truffles. I pop one in my mouth and god, it's so heavenly I whimper a little bit. This calls for seconds.

After my bedtime routine, I cozy up in bed and am nearly ready to visit dreamland when my phone buzzes. I snatch it off the nightstand and with one scroll see a by now familiar number.

Sweet dreams, cupcake.

I don't respond, but I can't help smiling as I drift off to sleep, thinking of Luke and cupcakes and all things sweet and dreamy.

Chapter 7

I made it through Saturday with determination. Luke may be persistent and border-line stalkerish, but I'm resolute. I'm hoping he'll realize I have no interest in going out with him. I'm hoping he'll conclude it's futile to try to win me over. He's only here for a few days leading up to the wedding, and then he'll be back in London. What would be the point anyway?

But it appears Luke and I don't see eye to eye on this topic. I'm just about to head out for my morning run when an incoming text startles me.

It's a new day. Go out with me. Please.

I give it a moment's thought. But alas, just as it did last night, logic prevails.

Not in this lifetime.

We'll see.

Whatever. I have an urge to respond with a snarky reply, but I don't. Instead, I head out of my apartment and do what I enjoy every morning. I'm not going to let some guy take over my thoughts. Not going to happen.

This morning's run is kind of frustrating, though. I can't shut off my brain like I normally do. Some annoyingly hot guy's taken over not only my dreams, it appears, but also my thoughts. When I get back, the first thing I do is sit down and write a list. A list of pros and cons of saying yes to a certain someone's offer. A list will help me keep things straight and stay strong in case there are any additional attempts by said someone at wooing me again. The flowers and chocolates were a nice touch, though.

"I'LL BE RIGHT BACK," I SAY TO ROSE AS I MAKE MY WAY to the front of the store carrying freshly baked cupcakes. I'm wearing my favorite pink apron, which has "Life is sweeter with a cupcake!" written across it. That's my motto.

As I put the cupcakes into the display case, I manage to get some strawberry icing on my index finger. I take a quick lick, savoring the sweetness, just as the front door chimes.

"Hey there, cupcake." I hear a deep voice, the one I could recognize in my sleep.

I look up and freeze at the sight of two familiar eyes locked on me and my finger-licking mouth. Oh god, he's here, in my little slice of heaven. And then my heart kicks in, feeling like it's ready to jump right out of my chest. Not surprisingly, the insta-lust kicks in too. Especially since I've seen his you-know-what.

An image flashes in my head and I feel my body respond. And all he's done is said three words. *Three words.* I hate the fact I have so little self-control around him. Mentally I give myself a pep talk: He is not at all intimidating. I can do this. I can face him and not think of him in any way as delicious, sexy, hard… *Snap out of it, Conte.*

"Hi," I whisper, then gather the composure that was apparently taking a break. "What are you doing here?"

"You are one hard woman to convince. I figured an in-person visit may be my best bet. Though even that has proven to be harder than I thought." I smile briefly because obviously he was here yesterday and he's stopped by my apartment too, yet I've been able to evade him on both occasions. But I pull it back before it becomes a full-on grin. Self-control with guys like this is an absolute must.

"Try me," I challenge. I am so not going out with him. The list I made this morning flashes in my mind, the con side loaded with emphatic exclamation marks and heavily underlined warnings. I'm armed and ready.

Luke takes a moment, as if he's collecting his thoughts. It's kind of cute seeing him mentally struggle with his choice of words, when he normally just says what he thinks.

"Listen, I know you think I'm a prick for doing what I did." I interrupt before he's able to say another word. "I don't think it. You *are*." Point: Tessa.

"Right, right." He sighs. I think he realizes I'm not going to make this easy on him. "I *know* I'm a prick for doing what I did, for leaving without giving you any kind of explanation."

"I'm all ears." My arms are crossed and my expression is stoic. On the surface, at least.

"I'm sorry for how I left things. I'm sorry I didn't have the guts to explain, but I didn't really have a choice."

He'll have to try harder than this. "No," I interrupt again, "you did. You just didn't make the right one."

"It's just... What was I supposed to do? Call you and say, 'Hey Tessa, I'm sorry I left without saying a word after we fooled around. But you know, it was all in good fun. No hard feelings, right?' *That* would have made me sound like an ass."

"*That* is not helping you make your case."

"I know. I'm sorry. But it's not like I didn't try."

"Try what?" I'm confused.

"Seeing you again. When I came back around New Year's, hoping that I would see you, *in person*," he makes a point as if to emphasize he didn't want to talk to me any other way, "your sister was kind enough to mention that you were away somewhere warm and sunny."

Oh, right. The time I actually decided to take a week off and spend New Year's in Costa Rica. I may have been under the influence of the guy who's standing in front of me and his outlook on life. So I decided to take an actual vacation and travel somewhere new and exciting. Unfortunate timing. Clara never mentioned anything either. He must have asked very inconspicuously for her curious mind not to catch on.

"It's been eating at me, how I left things that night. Trust me, I wanted to set things straight, but it just never worked out. I really am sorry for what I did, for how things played out, but I couldn't help it. Your scent, your lips, your body... God, everything about you that night was so tempting, so difficult to resist. Everything about you still is. I've fantasized about you before, but nothing even came close to what you did at the club. Something about you just does things to me."

He looks down, like he's unsure of himself, of how I'll react to his confession. That is not the Luke I remember. This little glimpse of vulnerability, combined with the feelings he's just spelled out, is kind of … hot. The fact that he fantasized about me – even hotter.

He's genuinely trying to apologize. Isn't that all I wanted from him in the first place? I've known for a while now that he's in London. I also know I'm probably not being entirely fair to him. I just didn't want him to be *that* guy, the guy who fools around and then makes a clean getaway. A player. We'd made such a connection – in the car, during dinner, and, well, after – that I guess I'd foolishly thought he couldn't possibly be that guy. I'd hoped he'd find a way to prove he wasn't. I wanted to hear him say he's sorry. But now that he has – now what?

"If it's any consolation, I'm here now, and life is sweeter seeing you again, Tessa. And don't even try to deny that you don't feel it too. I can see it in those gorgeous eyes of yours. Every time you look at me."

Look at that – the confident Luke is back. And just as hot.

"I'm not sure what I'm feeling … yet." I'm confused by my own emotions, my own thoughts. Is it anger? Lust? Infatuation? Fear?

I'm pretty sure I'm past anger at this point. I realize that was kind of childish of me. I'm twenty-six, not sixteen. I'm also pretty sure that I've been craving Luke, even though I've tried very hard to suppress that notion. So, definitely lust and infatuation.

I take a moment to glance over at him, and what I think I see is a hopeful look on his face. He really wants another chance. Can I give it to him? Is there any point? Am I ready to open myself up to the possibilities? Or am I just opening up a Pandora's box of memories and emotions I don't ever want to experience again?

Definitely fear.

Luke must see right through me. It's like he senses my quandary, because he doesn't let me delve a moment longer. "Can we just start over again, please? One date. That's all I'm asking for. After that, you can decide if you want to see me again or if you'd rather send me packing. And I mean that in the most literal sense."

I'm well aware that he'll be packing in just over a week. Whether or not I want him to. That's exactly the problem.

So of course it's not surprising that I can almost hear my mind screaming, *"For your own sake, Tessa, don't go there!"* Meanwhile, my panties are, well, panting, *"Yes! Yes! Yesss!"* This is quickly becoming a familiar and nerve-wracking pattern. I need a minute to process.

His proposition is tempting. I know I said I wouldn't cave – in fact, I have a whole list of reasons why saying yes to Luke is a bad idea. I remind myself of a few so that I can stay resolute: He exhibits player-like tendencies (though I do need to confirm my presumption). He messed with me once; he may do it again. He's stubborn. He's physically unavailable (he lives across the Atlantic, after all); emotionally too, perhaps. He's too easy-going and too impulsive – I doubt he's ever thought of making a list about anything. He doesn't seem to think about the consequences of his actions, or at least that's what I thought this morning.

But I would be lying to myself if I didn't acknowledge that I do feel something too. After all, the list did include some pros of saying yes to Luke. Several, actually. He's kind of hot (okay, a *lot* hot). He's educated. He's adventurous. He's fun to talk to, easy to listen to, and quite charming. He can *really* dance. He's hot. (Yes, it was worth jotting down twice). He also has magic fingers – at least that's how I remember them. Oh, and a giant cock that I seem to really enjoy (bonus). He smells yummy and loves cupcakes. Extra points for that. He did come looking for me, and he apologized. *Genuinely* apologized. Maybe he does have a conscience after all.

Perhaps, in the spirit of fairness and as per my list, I should give him a chance. Without committing to too much. But I can't come across as too eager. It would quash everything I've worked so hard for.

"Okay. Fine."

"Fine?"

"Fine, I'll go out with you. One date. That's all I'm committing to."

"I'll take it." He's grinning. Like a smug I-knew-you-were-going-to-cave-eventually kind of grin.

"That smirk looks too cocky," I point out. "Better take it down a notch. You wouldn't want to get your hopes up, now, would you?"

"Oh, my hopes have been up for a while now. Can't help it. I like when things work out my way."

"I said just one date, didn't I?" I need to show him I control the outcome.

"You did. But I don't think you'll be able to resist my charms."

"Pfft. Whatever." But what I'm really thinking is, *God, he's so delicious. How will I ever say no to him again?*

"Maybe we can have dinner?"

"Sure. When?"

"Tonight."

"Tonight?" I didn't expect it to happen so soon.

"Need I remind you I leave for London next Monday? Really working against the clock here."

"Right. Makes sense. Tonight it is, then."

"I'll pick you up at six thirty?"

"Sounds good. So…" I guess this is it? I don't want him to leave just yet. Because he's sort of pleasing to the eye. I scramble to find something else to say. *Just think of him as a customer.* "Is there anything else I can help you with today, seeing as I've already been more than helpful in responding to your needs?"

He chuckles. I wonder if he finds me funny.

"You most definitely can. I may have a soft spot for cupcakes. And icing. Kind of obsessed, actually," he says with a crooked grin, his eyes never leaving mine, making my cheeks flush. "Any suggestion on which one I should get?"

I definitely have a suggestion. I point to the display case. "Strawberry chocolate is one of our bestsellers and my favorite."

"I think that may actually be just what I'm after."

"Great. One cupcake coming right up." I lift one out, place it in a box, and seal it with one of our Lovely Cakes stickers. "Enjoy!" I say with a sweet smile as I hand over the package, my fingers trembling ever so slightly. *Calm down. It's just a date.*

"Oh, it's not actually for me." I give him a confused look. "I mean, it kind of is. Never mind. I'm sure, though, it will be enjoyed. Plenty." He winks suggestively.

My curiosity is piqued, and I wonder who the cupcake is for. He's probably visiting an old friend, or maybe his grandma. I bet she'll enjoy it. But I don't want to pry, so I leave it at that.

"Well, I guess I'd better make you pay. For the cupcake, that is." I grin devilishly because, let's face it, I've already made him pay enough.

"Of course. I'd hate to be an asshole who runs off without paying." He totally gets it.

When he finishes paying for the cupcake, I'm caught off guard by what he does next. He leans over the cash register and, with the tip of his thumb, reaches for the corner of my mouth, sweeping against my lips. The rest of his fingers cup my chin while he rubs my lower lip with his thumb. I stand there, captivated by his touch, unable to move. My toes are curling and my skin is tingling. I can't help it. My mind wanders off, remembering what his fingers did to me months ago, and I want them again. Down there. *Ugh!* He's trouble.

Luke's deep voice quickly brings me out of my daydream and back to reality. "A bit of icing. There, all gone now. Seems as though I'm always rescuing you from messy situations." He smirks, leaving me dazed and speechless. The slightest touch from him has such a profound effect on me. "Mmm, that's sweet," he says as he licks the little bit of icing that's stuck to his thumb.

This is when I know I'm overly analytical, because I start to wonder if he's referring to the icing he just tasted or the taste of my lips on his thumb. I mean, it's almost like we kissed. And then I'm blushing, not because of the sensual display in front of me (well, maybe a little bit), but because I realize I must have looked like a dork all this time, talking and grinning with pink icing stuck to my mouth. *Note to self: Install a mirror above the sink.*

"I'll see you later, then," he says as he backs away and walks toward the door.

"Later, stranger." I stare after him, enthralled.

Oh shit. Where is he taking me? What should I wear? A list of questions fills my head. Before I'm able to ask him, he's out the door. I hate not being prepared. But my phone buzzes, and this time I'm actually hoping it's from him.

Wear something as pretty as your eyes.

I smile at his text. He thinks I have pretty eyes. And then the nerves hit me. How am I going to get through the day knowing I'm going out on a date, an actual date, with none other than my delicious stranger?

Chapter 8

"You need to loosen up, Tessa, or your brain's going to explode all over the bakery, and that would not be pretty." Rose interrupts my thoughts, which is welcome because the day seems to be dragging on as I try not to think about seeing Luke tonight. And fail. I'm excited and nervous and having trouble focusing. I'm a wreck.

"Umm, gross. Thanks for painting that picture." I grimace in disgust.

"Relax. I'm sure it will all work out fine," she continues.

How can she be sure? So far our encounters have been physical and intense. I still can't quite figure out who Luke is. My mind is telling me that he's a player and that I should tread carefully, but it's also telling me he's anything but. The pull I feel when I'm around him is indescribable. He's like a magnet, and I am undeniably drawn to him. When we're together, everything else seems to disappear. It's just him and me and our little bubble, though so far it's been a very sexually charged bubble. I need to know if there is more to him, to us, than pure physical attraction.

"You're right. I'm just not sure what to expect. What if we totally don't click and end up sitting through an entire dinner with nothing to say? God, that would be horrible." I clench my teeth, feeling a sense of panic. I hate the quiet. It makes me uncomfortable. No matter who I'm with, I'm always nervous that there will be that weird silence and we'll have nothing to talk about. So I compensate by over-sharing – anything to keep the conversation going, even if it ends up being one-sided. And I hate when that happens even more.

"Tessa, you obviously like him," Rose says matter-of-factly.

"Is it *that* obvious?"

"A little. You wouldn't be this frazzled if you didn't. Have you considered just going with the flow and not stressing out over what's going to happen tonight?" It's easy for her to say. She's an expert in first dates.

"Trust me, I have, and I wish it were that easy for me. You know how obsessive I get. I overthink pretty much everything that has any importance in my life."

"Are you suggesting that he's important?"

"I don't know. Maybe?" I'm unsure of my own answer because he can't be. I barely know him. "It sounds so ridiculous, but I've thought of him pretty much daily since the first time I ran into him. And even more since the last time I saw him. I seriously think there's something wrong with me. But then I thought I had it all figured out and under control. I thought I was going to be able to break free. And now that he's here again and has asked me on a date, I'm going crazy wondering if I've been given yet another chance with him for a reason. I don't know if I can trust myself not to ruin it all with my inability to just let things play out." I ramble on in a state of panic as the messy emotions that have built up over the last few hours explode. "And what should I be expecting from all of this? He's only here until after the wedding, and then what? He'll be gone, and I'll be left wondering why I wasn't able to reason myself out of feeling anything so that I could just go on with my life as if he'd never entered it in the first place! I don't want to have to go through that again."

"Okay, now look at me." Rose grasps my shoulders and looks me straight in the eyes. "Take a deep breath. Here, have a sip of water." She hands me a glass that I don't even recall her filling. I nod and do as I'm told, feeling slightly more under control. Slightly more like normal me. Where did that Tessa disappear to just a moment ago?

"Tessa, you can't predict what's going to happen. You don't even really know Luke. The one thing you should know is that he's not Jason. And I'm telling you right now, you would be crazy not to let yourself take a chance on something that could turn out to be fun. And who knows, maybe even something you'll be able to hold on to? This is only going to get as serious as you make it. Even if it ends up being just a fling, so what? Give yourself that chance. Live a little."

A fling. That's probably all this could ever be. That's all I can take right now; that's all I can give. That's probably all Luke is really thinking too. There's no way he's even considering an emotional attachment of sorts.

Rose is fully aware of my experience with Jason and my resulting aversion to the opposite sex, though there's no way she could quite understand how frightening it all sounds to me. But it's like she's the voice of reason I'm currently lacking. I know I have to do just as she said. The fact that I just blew up in front of her means I am far less likely to freak out in front of Luke tonight. Good start, at least.

"Thanks. You're always able to put things into perspective for me. And you're right. I have to give this a chance, for whatever it's worth. Even if it is just a fling."

WHEN FIVE O'CLOCK STRIKES, I RUSH HOME LIKE someone's chasing me. As I shower, Luke's words echo in my mind: *Wear something as pretty as your eyes.* Translating guy-speak into an appropriate wardrobe selection is not as easy as I thought it would be.

I methodically select a few dresses that seem to fit his request, but I can't decide what I want to wear. Is the dress too casual, too formal? Too sexy, not sexy enough? Do I want him to drool or do I want to have a meaningful conversation? Is the color right? Ugh.

Eventually, I settle on a flowy, knee-length dark red dress that complements my eyes. The bodice criss-crosses above the wide-banded waist, leaving sexy openings above my belly button and my lower back. It's pretty but flirtatious enough to make Luke drool. I hope.

Wait, why do I hope? I'm analyzing this when my intercom buzzes.

"I'm downstairs. You ready?" Luke asks.

The heaviness of his simple question resonates with me. Am I ready? Yes, I'm dressed and dolled up, but am I really ready for a date with Luke? My heart is pounding with anticipation and panic at the same time. I try to steady my voice before I respond, "As ready as I'll ever be."

"Good. Because I can't wait to see you."

I realize I'm grinning like an idiot as I buzz him in.

When I open the door, I'm faced with Mr. Delicious. He's looking down at me, his shoulder pressed against the door frame and his legs crossed casually. He's handsomely put together in a light pair of pants and a dark button-up shirt with rolled-up sleeves that accentuate his muscular forearms. I inhale that freshly showered scent of his and instantly feel weak at the knees.

"Hey, stranger," I breathe, clearly smitten.

"Hey." His eyes are on me, traveling from top to bottom. "That's quite the dress."

I can't help but smile. "You like?"

"Like? Tessa, you look incredible."

"Thanks." I feel myself blush.

He takes a step closer, and then his lips meet my cheek. His kiss is short, but lingering. When his lips leave my skin, the spot burns. I open my eyes and see him smile smugly. He's such a tease.

When we get to the car, which Luke has borrowed from Marcus for the night, he opens the door for me. As I'm about to sit down, I notice a shiny silver gift bag with a pink twirly ribbon on it waiting patiently on my seat.

"For me?" I point to the bag before sitting down.

"Maybe," he teases. I'm starting to realize Luke likes being playful, and I also realize I most definitely like it. "If all goes as planned."

"Oh, I see." I pause, mulling over my response before saying it out loud. I go for it anyway. "For what it's worth, I really hope it does. Otherwise, I'm not sure I'll be able to go on with my life wondering what could have been." I gaze longingly at the gift, wondering if he gets the double meaning.

"I'm sure it will, so no worries there. I have a good feeling about tonight."

Chapter 9

Luke's made reservations at one of my favorite Italian restaurants in the Loop. I'm guessing he picked up that little factoid from Clara along with all my other vital statistics. Or maybe I just need to stop analyzing every move he's making and go with the flow. It's just dinner, after all.

The restaurant is authentic and romantic and it smells like heaven. I'm immediately taken back to childhood memories of my visits to Italy, of the charming beauty of the Italian Riviera, of the countless summer days spent at Nonna's house.

While we're deciding what to order, I take a moment to peek at – or, more accurately, swoon over – Luke while he's analyzing the menu in front of him. He's rubbing his index finger against his lips, deep in thought, as his chin rests on his thumb. God, those lips…

Luke peeks over his menu, catching my not-so-subtle ogling. I'm so busted.

"Are you secretly spying on me?"

"Who, me?"

"Yes. You."

"Hmm, maybe."

"You see something you like?" he asks, his index finger still rubbing his lip absentmindedly. He really needs to stop that. It's kind of distracting. It's a good thing the table is separating

us, because I cannot be held responsible for any socially inappropriate actions when faced with this male form of sex-on-a-stick. "Maybe a bit more than I anticipated." I smile while holding his gaze, then say flirtatiously, "I'll have the lobster risotto. Mm-hmm, I'd definitely like that."
"Well played, Ms. Conte."
"There's more where that came from."
"Then tell me more. I'd really like to know more about you, Tessa."
This is one of the reasons I was panicking earlier today. I knew this question would probably come up at some point tonight. I thought about what I would say to make sure I didn't come across as, well, me. But I am who I am. No need to hide. Though I can't help but wonder if my response might scare him off before the main course arrives.
"There's not much to know. I'm twenty-six and I'm single. I'm an obsessive overthinker, planner, and perfectionist. I make lists – for *everything*." I might have made a list of key points to discuss tonight in case things got awkwardly quiet. Not that it's one of those moments right now, but it's good to be prepared. "I very rarely let emotions get in the way. I like my personal space. I'm generally talkative, especially when I'm not smitten by delicious, sexy strangers." Luke smirks. He's fully aware which sexy stranger I'm referring to. "And as you probably already know, I'm pretty creative," I say matter-of-factly, nervously picking at my polished nails. "So yeah, that's me."
The hills are waiting. Run for your life, Luke. But he doesn't.
"That all sounds very appealing to me." He's actually dead serious. "Especially the 'single' part. Thinking things through just means you've got a good head on your shoulders, which I admire. Emotions can cloud judgment, so I can understand that. You're adorable when you talk, albeit inarticulately at times, to delicious, sexy strangers. Your creative side … I can think of a few things we could do with that."
I like where this is going. I also like how forward Luke is, how comfortable he is saying whatever's on his mind. And

frankly, I'm a little bit shocked at how accepting he is of me and my quirks.

"But what intrigues me the most," he continues, "are the lists."

Of course.

"It's just a little something to help me keep my life organized, to help me make decisions. No big deal, really. It's just the way I work." I smile, trying not to make it sound like I'm some sort of freak, when clearly I may need help.

Luke is contemplating something, I can sense it. "So, is there a list for me? Did you make one to help you decide whether to go on a date with me?"

He's so intuitive. To tell the truth, or not?

"There may be a list." I smile. "Or maybe two."

He's about to say something else, but I stop him before it comes out. Because it doesn't take a rocket scientist to know what he's going to ask next.

"No, no, no. There's no way."

"What?" he pleads innocently.

"There's no way I'm letting you see the lists." I should have lied.

"I wasn't going to ask, I swear," Luke laughs. "I think it's kind of cute."

"Sure you weren't. You make me seem like less of a freak, but you should really run for the hills," I suggest, giving him one last chance.

"No way am I running from you. I think you're kind of stuck with me, whether you like it or not," he jokes. But underneath that sexy grin, he seems more serious than he lets on. Maybe he really isn't a Jason. Maybe he's more of a Luke.

"Suit yourself, and don't say I didn't warn you."

"Duly noted." He doesn't seem to be taking my warning seriously, at all. But that doesn't really surprise me.

"So how about you?" I ask, hoping to move past the topic of lists.

"Let's see. I'm twenty-eight and single. I let emotions guide my decisions more often than I care to admit. I like to cuddle – *a lot*, but mainly with Elsie. My Lab," he clarifies, after catching the confused look on my face. "I act on instinct, I say what's on my mind, and I love adventures of all sorts." He's nothing like me, yet I'm intrigued because he's so different. "Oh, and I'm also pretty stubborn."

I'm guessing he's referring to his persistence in coercing me to go on a date with him. Hmm. Maybe *I* should run for the hills.

"That you are," I reply, earning a mischievous smirk. Those really look nice on him.

"It's served me well. Especially leading up to tonight."

"One date," I remind him.

"That remains to be seen. If you ask me, I think we may just be cut out for each other."

Perhaps he's right. Perhaps we may in fact be right for each other. I am endearingly attracted to all things Luke, it appears. At least from what I've been able to learn in the short time we've know each other. Which really hasn't been very long at all.

"Perhaps." Luke may act on instinct, but I, on the other hand, need solid proof.

"I bet if you found out more about me, you'd like what you saw. I know we don't have a lot of time, so we could pretend to be on one of those speed-dating dates. I ask a question, you ask a question. No rules."

"Okay. That sounds like fun." Rose's stories have left me apprehensive about this sort of thing. She's met some less than stellar men, so they don't seem to produce any lasting results for her. But I'll give Luke a chance.

"Ready?"

"As ready as I'll ever be."

"So, what I'm really, really dying to know is where you're most ticklish."

Well, that's different. Not the question I expected, at all, but not surprising either from this guy.

"Kind of everywhere, but especially around my belly button." I squirm just thinking about it. He smiles like he just got an idea. Possibly a naughty one. "You?"

"Below my ear."

I make a mental note. I could use it to my advantage.

"Okay, my turn." I try to think of a question that's as unexpected as his was, but can't come up with anything better than, "Are you a morning person or a night owl?"

"Definitely a morning person. I like to get my morning started bright and early. Get on with the day. That's when Elise and I normally go out for a run." So he is a runner. I remember the way his muscles felt under my hand at dinner on Friday night. I remember wondering how he got so fit. I'd like to feel the weight of those muscles on top of me, skin on skin. Focus!

"How about you?"

"I'm not really a morning person." I grin. "I kind of like my sleep. But still, I stick with morning runs too. They're energizing, and part of my routine."

"We should do it together sometime."

"That would be nice." Yes, so very nice. Running together. Seeing him breathing hard. Sweaty. Focused. While we take a detour. Oh my gosh, what is wrong with me?

"My turn." Luke's obviously not thinking of detours. "The most spontaneous thing you've ever done?"

"Hmm, that's a tough question."

"Really?"

"It is. For me."

"Because you like your lists." I know he's teasing, but I don't mind it.

"I do like my lists. I think I was more spontaneous when I was younger. Though Clara was the impetus for most of it. I normally just followed suit." Not sure where that Tessa disappeared to over the years.

"We'll have to do something about those lists of yours."

"You don't ever make any?" He shakes his head. "For the love of cupcakes, how do you keep your life organized?"

He laughs. "I guess I just do what makes sense in the moment. It may get a bit messy at times, but ultimately, things line up and work out as intended."

"That's an interesting perspective. Have they? Worked out, I mean."

He thinks for a moment. "For the most part." But there's a hint of hesitation when he says it. I wonder why. "But back to the question. Anything?"

Now I'm the one thinking for a moment. I know exactly what it is. And I'm about to admit it ... then hope I can escape unnoticed. "Fine. The movie. Your magic fingers." I feel myself blushing.

That earns me a sly grin. If I'm reading him correctly, he may be just a tad bit proud that's the case.

"*Magic* fingers?"

"Yes. I've thought of them a lot over the past several months, actually. I may have been craving them since. So yeah, magic." And I should probably stop spouting words before I embarrass myself even more.

"Good to know." That sly grin is still plastered on his face. And I'm a little frazzled. Because one, his smile makes him way too attractive, and I can't seem to take my eyes off him. And two, we're talking about his fingers. Enough said.

"How about you? Any spontaneous experiences?"

"Lots," he states matter-of-factly. Just as I thought.

We continue our conversation with ease. No weird silences that I want to fill with irrelevant nonsense. Luke's engaging, easy to talk to, and easy to listen to. He's thoughtful and funny and bright. Also, too good to be true. Why is he still single?

We talk about everything, from his life in London, his work, and how much he enjoys traveling to my love of baking, opening my own business, and what made me do so in the first place. I tell him about my childhood summers in Italy and how I learned the art of baking and cake decorating from my nonna. I tell him about how much I loved visiting and how much I miss being there.

Luke studies me for a minute, his eyes searching mine, taking me in.

"Tessa, I really, really like you." He reaches for my hands and pulls them toward him, entwining his fingers with mine. His touch feels so welcoming to my skin, it's arousing all my senses. He's opening up some very foreign feelings that have been tucked in neatly for years. I don't know if I should embrace them or escape through the washroom window, head to Lovely Cakes, and bake a cake instead. My safe house.

"And forward," I say after a moment's thought. He looks at me, confused. "Another trait of yours," I explain. "You're very forward, but I don't mind it one bit. I'd rather you be honest and open with me than hold things back."

Jason was never this forward. That's why his decision to move overseas totally took me by surprise. That's why the fact he never came back was a difficult pill to swallow. I don't think I ever knew the real Jason. I feel like I've gotten to know Luke in the few hours we've spent together better than I ever knew Jason. They are complete opposites. Luke's forwardness, his honesty – it's refreshing.

"See, you already know me so well."

"Maybe." I smile as I take a bite of my dessert. "Oh my god, this is so good. You have got to try this."

He's looking at me weirdly, but I'm probably just misinterpreting his expression. Maybe it's curiosity. Or something else entirely. After all, it's hard to know what exactly is going through another person's mind.

"Sorry, I'm talking too much, aren't I?" I ask with an embarrassed smile, noticing his eyes are directed at my lips. Just that look, the way he's watching my mouth move, it's deliciously unsettling.

"Not at all. I love listening to you talk and watching the way words roll off your lips." He grins a sexy, crooked grin that nearly leaves me breathless. I instinctively touch my bottom lip, imagining his touch. "Speaking of lips, I'd kind of like to kiss yours. I bet they'd taste fucking sweet as icing."

I am so caught off guard by his comment, I struggle to respond. All that repeats in my mind are his words. The memory of him wiping icing off my lips crosses my mind, and suddenly all I can think of is how much I want to taste his lips too. I'm also suddenly very, very hot. Isn't the air conditioning on in here?

"And yes, I'd very much like to try a bite. Of the dessert."

"Oh, dessert. Right," I mumble, and Luke chuckles. I forgot I made an offer in the first place. I extend my fork and he takes a bite. Like, in slow motion, or at least it appears so in my possibly distorted reality. All I can focus on is the way he tastes the cake. I wish that fork was my lips. Or my nipples. Or my...

"How's the dessert?" The waiter's words pull me out of my trance. The timing cannot be more unfortunate, but also perfect, because it's just the break I need to cool off. The cooling-off means my brain has a chance to think. Though that's not always a good thing.

Case in point: My insecurities get the better of me and I can't figure out whether Luke is being genuine or whether he just wants to get into my panties. I remind myself that I really don't know him that well yet, and from what I recall, he did play me, despite his excuse. He's also very charming – probably something he's practiced and perfected over time, right? Though for whatever reason, I'd like to think his words are real and meant just for me.

"Is this how you get all the women to fall for you?" I'm sure he notices the unease with which I ask. I fully expect that he uses his charm to make women swoon. He certainly has that effect on me.

"What do you mean?" He appears to be genuinely taken aback by my question.

"You know, saying all the right things?"

"Tessa, don't even think that, not for one fucking second." Uh-oh, I may have hit a nerve. He sounds annoyed. "What I say is meant for you and only you. You should know by now that I say it the way it is."

"Sorry, it's just ... it's hard for me to know. I've only known you for a couple of days, and I'm not sure what to think," I clarify.

"Don't overthink it. Just take it for what it is."

As if that's ever been easy for me. "Okay," I say softly, but I struggle to convince myself.

"Does this mean you're falling for me?" he asks, grinning ear to ear.

Yes ... no ... maybe? Just this morning I was sure I wasn't even going to go out with him, even though I've secretly obsessed over him for too long. But the bubbly feeling in my belly is telling me that maybe I am. Of course, there's no way I'm going to let him know that. He'll have to try harder to convince me.

"Me? Never," I tease, taking a forkful of cake.

"Never say never, Tess."

Tess. Only my dad has ever called me by that nickname. As a matter of fact, I'm pretty sure that if anybody else tried to, it would bother me immensely. But Luke saying it feels nice. So I don't try to correct him. I just let myself be Tess to him.

"Umm, so where were we?" I'm trying to get back to what we were talking about just a few minutes ago. Honestly, I haven't the slightest clue.

"You were telling me about your summers in Italy," Luke acknowledges.

"Right, Italy," I confirm, clearing my throat.

"So when's the last time you visited?"

"It's been a while. We haven't been back for several years. Since before my dad died."

"I'm sorry to hear about your dad, Tess."

"Life happens. Sometimes not quite the way we expect it. Good and bad." I don't want to get into the details of my dad's death at this time. I don't want him to know just how much it affected me emotionally.

"Yeah, tell me about it," he says, as if he knows exactly where I'm coming from. I wonder what's behind the understanding that I recognize. I want to find out more, but at the same time I don't want to pry.

It's like he can read my mind, because the next thing he says is, "I know what it's like to lose a parent."

"Oh?"

"Not in a literal sense. Not like when a parent dies. But my mom left, so ... it might as well be the same, only it's different, because it was a choice she made." There's a roughness to his voice that betrays his anger.

"Left?"

"Well, cheated on my dad first. Then took off without so much as a goodbye."

"I'm so sorry to hear that." It's difficult to imagine that someone who comes across as confident and lighthearted as Luke has been affected by something so difficult.

"Hey, let's just forget about it, it's not important." He's closed himself off, uncharacteristically, but I can sense it's more important than he's letting on. Losing a parent, no matter how, is a traumatizing experience. He's not showing it, though. And although I know there's more to this story than he's ready to share, I don't want to open up the wounds any further. His or mine.

"You were saying," he prompts.

"My nonna passed away a couple of years before my dad," I continue, "so we haven't visited since."

"How come?"

"It just never seemed like a good time to go back. But I really miss it sometimes, you know? I miss being there. It was just such a big part of my childhood. It really shaped who I am today."

"Do you speak any Italian?"

"I do some, but not so much anymore. I understand most of it, but it would take a bit of a refresher to speak it fluently again. Since my dad died, there hasn't been much Italian spoken around the house."

"Well, I'm sure you'll make it back for a visit one day," he says reassuringly.

"I hope so. But I'd like to see more of England too. I don't remember much of it from the one time we visited. I've been meaning to go back."

"Tell you what. I have yet to visit Italy. You haven't been to England in a really long time. We could do it together one day. We'll make it a three-week date. That way you'll have your personal tour guide, and I'll have mine. You can show me all that is beautiful about Italy and I can show you all there is to see in England." He's positively excited, our previous conversation forgotten or purposefully strayed from. "What do you say?"

"I thought we were starting with one date. Here you are planning three more weeks? Pfft! I'm not that easily convinced," I tease, but it's just a way for me to deflect the girlish infatuation I'm feeling with the idea. Is he being serious? The thought of spending more time with Luke, and the thought of it being on a trip through Europe, is enticing, I have to admit. He'd be a very sexy– I mean informative tour guide. Especially if the tour involved exploring more of Luke, and his body, and his cock– *Argh!* I mean Europe.

"Then I'll make sure I spend the rest of the night convincing you."

See? Unfazed. I love that about him. No no no – I mean I *like* that about him. Love is too scary a word for my vocabulary.

Chapter 10

"Oh my god, you look hilarious." I'm laughing like I haven't laughed in a while. My stomach actually hurts. We're at the Bean, since we decided to visit Millennium Park after dinner, and Luke is making silly faces in the mirror-like surface of the sculpture.

"You mean like this?" He exaggerates the look on his face even more. He's eyes are huge, his tongue is hanging to the side, and he's making Dumbo ears. I'm barely able to keep my hands steady as I try to snap a few photos of him on my phone.

"Yeah, just like that." I laugh as I try to copy his expression.

"I may look hilarious, but somehow you still look cute when you do that."

"Yeah, right. I most definitely do not look cute."

"Then you most definitely need glasses."

I nudge him in his ribcage.

"Hey, come here, you," he pulls me into him, then grabs my phone and snaps a few selfies of us together. Some are ridiculously funny, some are totally serious, and others just lovely. I may be inclined to stare at these for hours.

"I'm really having a great time," I say through laughter, without much thought. There's a good chance he'll use it to his advantage and challenge me on my one-date commitment, and I'm not sure a second date is the best idea. I'd be in danger of having too much of a great time. It's not like he can't tell from my massive smile, but if he wanted to test my resolve, I've just made myself vulnerable.

"I'm glad to hear that. I'm having a great time too," Luke acknowledges, then follows with, "So does that mean that you may want to spend more time with me this week?" I knew it.

"I'm still undecided. This may require another list."

I'm joking. But only a little. That may be how I operate most of the time, but what I do next surprises me, because it's spontaneous and quite out of character. I wrap my arms around Luke's waist, lean into his chest, and hold him close. His arms reach around me and he rests his chin against my hair. His chest lifts up and down against my cheek, his breathing deep and calculated. There are people around us, but I don't see or hear them. I just want to hold onto this moment of quiet, this soothing embrace, for a little longer. It feels natural – where Luke begins, I continue, and where I begin, he ends. It's like we're seamlessly molded, just like the sculpture we're standing in front of.

"Where did this come from?" Luke finally interrupts.

"Just felt like it," is all I say.

He shakes his head. I'm probably confusing him, given that my words and actions are a paradox he's yet to completely unravel. A paradox I may have to unravel just as much.

"Let's go see the garden," he says as he pulls me by my hand. And that's how smooth he is. Because his hand doesn't leave mine. Last time I held hands with a guy? It seems like a lifetime ago. It's the simplest caress, the lightest brush of his fingers over mine that makes our hand-holding even more intimate, somehow.

We make our way toward Lurie Garden, and after strolling through the beautiful sanctuary, we sit down on one of the benches. The view in front of us is illuminated only by the shimmering lights of the city.

"I want you closer," Luke says as he reaches under my knees and lifts my legs across his. His hands linger on my knees, just under the hem of my flowy dress, the spark from his touch always so welcoming to my skin. I can't help myself from trailing my fingers up and down his stomach. Meanwhile, I'm contemplating how to snap the buttons off his shirt so I can touch him bare again. The image of his naked torso from Friday night is still very, very fresh in my mind. And very enticing.

He grins as his darkened eyes meet mine. He brings his index finger to my face to brush away a strand of hair that's dancing freely in the breeze. And just like that, I lose track of everything around us and anyone who may be passing by. It's just Luke and me ... and that gift bag he's been carrying ever since we left the car. I was certain he was going to let me open it during dinner, but he didn't. I really, really want to kiss him, but I also really, really want to know what's inside that damn bag. I'm so torn. Why can't I just be more of an in-the-moment kind of girl? But my brain just can't let it go. My curiosity wins.

"Okay, you're killing me. I really want to know what's in the bag," I say impatiently. "You've been carrying it around the entire night. I'm dying to find out what it is!"

"You'd like to know now, wouldn't you?" he teases. I nod. "Ask me nicely," Luke demands, and it's so sexy.

"Please?" I beg candidly, fluttering my eyelashes, giving him the most adorable expression I can manage. His laugh is so charming.

"Okay, but only because you asked so nicely. Close your eyes." I do as I'm told, squinting to steal a look. "Hey, no peeking!"

"Fine," I mutter. This time I comply. I gently close my eyes and giggle a little as the excitement of the impending surprise looms. I hear him open the bag and pull out whatever is inside. My senses are hyperaware of all things Luke. The next thing I feel is his finger on my lips, tracing the line of my mouth corner to corner. Top first, then bottom. My body tenses as sweet sensation starts to build low in my belly. This has got to be the most erotic feeling ever. And we're not even naked.

"God, your lips Tess..." Luke trails off, and I'm ... oh, God, I'm a mess of emotions. Need. Anticipation. Lust. All I can think about is *his* lips. We've done some very – how shall I put this? – adventurous things, but we've yet to have our first kiss. I just about decide that I don't care about the gift anymore because all I can suddenly think about is how much I want to kiss him and how much I want him to kiss me. Will his lips be soft and caressing, or will they be needy and passionate when they first meet mine? Will his tongue gently find mine, or will he greedily take it?

I'm holding onto my composure with less than an ounce of control and, rather impatiently, waiting for further instructions. His finger leaves my mouth, and I'm bummed out by the sudden loss of contact. A moment later I feel his finger on my lips again, but this time there's added *something*. Something creamy and buttery and ... sweet, I realize as I suck on my bottom lip. Strawberry icing. Belonging to the cupcake he bought earlier. *He picked it out for me!* With my eyes still shut, I savor the sweetness of my own creation.

"Mmm. *So* good," I purr.

I open my eyes and am drawn into his gaze. He's looking at me as if he's memorizing my face. There's so much emotion, so much sincerity there, so much desire. He cups my cheeks in his palms and I lean into him. He looks down at my lips, and the moment I've been anticipating, the moment I've imagined a thousand times over, is so close I can almost imagine the taste of him. The sounds that surround us are faint. I can hear only the whispers of our breath.

"No, *this* is good," he breathes, and then his lips lunge greedily against mine. Best. Present. Ever. His lips are full and tender – sweeter than the icing I just tasted. His kiss is gentle and hungry, utterly consuming. My mouth lets his tongue in as he urgently searches for mine. The sweet sensation that started to build moments ago is now fully engaged.

I give in to his hunger and give back just as hungrily. My fingers travel to his hair – playing, tugging, stroking. He pulls on my bottom lip with his teeth and I moan softly. I am so aroused and lost in the feeling that I'm not really thinking. I lean against him and am rewarded with a low growl from Luke. My body's giving in, and I feel weak all over. We should so be naked right now.

"Ahem," is a faint but distinct sound that registers from a passerby, and I feel myself blush. I'm sure in the daylight I'd be bright pink from embarrassment. We both pull away slowly and grin at each other, nearly laughing. We are, after all, in a public park. I might have completely forgotten that little fact. Because – kissing Luke.

"Uh-oh," I giggle. "I think I got carried away."

"I beg to differ. I think I did," Luke counters while looking at me like I'm candy. "I've been waiting to lick icing off your mouth for over a year now, Tessa. Your lips taste so fucking sweet." He sneaks in kisses between the last three words, and I am in heaven. At least that's what I imagine heaven would be like for me.

"Yours too," I whisper.

He leans his forehead against mine, the tips of our noses touching affectionately as we experience the aftereffects with measured breaths.

"What you do to me..." he remarks absentmindedly, kissing my forehead. If he only knew what he does to me too.

How did you get here, Tessa? Just a fling, remember? A charming, sexy fucking fling. A fling that appears to be quickly veering out of my comfort zone of predictable control.

"Cupcake?" he offers with a smile. "Don't want it to go to waste, after all."

"Only if it comes with more of this." I smile, then kiss his mouth softly. We continue this game of cupcake kissing back and forth, with small pecks and intense make-out sessions in between bites. I have to admit it's one of the most delicious games I've ever played. And when the game's done, I snuggle up against Luke, and we just gaze at the night sky above us and the serene beauty of the garden.

"SO, HERE WE ARE." LUKE STATES THE OBVIOUS WHEN we pull into the visitor parking spot of my building, letting the words hang suggestively in the air.

His hand is on my knee, touching my skin gently but purposefully. It's been there most of the ride back. His closeness, his scent, the slightest touch of his fingers – all are making it extremely difficult for me to stay on my side of the car. I'm not sure that just-a-kiss will do it for me tonight. I really, really want more than kisses from Luke. But my mind and its innate ability to overthink almost everything messes with my head. *Play hard to get. Jump him! Make him really work for it. Don't make it too hard! Ugh!*

"Mm-hmm," is all I manage.

"Come here," he says as he reaches his hand behind my neck, his fingers tangling in my hair, bringing my face within inches of his. He doesn't wait a moment longer. Unlike me, he knows exactly what he wants to do and just goes for it.

His lips lock with mine and his tongue searches, explores. I lose myself in the embrace and react, guided only by ecstasy. I fumble with my seatbelt, then jump onto Luke's lap, wrapping my legs around him as best as I can. It's not extremely comfortable, but that thought evaporates before I fully process it because I'm instantly distracted. I feel him thick and hard through his pants, pressing against me in just the right spot. He feels like he's ready to burst at the seams.

His hands fumble underneath my dress and then grab at my butt cheeks, his fingers interlocking with the lace of my panties. My body gives in to an uncontrollable need as I rock against him. My fingers are making a mess of his hair as our tongues continue a tangled and urgent make-out session. God, I love the way he kisses me. I moan as the friction stimulates that very sensitive spot in my panties. I'm impatient. I reach down to his belt buckle and try to get it undone.

"Fuck, Tess," Luke says almost breathlessly as he pulls away from my face suddenly. "We can't do this now. Not like this…" He's clearly turned on, so his words confuse me. He must sense it because he tries to explain himself. "Tessa, I'm just trying to be a gentleman tonight," he clarifies. He's obviously still feeling guilty about the movie incident. "Trust me, I want you so badly right now," he continues, as he pulls me closer, "I can't even begin to describe. But I don't want to fuck it up this time around. I don't want our first time to be in the front seat of a car – a car that's not even mine."

"Oh, okay." I'm surprised, but I also understand his hesitation. Now that I have a moment to process, this isn't the place I want it to happen either. And I know I'm not ready to have him come upstairs. That would be committing to too much, too soon. I have yet to have a guy stay over at my place since Jason left. And I don't really want to think about *that* jerk right now.

The reality is that Luke and I barely know each other. I know having him come up would be too fast, too fuck-the-consequences for me. Not how I normally do things. So yeah, just-a-kiss will have to do tonight.

"I have some catching up to do with Marcus tomorrow, but I really want to see you after I'm done. Can I? See you again, I mean?" He holds my gaze, his eyes expectant.

"Yes, yes, please," escapes me without much thought, and I'm not sure if it's because I'm so in lust with Luke right now or because I have subconsciously decided that spending more time with him is in fact what I'd really like to do. Maybe a combination of both?

He smirks like he's got his way again, and I wonder if I am ever going to be able to resist him, given how easily I've managed to change my mind at every crossroad so far.

"You've got yourself a second date, stranger. Gloat all you want." I'm a weakling.

"Oh, trust me, I'm gloating. Told you I had a good feeling about tonight. I always trust my instincts."

A realization hits me. "I guess I need to trust my instincts more."

Luke kisses me in response. "That may be an idea worth considering. Do you want to come by my place tomorrow evening?"

"I'd love to."

"I'm staying at my dad's condo for a few nights. He's away until Tuesday night." I'm by no means ready to meet Mr. Callaghan Senior, so that added intel for clarification is welcome and very considerate. "I'll text you the address. Seven o'clock?"

"Sounds good."

"It *is* good. Otherwise I would have been deprived of this," he kisses my mouth, "and this," he kisses just below my ear, "and this," he trails kisses down my neck, "and a few more things I can think of. And that would have been one fucking problem," he growls.

I really like the sound of that. Flashes of what tomorrow night will likely bring cross my already over-stimulated mind. Tomorrow suddenly seems like such a long way away. I would have settled for a sequel to the movie incident right now, but since Luke is trying to be a gentleman tonight, I guess I should hold back too.

"Definitely a good thing," I whisper in his ear, and then I nuzzle against him.

"Tomorrow, okay?"

"Okay."

He gives me one last kiss before opening the car door. "I'd walk you to your door, but that would only lead to trouble, so you'd better go before I change my mind and have you rough and hard right here," he commands in that deep voice. The thought of the scenario he just painted so clearly makes my head spin. In any case, the trouble will have to wait until tomorrow.

"Fine, till next time." I smile.

I can barely find my feet as I walk toward the parking garage elevator. My body is trembling with the aftereffects of the evening and with the anticipation of what's to come. When I finally find myself in my apartment, I shut the door behind me and lean against it, taking a deep breath, debating what to do next. I am so worked up, I can feel the heavy wetness in my panties. But I don't want to have a fantasy of Luke be the end of it for me tonight. Not when I know now that Luke is real and back in my life. And I am going to see him again. Elated, I go to bed, very much looking forward to tomorrow night. And my dreams? *Very* interesting and definitely NSFW.

Chapter 11

I feel the warmth of the sun's rays poking at my face through the shades, awakening me from my slumber. I'm rested and excited. No, ecstatic. My date with Luke was the best first date ever. I can't wait to tell Rose all about it. She'll be so happy for me, although I bet she'll hate me just a little too. She's the queen of worst first dates, seriously.

As I'm thinking about last night, I feel a hint of panic. Did I imagine it all? Am I going crazy? God knows how many times my fantasies have gotten the better of me. For a minute I worry that the date with Luke was just a dream. I close my eyes and try to picture it all in my head again so that I can hold onto it for a moment longer.

My phone buzzes, bringing me back to reality. Crap, it was all just a dream, wasn't it? I grab the phone off my nightstand and read a text that makes all the particles of my fragile universe fit into a perfect realm again.

Hope your dreams were as sweet as mine.

I can't help but smile. Oh, they were sweet. I touch my lips, feeling a lingering swelling.

Even sweeter, I type back excitedly.

Can't wait to see you tonight, cupcake.

I can't wait either.

I bolt out of my bed and nearly face plant as I trip over my own feet and catch myself inches above the floor. *Epitome of grace, Conte!* I shake it off and hurry to the bathroom to start what I can only anticipate is going to be yet another exhilarating day. Because I'm seeing Luke again tonight. Tonight!

I'm like the Energizer Bunny, too excited to stand still. I put on a pair of running shorts and a sports bra and head out for my morning run. I know I'll have to keep myself busy throughout the day as I count down the minutes to our date. I know that the nerves are eventually going to creep up on me the closer it gets, so I have to remind myself to think of anything but until such time as it is absolutely necessary. Of course, that's easier said than done.

My morning high funnels into one of the fastest runs I've ever done. Just as I'm getting out of the shower, my phone rings, and I notice it's Clara. *Shit!* In my bewildered obsession with Luke and all that's happened, I completely forgot about the promise I made to her before I left the club Friday night. I was supposed to call her. Two days ago. I'm surprised, actually, that she lasted this long.

"You never called me back," she says without even a hello.

"Hi, Clar." I try to sound cool and collected. "I know. I'm sorry, I've just been ... busy." *Very convincing.*

"Sure you have." I know my sister well. From the way she says it, I'm pretty sure she's implying something. How would she even know?

"I have been. Weekends are always crazy at the bakery, and with your wedding a week away..." *Ugh!* It's no use. When Clara makes up her mind, she's made up her mind.

"Mm-hmm. Busy with Luke?" She cuts straight to the chase, just as I expected.

"Luke?" I'm failing miserably to sound unaffected. The eagerness in my voice betrays me.

"Come on, Tessa. He called me on Saturday, clearly smitten, wondering where he could find you – where you lived, where you worked." So it was Clara, giving Luke all the intel he needed to practically stalk me. Just as I expected. "I know you said nothing happened between the two of you before, but I caught more than a few glances between you guys on Friday night. And I saw a spark in your eyes I haven't seen before. Like, ever. So something tells me there's a 'you and Luke' conversation to be had."

She's good. Perceptive. After all, Friday night I was working really hard on what I can now only refer to as the Flushed Down the Toilet Plan. I wonder what I should tell her. Should I tell her anything? Normally I would, but it's never involved anyone she knows before. Especially someone who's one of her future husband's best friends.

I have to come clean. Otherwise, she'll just dig up the truth herself. And the last thing I want her to do is harass Luke about it.

"Fine, you got me. Things got a little heated between Luke and me on Friday."

"Oooh. How heated? Like 'we kissed' heated, or…?"

"Um, more like 'I was doing most of the kissing' heated." I let that sink in for a moment.

"What? Tessa! You didn't!"

"I kind of did." I hurry up and add, "Oh, and we went on a date last night," hoping she'll take the bait because TMI is never enough TMI with Clara. She'll want more.

"And?" she continues expectantly.

"And we're having another one tonight." There it is again. My voice is overly enthusiastic. What is wrong with me?

"And? How did it go?" She's persistent, as always.

"And … we've kind of hit it off."

"Oh my god, Tessa, that's great!" she squeals in her typical over-the-top reaction to just about everything. Coincidentally, that's one of the reasons I love her. "I want to hear more, please please please? You've gotta give me more."

I take a steadying breath before saying what I haven't acknowledged out loud before. "I think I really like him. And I'm going a bit crazy," which is the understatement of the century, "because I'm really scared that I'll end up getting hurt again."

"Tessa, how many times have we had this conversation before? Honestly." She sounds exasperated. "You can't just shut down every guy who has even the slightest interest in you because of what that jerk did to you three years ago. You need to relax and let things play out. Let go of those inhibitions and find that heart of yours again." She says it with such sincerity that she nearly has me convinced. Maybe I can in fact find my heart this time around. "I don't want to sing it, but I will if you need more convincing. Let. It. Go."

"No no no. Please don't sing." I laugh and stop her before she starts. Clara is tone-deaf. Horribly, brutally tone-deaf.

"Fine, I'll spare your ears this time. But take this as a warning. Next time you won't be so lucky."

"Point well taken."

"Good. I'm just so excited for you and Luke, I want to squeeze the life out of you right now." Clara's hugs can in fact be suffocating. "Wouldn't it be great if things worked out?"

"*If* they work out, then I'm dating someone who lives miles away, all the way across the Atlantic," I reply. "That's exactly why I'm questioning whether this is something I should be getting myself into in the first place."

"What you're getting yourself into is a fun little fling, and if it turns out to be more than that, well, then you can figure it out. If it doesn't, then who cares?"

Apparently I'm the only one who cares, since Clara and Rose both seem to have the same idea. I'm starting to realize I may not be a believer in this fling thing that I've somehow convinced myself into. Even though I have yet to admit it to myself, I feel like I'm crossing that imaginary boundary faster than I ever thought was possible and heading into uncharted territory. The closer I get to moving past it, the more it's making my heart ache, my head hurt, and my fears resurface. But the sexually stimulated parts of my body – they most definitely want to cross it. Tonight.

"I just don't want to make things awkward, you know?" I admit. "I mean, your wedding is less than a week away, and I don't want to mess things up for you and Marcus. It's your day, and I don't want anything to overshadow it."

"God, Tessa, stop being such a drama queen. We're all grown-ups here. Whatever happens, happens! I'm just glad to hear there may finally be someone out there who you are even remotely interested in, enough to at least try. So just go for it. I couldn't be happier for you if Luke turns out to be the one."

The One. Clara has always believed in true love, in finding that mythical creature. Even with bumps along the way, she's finally snagged a One for herself. Her new goal in life, it appears, is to find Ones for her dearest friends and, especially, her sister. I'd never let her know, but sometimes, against my nature, I even get caught up in it and find myself believing in The One. Unicorns, however, can kiss my ass.

So I have to remind myself to take baby steps. Even if those baby steps are happening slightly faster than I anticipated or can control.

"You always make things seem so simple. How do you do it?"

"It really isn't as hard as you think it is," she replies, deadpan.

"Very funny. Okay, I'll try," I say as convincingly as I can manage.

"And you need to fill me in on all the details," she warns.

"Of course."

"And don't forget – you've still got one amazing cake to make!"

"I haven't forgotten, and amazing it will be, don't you worry."

"I know it will be. You're awesome. Talk soon, okay?"

"Okay. Love ya."

"Love ya too," she says and then hangs up.

My sister's words of wisdom might be just what I need to convince myself that I am not at all crazy to be getting involved with Luke. As a matter of fact, as if I couldn't be more excited already, I'm distractedly giddy with the thought of seeing him tonight. Clara is right. I need to put myself out there and trust Luke more than I've ever allowed myself to trust the opposite sex before. And that – that is going to be one of the hardest things to do. After Jason, the one thing I learned was to trust no one but myself.

I'M HONESTLY HOPING TO KEEP MY MIND OFF LUKE SO the day isn't torture, but Rose is at Lovely Cakes when I arrive, waiting like a hawk to hear how last night went.

"So?" she asks while handing me a cup of strawberry-peach white tea, my favorite summer blend.

"So?" I question back, taking the warm cup from her and holding back the grin that is nearly ready to burst on my face.

She gives me the you-know-what-I'm-talking-about look. "Sooo ... how was last night?"

"Wonderful." I smile from ear to ear as I take a sip of the fruity, sweet, fragrant goodness.

"I'm so happy it went well, considering how anxious you were yesterday."

"Me too."

I tell her about the dinner, the walk through Millennium Park, the cupcake, our first kiss, and the kissing that followed (because there was a lot of it). Like a sponge, Rose is soaking it all in.

"And?" she asks expectantly. I know where she's going with it.

"And?" I pretend to be clueless again. I love the worked-up look on her face.

"Did you guys *do it*?"

"Really, Rose? Remind me to talk to HR about appropriate conversations in the workplace," I tease, and she just shrugs like she's not bothered by it at all. Of course I knew she was going to ask. Our relationship crossed the employer–employee boundary long ago, and having her as a friend is really quite nice. But sometimes I forget how no-nonsense she can be. "No, we didn't. But it was close." I grin. "Luke was being a gentleman and thought we should hold off until we're in a more appropriate setting. Doing it in the car wasn't quite what he had in mind."

"Isn't that sweet." She's being sarcastic. I think she may dislike Luke just a bit for how he treated me in the first place.

"*I*, likewise, didn't think a car was the place to, you know... I mean, it was a joint decision." Why do I even bother explaining myself? I would have totally done it in the car if he hadn't been so conscientious. Fuck his gentleman-ness.

"So does that mean there's another date?"

I nod. "What can I say? He was pretty convincing. I had no choice but to give in." I'm a weakling, is what it is. When it comes to Luke, "resolute" doesn't seem to exist in my vocabulary.

"Of course you didn't."

"Rose," I warn. I'm walking a fine line between being a friend and being a boss.

"Just sayin'. Anyway, when's the next round?"

"Actually, tonight. I'm meeting him at his dad's place."

She gives me a questioning stare.

"His dad's out of town," I clarify.

"In that case, sounds like there may be an action-packed night ahead." She winks playfully.

"I wouldn't be surprised, especially after last night. I think I'm going to be a nervous wreck the entire day knowing promises were made. The anticipation is killing me already, and I have a full day to get through before seeing Luke again."

"Tessa, relax."

"I know, I know. I should probably get my head back out of la-la land and focus on work or I'm going to drive myself crazy."

"Yeah, you do that," Rose says. "Or maybe make a list. You know. About how far you'll let Luke go tonight."

"Whatever." I stick my tongue out at her. Although it wouldn't be a terrible idea.

"I'm just gonna stay out of your way." She knows just what I need. "We've got work to do."

"Thanks for the reminder, Mom. You know me better than that, Rose; you know that work is my life. A guy's not going to stop me from doing what I enjoy the most."

I'm not sure that I've convinced her. Or myself, for that matter. Because last night, I may have enjoyed kissing slightly more than work. A lot more, actually.

SURPRISINGLY, THE DAY FLIES BY QUICKER THAN I anticipated as I keep myself busy with Clara's wedding cake and customers dropping by to pick up orders or indulge in a tea/dessert combo. It's not like my mind doesn't take a few detours. The excitement's building deep down in my belly; the anticipation's burning within me. The later in the day it is, the more nervous I get about the night ahead. And this time, it's not all about seeing Luke again. It's quite possibly because I haven't had sex in almost six months. And the last two times were merely attempts to get Luke out of my system. Very futile attempts at that.

The first time was with a guy I met on one of my morning runs. The experience was so forgettable that I can barely remember his name. I think it was Mark. Thoughts of Luke and his magic fingers were re-playing in my head and I needed to figure out how to, well, get him out of my head. So I figured maybe going out with another guy would make it happen.

Mark and I went out on a couple of dates, which were fine, but the sex turned out to be a fucking disaster. Pun intended. The guy was big on words, small on everything else. And it lasted all of a few minutes, barely enough to get me worked up. Of course I faked it, then had to finish the job myself with the help of my four-speed BFF and memories of Luke. After that, I changed my running route for the first time ever and never ran into Mark again.

The second time was a few weeks later, and yet another disaster. This time I really have no clue who the guy was. I might have been slightly drunk. Okay, a lot drunk, which has happened only twice in my entire life. That particular night was the night of my twenty-sixth birthday, just a few days before the Christmas holidays. I normally don't like the loss of control alcohol creates, so I try to pace myself. But that night was different.

Clara and Rose had made it a point to take me out clubbing to celebrate. Not how I'd planned to spend my night, but they were able to drag me out of my apartment cave, so I just went along with it. My sexual frustration at that point was at its peak, and after celebrating with a few shots, my need for sex only intensified. I wanted nothing else but to put out the fire that Luke's lingering fingers had set within me. I had a few more drinks, and I think, from the very little I recall of that night, some guy flicked me a sexy look, one thing led to another, and we ended up going at it in the back seat of his car. Terribly cliché.

Just the thought of it makes me cringe. It was so unlike me, and even now I feel painfully embarrassed about being so senseless. It was short, rough, and disappointing; I can't even remember if I actually climaxed. Which really was the whole point of the exercise – to release the built-up tension. To make things worse, the next day I had to deal with the consequences. One: a major hangover; and two: sheer panic. It was so out of character for me to fuck a complete stranger. Then again, I was under the influence, so I guess it wasn't surprising that I felt less inhibited than usual. Normally I at least like to get to know the guy enough to make sure he's not a serial killer. Even though we used protection and I was on the pill, I ended up getting myself tested for everything under the sun that same morning. I was glad that I didn't have to deal with any undesirable long-term consequences and certain that I would never do anything like that again.

Of course, I blame Luke for all of it. For how sexy he is, for my frustration, for the incompetence of any other guy. If it wasn't for him and our fateful encounters, I would have been fine. Peachy, even. I would have just done what I always do and gone on with my life as before – met a guy, went on a couple of dates, released my sexual tension, and then cut all ties. "Break, detach, run" – that was my mantra during the pre-Luke era, ever since Jason the Jerk turned me off relationships. But Luke's captivating grin, his beautiful eyes, and his skilled fingers fucking ruined me.

I have endured this constant battle, trying to decide if I was angry at him, if I despised him, or if I was bewitched. I think I finally figured it out last night: *definitely* bewitched. The promise of more than a kiss, the anticipation of finally being able to quench my thirst for Luke, has my body quivering. Yup, I'm literally aquiver as I think of all the naughty things we could do, all those things that only my imagination has allowed me to indulge in so far. I'm positive I need no list to help me decide how far to go tonight. I am going all the way.

Chapter 12

These dates with Luke are going to be the end of me. Here I am, yet again, obsessing over what I should wear for our date. I want to make sure it's just right, especially after the unspoken promises that were made in the car last night. I have chosen lacy black lingerie that accentuates my rather full breasts, naturally. After changing my outfit three times, I've finally settled on a sleeveless, deep-eggplant cocktail dress that defines my curves. I take one last look in the mirror, satisfied with the final product and momentarily dazzled by the gems in my earrings, before I head out of my apartment wearing my favorite pair of ankle-strap stilettos.

My stomach is in knots with cautious excitement. It's not like me to be so emotionally invested in what is officially only a second date. I'm confused by whatever it is I'm feeling. It can't possibly be love, of course, so it must be an intense form of like, with a heavy dose of lust. I decide to let myself embrace this side of Tessa, one I haven't seen in ages, and take it one step at a time. At some point, I figure, things will just fall into place and it will all make sense. At least that's what I tell myself.

As the cab pulls up in front of the condo, I notice Luke is waiting for me outside the building. I ogle him for a moment, secretly spying on him. The top two buttons of his dark-gray shirt are undone, and my immediate thought is how much I want to taste the skin that's exposed there. Or the skin further below. Or his cock.

Our eyes connect, and from the way he smiles I bet he's thinking of how much he'd like a bite of me. He walks up and pays the cab driver, then takes my hand and twirls me around. And I giggle like a schoolgirl.

"God, Tess," is all he says, and seconds later his lips are on mine. My head swirls and my knees weaken. I'm fuzzy and warm and gooey. And when the kiss is over, I want to push rewind and play again. Over and over. I want this man, this sexy creature, whose pheromones do crazy things to me. *Control, Conte!* Dinner first. Then dessert.

Luke's dad's condo is quite the space. The first thing I notice is the beautiful view of Lake Michigan through the massive windows. The second thing I notice is that there are two bedrooms, which is a relief. The place is modern, minimalist, almost sterile. I think his dad and I would get along.

"Wow, your dad's place is so clean." I say the first thing that pops in my mind.

"Yeah, he likes to keep it that way." I can't tell if Luke thinks that's good or bad. I wonder what kind of place Luke has in London and whether he's inherited his dad's cleanliness trait. "He's a retired doctor."

"Oh, I see. When did he retire?" I ask out of courtesy, but the way Luke is looking at me, I have a feeling talking about his dad's career is the last thing he wants to do right now.

"A few years ago. He lived here mainly when he worked at Northwestern Memorial. Now he spends most of his time at his cottage."

"Having a condo must have been convenient and probably something he…"

Luke interrupts my rambling with a simple, "Come here," as he grabs me by my hand from behind and twirls my body toward his. "I don't want to seem impolite, but I'd rather talk about you and me then my dad tonight. And I'd much rather do this," he says as he cups my cheeks and kisses me. I'd much rather be doing this too. He tastes sweet like sugar. My personal dose of calories.

"Okay, Callaghan, you need to control yourself," Luke mutters to himself when he breaks away. "I think we better get to our dinner before I completely lose it and have you instead."

I don't tell him I wouldn't complain.

The table is set and the aroma coming from the kitchen is intoxicating. "I'm starving," I say. My stomach is in fact growling. I realize I've barely eaten today. Instead, the nerves ate away at me all day long.

"Then let's dig in." Luke places pan-fried fish, steamed vegetables, and roasted potatoes on the table.

"Wow. This looks amazing."

"I thought you might like fish." He clearly took notes from our dinner yesterday.

"I do. Did you make this?" I point to the vast display.

"I most certainly did."

"I have to admit, that's impressive. When did you learn to cook like this?" Being that I'm a professionally trained pastry chef, my culinary standards are slightly higher than that of the average crowd. I'm glad he can put together more than grilled cheese.

"It's just something I had to learn when my mom left. Dad wasn't a great cook, so I kind of took it on. Otherwise, I think I would have likely grown up on Happy Meals." He chuckles. "But I enjoy it, so it's all good."

He can cook. Definitely a plus. When I take a bite, I find out just how good his cooking skills actually are. I'm in love. With the food I'm tasting, that is.

"This is delicious."

"Thank you."

"No really, I'm more than impressed. You get cupcake points for this."

He laughs. "Cupcake points?"

I nod as I take a bite. I'm nearly moaning it's so good.

"Good thing, I assume."

"Very." I take another bite, and this time I actually moan.

"You can't be doing that."

"Hmm?"

"The moaning. It's kind of distracting."

"Oh, I'm sorry."

"Don't be. I meant distracting in that I may not be able to finish my dinner because I'd rather have you."

"Well, you're more than welcome to take a bite."

"I told you, I'm trying to be a gentleman." I make a pouty face, and he laughs. "Don't worry. I'm definitely going to take a bite. Just ... later."

"I'll take you up on that offer." I raise my glass, and we clink our glasses together. "To later."

"To later," he repeats.

We eat in comfortable silence for a few minutes, with only quiet music playing in the background. I normally hate the silence, but this is nice. Intimate.

I sense Luke's eyes on me, watching every bite, every movement of my lips. He really is obsessed with my lips. Not that I mind.

"What's up, stranger?" I look up at him, wondering what he's thinking.

"I'd really like to get to know you better, Tess. I know we shared a lot last night at dinner, but I want more."

"I'd like that." When what I'm really thinking is, "I want more too."

"But this time, let's make it more fun."

"Okay."

"First kiss?" Luke asks.

Oh, *that* kind of fun. I'll play. "Grade eight dance. Just a boy, nothing special. A bit sloppy, if I recall correctly." Luke laughs. "Yours?" I ask.

"The girl next door, when I was ten or so. It was nice, but nothing special. Best kiss?"

"Hey, I thought it was my turn," I protest. I was really hoping not to have to go there.

"It's basically the same question, so still my turn."

God, this is so embarrassing. "Yours," I whisper, and look down, picking at my nails. I can't bring myself to ask him the same question. I worry my kiss, us making out, will fail in comparison to his prior experiences.

He leans across the table and brings my chin up. I look up to see his eyes full of amusement. It's like he can read my mind and knows exactly what I want to know but am too afraid to ask. He brings his lips closer to mine, but before he moves closer, he brushes his finger across my bottom lip and whispers, "Yours ... only yours," then plants that "best kiss" on my mouth.

As if he could be any more perfect. Honestly.

"Definitely," I breathe when he pulls away.

"Definitely," he confirms and smiles back.

"Okay, my turn now. Your first time?"

"When I was fourteen. My grade nine welcome."

"Ew, that's kind of gross. Was it any good at least?"

"Back then, yes. She was a couple of years older. More experienced. Looking back on it now – nope. Not even close to the experiences after her."

Shit, now I am really worried that I won't be up to par. *If* we do it. No, *when* – because it's happening.

"How about you?" he asks.

"I was twenty-one. Late bloomer. I guess I always thought that I needed to be in love when I first did it."

"Were you?"

"What?"

"In love?"

"I thought so back then. I'm not so sure now." I'm so torn as to whether I should share more with Luke. I want to tell him, but I don't want Luke to think I still have feelings for Jason. I'm certain I don't. Not the love kind, anyway. "Your turn to ask," I prompt. If I'm lucky, he'll think of something easy to ask and I'll have a few more minutes to decide how much more I should divulge.

"Last time?" he asks.

"Just over six months ago, on my birthday," I admit. "It was kind of embarrassing, though. I was drunk. Only for the second time in my life, however." Of course I neglect to say why I was drunk in the first place and that the reason for my sexual frustration was him. "You?"

"It's been several months. Longest drought ever," he jokes, and I smile because I can't believe it's been so long. He doesn't strike me as the type to not have casual sex.

"How come?" I can't help but wonder – hope, even – that it just may be because of me.

He looks at me with eyes that undress me. "Some brunette's got my cock wound up so hard, I've barely been able to focus on anything but her."

Huh. Had I known this months ago, it would have spared both of us a lot of headaches.

"Well, that's good to know." I think my smile must be the size of a watermelon slice. But I don't probe further because I'm still not sure how to respond to that revelation. "Moving on, then: longest relationship?" I really want to know if there's been a Jason equivalent in Luke's life.

"You really want to know?" I nod. "I don't think I've ever been in a serious relationship."

Uh-oh. "Oh. That sounds somewhat non-committal." Who the heck am I getting myself involved with? *A player*, my conscience reminds me.

"I know what it sounds like, but it's not like that. Really. It's not that I didn't try. Things have just never seemed to work out, for whatever reason. If it wasn't one thing, it was another. And I wasn't always the one breaking things off. But I've never had my heart broken, if that's what you really want to know."

That is exactly what I wanted to know, but his answer is troubling. On the one hand, I'm glad, because that means there's no other woman in his life that he may still have feelings for. On the other hand, it's disconcerting, because let's face it: he may not be a player, but he might as well be. If he's never had his heart broken, how will I ever know if he's serious enough about me? Would he be willing to put his heart on the line for us? I guess I should look in the mirror. I might as well ask myself the same question, and yet my heart was broken once.

"It is," I say, still not sure how I feel about his response.
"How about you?" he asks.
I knew this was coming, since I asked the question. In the meantime, I've thought about it, and I think I'm ready to give him a snippet. Jason's long gone from my life. Not telling Luke would make it seem like he still has control over my feelings, which he doesn't.
"Three years," I admit.
"That sounds *somewhat* committal." I'm trying hard to figure out what his expression is telling me, but I can't. If he's at all concerned, he doesn't show it.
"I thought so too. But it didn't work out. Obviously." I snort because I feel a little nervous talking about it. Classy. But beside my mom, my sister, and Rose, I've never shared this story with anyone else. Especially not with another guy. And I'm about to.
"What happened?"
"I thought what Jason and I had was going to last forever." *Great lead-in, Tessa.* Explaining this is going to be harder than I thought. I take a moment to collect my thoughts. "We started dating while I was in college. He was a couple of years older and I was so head-over-heels for him. I thought I loved him, and I probably did on some level. But it turns out I was so infatuated that I failed to see anything. I had no idea that he'd decided to move overseas to do his masters until he called one day to tell me he was leaving. And that long-distance wouldn't work for him. He basically broke things off on the phone." I take a sip of my wine; I need to continue this calmly, even though I still seem to feel this anger inside whenever the topic of Jason comes up. *Jerk!*
"He was supposed to be gone for eight months. For weeks I held out hope that he'd miss me, that he would realize he was wrong and come back. But he never did. So you can see how I may have a slight problem trusting men. Especially those across the Atlantic." I laugh nervously again, as I'm sure the irony of the situation is not lost on Luke.

"I'll keep that in mind," he says, trying to make light of the situation. "And I'm sorry things didn't work out, because I know that must have been hard on you. But I'm kind of glad."

"You're glad?"

"I am. Because you're here now, and I have a shot with you. Because I get a chance to show you that not every guy is like Jason. Because I can make you believe again."

"Believe?"

"In love."

Chapter 13

By the time dinner is over, there is so much I've learned about Luke, so much that I really, really like. And a few things that absolutely petrify me. But there's still so much I want to find out and that I know would complete my picture of this intriguing person who's sitting across from me. I'm beginning to realize that my infatuation with Luke is more real than I thought.

Luke is studying me intently and looking at me like he wants to devour me bite by bite. He reaches for my fingers across the table, and without letting his gaze leave mine, he stands up, comes around to me, and pulls me up by my hand so that I'm face to face with him.

"Let's dance," he whispers, and then his arms wrap around my back and mine instinctively wrap around his neck.

I haven't been paying attention to the music in the background, but as the acoustic version of Sam Smith's "Latch" starts, I can't help but wonder if he chose this song to dance to on purpose or if it just happens to be playing. My brain is wired to analyze every situation, and right now I'm wondering how reflective the lyrics are of us. Can I take this chance with Luke when I haven't taken a chance on anything even remotely similar in years? Will I be able to commit to him when my last committed relationship blew up in my face?

This insta-lust I'm experiencing kind of sucks. I mean, not really, because *duh*, who wouldn't want a bite of Mr. Delicious? But it does, given our less than ideal situation. Why do people fall like this? So suddenly, so unintentionally, when it's least expected? I realize my experience with Luke is in direct contrast to how I've lived my life so far.

It's like he can read my mind; as the song ends he whispers, "Give us a chance." We're barely moving now, yet somehow still dancing in the quiet, our foreheads touching, our bodies still connected.

"I'll try," I whisper back, realizing just how much I want to, and hoping I can actually deliver on my words.

The soft promise is all the reassurance Luke needs, it appears, because he doesn't wait a second longer. Instead, his mouth finds mine and his hands tangle in my hair. His kiss is impatient and laced with need. I close my eyes and let out a soft moan as I lose myself completely in the way his tongue dances with mine. It's tango and rock and waltz, all in perfect harmony.

As the intensity of our kiss grows, Luke scoops me up and carries me to his bedroom. I cling to him until my feet find the floor next to his bed. I'm so ready to take our mouth-to-mouth dance to that next step – I've been ready for a while. And from the raw need in Luke's eyes, from the ragged breaths that escape his chest, it seems like he's been ready for a while too.

He unzips my dress, and it slips down so that all I'm left with is the black lace lingerie that I selected for tonight. Goose bumps prickle my skin, and I'm not sure if it's because I'm almost naked or because the way his fingers trail down my skin is causing them to surface. Actually, I'm pretty sure it's the latter.

"You're beautiful, inside and out," Luke murmurs, his eyes glistening with what I can only decipher as admiration mixed with lust. I wonder how many times he's thought of me like this, nearly bare and feverish with need. I wonder how many times he's imagined us like this, in the moment before we really connect. I've thought of these moments, dreamed of them. Now I want the real thing. I don't want to wait a moment longer.

I unbutton his shirt with hurried movements and pull it off him, then place the palm of my hand on his chest. He sucks in a deep breath, like my touch is enough to light his skin on fire. I feel the beat of his heart bounce off my palm, and I recognize that my heart beats at the same exhilarating speed. It's ready to jump out of my chest.

"God, Tess, I want you so fucking bad," Luke growls, and I'm almost undone just by the sound of his rough voice. He pulls down my panties, and I step out of them while he takes a moment to undo my bra. Now I am definitely naked and completely aware of how Luke's proximity makes me feel. Flushed. Frenzied. Exposed. My nipples taunt him, I'm sure, because he grins, seemingly enjoying the display. I smile back, but my smile quickly turns into a moan as Luke cups one breast and then pinches my nipple between his fingers. My body reacts and I'm quivering with the need to have him. Self-control is at a premium right now.

With pained restraint, I manage to find the focus I need to undo his belt and unbutton his pants. I'm a bit clumsy, but it's only because if I had it my way, I'd tear them right off him. Or maybe if I had a magic wand, he'd be naked and in me. Like, right now.

Luke chuckles at my impatience and helps me by pulling his pants down along with his boxers. And there he is. Thick, hard, totally erect. I may have missed him a little since Friday. Or a lot. Either way, my eyes are stuck on his cock like it's a shiny new toy I saw in a store, played with for a few minutes, and then didn't think I'd ever see again. Until Christmas morning. Oh, how I *love* Christmas morning.

"You're so hard." I point out the obvious as my hand travels to grope his length. I have an urge to pet him, but not in a soft way. In a wicked kind of way.

"*You* make me hard." His voice is so rough it's driving me mad.

He lifts me and I wrap around him. Except this time I'm naked and can feel him right there, right where I want him. I whimper, demanding softly, "Fuck me, Luke."

He lays me down on the edge of his bed, and this is it. This is the moment. The one I've been secretly fantasizing about since I first ran into him. I'm about to have sex with my delicious, sexy stranger. Yay!

Of course, I should know by now that Luke prefers to keep me guessing. Instead of giving me what I've been craving for months, he stills, then smiles charmingly. "Not just yet. I want to take my sweet time with you. Discover every little freckle, explore every inch of your body."

I'm both astounded and exasperated. Really? How does he have any control when I am just about ready to fall apart?

As he begins discovering me, he leans over and takes a moment to brush his fingers against my lips, touching them softly, pulling on my lower lip. "Your lips … so fucking kissable, Tessa," he groans, and then he places a lingering kiss on them. I moan in his mouth and push my hips up so that I can feel him again. I'm in desperate need of more than just a kiss. And he's not letting me have it. This is so not fair.

"Nuh-uh, not yet." He traces his fingers down my neck to my collarbone, toward the middle and down my breastbone. His eyes follow his fingers, admiring every inch like he intended. My skin tingles; my body trembles. I kind of hate him right now. I mean, only a little. Even though he's not where I really, really want him, what he's doing is beyond arousing.

His next stop is my breasts. He circles them in admiration, then cups them in his hands, squeezing, kneading, playing.

"Your tits … mouth-watering," he growls, and then he brings his mouth down to one nipple. The feeling of his tongue on me is heavenly. He sucks, pulls, twirls, then moves to the other and does the same. God, that feels so good. I swear, it's like my nipples are wired directly to my pussy; I feel the wetness between my thighs and I'm certain I will break apart just from the action my breasts are getting. It's like he knows just what turns me on, what will bring me closer to that sweet oblivion.

"Please." The rasp of my voice is barely audible. My mouth feels so dry.

He shakes his head, not giving in, then continues trailing his fingers down, circling softly around my belly button. I can't help it. In the middle of his sensuous exploration of my body, I actually giggle.

"Is this that ticklish spot of yours?" He's grinning like he's found a pot of gold nestled in my belly button. I nod.

"Right here?"

"Very."

He hums and gently kisses the spot. Surprisingly, it's no longer ticklish. It's pure delight. And I'm no longer laughing. I'm back to being crazed and hot in anticipation. As he's kissing my belly button, his fingers travel lower ... and lower. I can't help but want to feel his fingers right where he had them once before. His mouth down there too would certainly be a bonus.

He lifts his head and looks at me with greedy eyes. He's so close to touching me again that I sense the control he's been so resolutely holding onto is starting to falter.

"Your pussy ... so fuckable," he breathes, his voice rough and deep, before he slides two fingers in me. I gasp as the warmth spreads through my body. It's sublime. I may have despised him because of this exact same feeling for the past several months, but I'd be lying if I said I hadn't missed it, hadn't craved it, hadn't imagined it over and over.

He grins impishly as if he's reading my mind. *Smug, sexy bastard.*

Then he brings his mouth on me, right in that sweet spot, while his fingers continue to explore, melting my brain a little. Coherent thought no longer exists. My back arches, and all I can do is writhe and whimper and beg him for more. His mouth and fingers are a near-lethal combination. He's licking and sucking my clit, while teasing my pussy with his damn magic fingers. I'm too worked up, too distracted to think of anything but what he's doing to me. My moans are becoming louder and louder – I have to bite down on my lip to suppress them from becoming full-on screams. I feel my toes curling, my fingers reaching for the sheets, grasping, trying to maintain some sense of control, an ounce of sanity. But it's too much, too soon, because I can't hold on any longer. The orgasm I've been waiting for impatiently while he was so purposefully discovering me finds me and brings me to pure bliss. My eyes close as I let out a gasping moan, and when I open them I see him watching me lose myself in him, his face lit up with a cocky grin.

"God, Luke, that felt so good," I sigh, still in a daze.

"You taste so fucking sweet." His voice is rough and crazed, and his eyes glow like he's high on me.

"I want more." I can't help it, I've waited too long. I need more than just his mouth and fingers. I want to feel *him*. "Please fuck me."

That's it. I'm officially begging. Enough with the games.

"Oh, I will," he growls, and then he reaches underneath the pillow and pulls out a condom. "Always good to be prepared."

"Yes, yes it is." How convenient, and how responsible of him. "Hurry," I mumble.

The moment he's neatly tucked in, he thrusts his cock inside me, claiming all that his fingers claimed just moments ago. He pushes in hard and growls, "Fuck, Tess," like being inside me, *finally*, makes him completely wild. The way he fills me… God, I want him in me like that for hours. I feel every inch of him as he drives in and out, and feel him deeper and deeper every time. He's relentless and tender; rough and gentle.

I grab his neck and bring him to me, and he's kissing me and I'm kissing him like we haven't kissed before. I don't know where his mouth ends and mine begins. We're immersed in each other. He's thick and growing and I'm crying, "God, Luke," and, "Please, don't stop." The rest are sounds that I would only ever make under a spell of ecstasy. Whimpers and sighs that state nothing comprehensible, yet say so much at the same time. I'm utterly lost in the sensations that consume me, bewilder me, and I don't ever want to be found. Not by anyone but Luke, that is. It's never felt this good, with anyone else, ever, but my brain does not have the ability at this particular moment to decipher what this may mean.

My eyes flutter open, then closed; I catch him watching me, drowning in me. I climb and climb and feel him climb along with me. The orgasm finds me and I swear I see stars and butterflies and cupcakes all at once. He's so close, throbbing inside me, and the pulsating sensation is incredible. Within moments, he reaches his climax, and I'm completely engrossed in the feeling. I take mental note of the moment, cataloging the way he closes his eyes, the way he growls, the way he fills me. And it's overwhelming how I feel watching him fall apart because of me. I'm elated and jittery at the same time.

It registers that I haven't felt anything about another guy the way I feel everything about Luke. I've always consciously thought of every move when I was with other guys, including Jason. I could never just shut off. But with Luke, there's none of that. Everything about our first time has felt natural, instinctive. I'm wondering if that's how it feels when two people are meant to be. I'm wondering if this is our beginning.

WE'RE RESTING IN HIS BED, OUR NAKED BODIES ENTWINED cosily. Luke's running his fingers up and down my arm, while I'm listening to the calming sound of his heartbeat. We're silent for a few minutes, reluctant to move, unwilling to interrupt this moment that feels like ours and only ours.

"You know, I've waited twenty-eight years for someone like you to walk into my life, and you literally did. More than once," Luke says, breaking the silence. "Only, I was being, well, me and didn't realize it. But after that night out with Marcus and Clara, something happened. I just couldn't get you out of my head."

"But it took you this long to make the connection. Why?"

"To be honest, I don't know. I think initially, for all I knew, I was never going to see you again. And I thought after a few days, my cock would calm down. *He* didn't. I swear, the guy's got a mind of his own." Luke laughs. I know he's trying to make light of the situation, but I need more than this to really understand where he's coming from.

"You're a guy. That's not at all surprising. So I'm not buying it. *Why?*"

He must be figuring out how to frame it, because he's silent for a minute. "I guess I just thought I'd go back to my pre-Tessa lifestyle. I thought a few random hookups would get me to forget you. But they didn't. In fact, the image of you losing yourself like you did that night kept on repeating in my head. And each and every time, you had less and less clothing on."

I pinch his nipple and he makes an "ouch" sound. "Luke, I'm being serious here."

"I'm getting there, I swear. I started to think of you – I mean, *you* as a person. You were intriguing. You were sweet and funny. Different. I was so confused and maybe scared on some level."

"Scared? Why?" Why would *that* have scared him?

"Scared that I would never see you again. And that I wouldn't be able to fully explore the possibilities." He looks at me with such tenderness as he tucks a strand of hair behind my ear.

I need some time to think about what he just told me. I've been so hung up on him for so long – I've thought of him, fantasized about him, pretty much daily. But now that he's admitted to going through similar feelings himself … well, that scares the hell out of me. I want to believe him and let him in, but my spidey sense is warning me to tread carefully.

"I'm not sure what to say. I … I had no idea. I wish you would have found some way to tell me all this earlier."

"Tess, I wanted you from the first time your beautiful eyes met mine. Icing and all," he teases, "but it never felt like the right time. I'm not sure if now's the right time either, but I say fuck it. I have at least the next few days to get to know you, to spend more time with you. One thing I do know is that I don't want to go back to London without trying. I know it sounds clichéd, but third time's the charm, right?"

"Right. I just wish I'd known. Then I'd have been able to tell you how much I wanted you, and maybe I wouldn't have spent the last few months so expertly planning how to get back at you."

"What do you mean?" He tries for a confused look, but he can't keep his face straight.

"Come on, you know exactly what I'm referring to."

"Was that all part of some thoroughly-thought-out plan of yours?" he mocks, and I nudge him with my elbow.

"Umm, yes. Evil, Kick-Ass Plan, actually. And it worked, didn't it? If I recall correctly, you came after me, didn't you?"

"Evil, Kick-Ass Plan? God, Tessa, you're adorable." He shakes his head and chuckles. "Maybe I have an Evil, Kick-Ass Plan to counter yours."

"Oh, you do? I didn't think you were much of a planner, if I recall."

"Maybe not. But I do plan on kissing you again. To start. I'll figure out the rest as I go."

I should give his plan a name. "Pure Action" would be quite fitting, because his lips meet mine, and within seconds we're right where we left off. I don't know what it is about his lips, but I can't get enough. I love kissing him. I love stroking his hair while we kiss. I love inhaling his fresh scent as I breathe. His mouth is greedy, needing mine the same way I need his. His hand travels up and cups my breast. He brings my nipple between his fingers, and as he pinches it, I cry out. My back arches and my pelvis pushes harder against his thickness. I am so turned on by him, I'm practically calling his cock to fuck me.

"Damn, Tess," he groans as he grabs another condom and rolls it on. This time he doesn't seem to have the patience to discover me. Instead, he brings my leg overtop of his hip and penetrates me.

"Oh god," I moan, and I hear him grunt in response. The feeling of him like this, while we're tangled in each other, is so intimate, yet intense. We find our rhythm and gain momentum. He's so slick, coated in me, as he slides in and out. It feels as though I'm in some sort of crazed state, feverish in response to how he feels inside me.

"You make me feel so good," I manage to voice in between his thrusts.

"I want to make you feel so good you'll never want to feel anyone else but me."

I don't think I will. Not after this. Not after the high I'm on, not after yet another orgasm shatters me.

When we've worked through his plan and are back to enjoying the comfort of tangled-body silence, Luke looks at me with drunken eyes and says, "Stay the night, Tess. Please?"

I probably should really think about what he's asking. I probably should evaluate the consequences. But right now, I am so comfy and cozy snuggled up right next to my stranger that my thoughts are focused merely on the here and now, and not on what I may be thinking tomorrow morning, when the aftereffects of Luke's presence wear off.

"Okay," I whisper, and I settle in against his chest. He kisses the top of my head. I imagine he smiles contentedly as he takes a deep breath. Then his breathing evens and his chest relaxes. And before I know it, we both drift off to sleep.

Chapter 14

I wake up in the middle of the night and feel unfamiliar warmth around me. The scent of the body next to mine is foreign yet familiar and so captivating that I'm in a momentary trance. As I blink my eyes open and take a few seconds to process where I am, last night's memories rush in. I can't help but smile when I realize the warmth that envelops me belongs to none other than Luke. His body is wrapped around me. He definitely is a cuddler. I have to admit, I'm enjoying the cuddling a lot more than I thought I would. He can invade my personal space all he wants. I can still feel the ghosts of kisses he left on me and retrace his lips touching my mouth, my skin, and the achy spot that seems to have no regard for my current state because it's screaming, "I want more!"

As I purr over happy thoughts of the night we had, out of nowhere a promise I once made to myself sneaks in. I don't date. I especially don't do long-distance romances.

No no no! I am not going there.

But the thought takes hold and nearly squeezes the air out of me. Near-panic strikes without warning, and I am back to being Rational Tessa, the Tessa I am so familiar with. That Tessa reminds me that Luke will be gone in a week and that this is just a fling. She reminds me that it's better to walk away before things get too serious. That Tessa slowly pulls out from underneath the strong arms that feel so incredibly warm and safe around her and decides that it's better to cut her losses. Break, detach, run.

Stealthy like a shadow, I pick my clothes up off the floor and start getting dressed, but I have no idea where my panties are. I remember is Luke pulling them down my legs, and then my mind goes blank for a moment. All I can remember is the ecstasy of the moments that followed; nothing else. I nearly feel the rush again. My heartbeat is speeding up like I'm being chased. Though, I try to reason, the sneaking out probably has something to do with that rush I feel.

Unable to find them, I decide it's best to go commando. The last thing I want is to have Luke wake up in the middle of my ninja-like mission. I pull my dress on and grab my sandals between my fingers so that I won't risk making any noise. Then I take one last look at the gorgeousness that is spread out on the bed. Too bad this is the end. But this is the rational thing to do after a hookup, right? I know he asked me to stay, but he was probably just high on lust. This is not the first time he's had sex with a girl – he's had plenty. I'm certain he didn't actually mean for me to stay, and he'd likely be wondering why I'm still here in the morning. *Awkward.*

Once I'm home, the sleep that I thought would so easily come does not. I toss and turn and stare at the ceiling, unable to process what I'm feeling. *Why am I feeling anything? We had sex!* I hate that I feel anything but relief for having left Luke's bedroom.

There's no point in trying to get to sleep once the first ray of sunlight finds its way through the blinds. I look at the clock; it's only six. Since I'm the one with the early shift today, prolonging this futile attempt at sleep is pointless. I take a long, hot shower, reminiscing about the kisses Luke left all over. I try to wash it all away, hoping the sensual feeling will just disappear.

But it sticks with me, even after I shower. I need a distraction, and I need it fast. Work is my salvation. I'm positive I'll have a productive day, especially since I'm going to try very hard to focus on nothing but work. I pull my hair back, put on a summery dress, and am at Lovely Cakes by seven.

I'VE OWNED LOVELY CAKES FOR CLOSE TO THREE YEARS now. After I got my BA – a "backup plan," as my dad liked to refer to it (he wanted to make sure both Clara and I had a formal education first and foremost) – I pursued a degree in baking and pastry. Two years later, I'd done it: I was a professionally trained pastry chef.

Even though my dad died unexpectedly, he'd made sure we were well taken care of. Mom, Clara, and I received a nice sum of money from his life insurance and the sale of his business. I invested my portion, and by the time I was done college, I had enough money saved up to start what I'd always dreamed of. The only thing I needed was the courage to make my dream a reality.

I don't know where he heard it, but my dad used to say, "In moments of decision, destiny is shaped." And he was right. After putting together an impressive business plan, evaluating the pros and cons of venturing off on my own, and figuring out the various scenarios of how I would survive financially, I took the leap of faith and Lovely Cakes was born. I haven't looked back since. It's been the biggest and best decision I've made thus far in my life. But a calculated decision. I knew the risks, and I did everything I could to make sure they didn't materialize. After all, I had a plan; I'd made a list. Both extremely useful, I might add.

I started small, barely breaking even the first few months, but I'd fully expected that would be the case. I focused on designing custom cakes and specialty desserts. I attended wedding trade shows, advertised in local magazines, and gave out free samples of my creations. I even offered cake decorating classes. To make the bakery more unique, I decided to incorporate my love of tea, undoubtedly my mom's British influence, to complement the sweets and treats – a perfect pairing. Sourcing local loose-leaf teas seemed like a great way to draw in added clientele and convert them into dessert lovers. Word of mouth spread quickly, and about six months later, things started turning around. I had orders coming in for weddings, birthday parties, baby showers, and all sorts of corporate events. And Lovely Cakes was bursting with both regular and new customers who enjoyed visiting the bakery to meet with friends, read, or just simply relax.

Since then, Lovely Cakes has grown significantly, but it hasn't lost its small-business charm. I have six part-time employees plus Rose, the only other full-time person on staff besides me.

I have a gift for creativity and have inherited the entrepreneurial gene from my dad. Sound business sense and planning skills have served me well. I know that I could never work for anyone else. I crave that sense of control, that knowledge that each decision I make is mine and mine alone. The satisfaction that comes from being successful because of the decisions I've made is extremely rewarding.

I'm proud of what I've accomplished in such a short period of time. I think I always knew I had it in me, but it wasn't until the first time I posted that OPEN sign on the door that I realized just how much influence my dad had on my decision to pursue this exciting venture.

My dad moved from Italy to Chicago full of big dreams, with even bigger holes in his pockets. But he was charismatic, smart, and ambitious. After trying out a few jobs over the first couple of years, he decided to start his own construction business and became pretty successful. I know I must have gotten that entrepreneurial spirit, that drive and passion, from him. Whenever he asked what I wanted to do when I grew up, I always said I wanted to run my own business, just like him. It's just too bad he didn't live to see me do it. But that was all the more reason I was determined to succeed.

I PLAN ON SPENDING THE DAY WORKING ON THE CRIMSON sugar roses and petals that will be scattered over the layers of Clara and Marcus's five-tier wedding cake. Antique Swarovski crystal brooches shaped like rosebuds are going to accentuate the sugar roses, bringing sparkle to the whole look. It's going to be amazing, and it's going to take time to put it all together the way I've envisioned it. Clara has no idea what it will look like, but I've incorporated all of her favorites – roses, sparkle, sinful red velvet and decadent chocolate – into this creation. I'm certain she'll love it. I also know it's going to take pretty much the rest of the week to perfect it.

First things first: I'm in a dire need of caffeine, given the less than restful sleep, so I go for a traditional English breakfast black tea this morning. While it's steeping, I put on my apron and get the mixing bowls and utensils ready. Just as I line up all the ingredients on the work room table, I hear a loud knock at the front door. Rose has a key; other staff don't normally come in this early. Who could it be?

Somewhat annoyed about being interrupted, but nevertheless intrigued, I go to the front door and what – rather, whom – I see is completely unexpected. What is Luke doing here? We're not even open yet. Perhaps he felt like having something sweet for breakfast on his way to work and decided to stop by? I don't think that's it, though, because his distraught face doesn't scream "I'm hungry." He's sporting jogging pants and a plain white t-shirt. He's scruffier than I remember him being last night, his eyes are wide and … hmm, furious? He may be angry, but all I notice is how sexy he looks. Really, it's not even fair. The man is more delicious than any of the cakes on display in the window.

Then I remember the likely reason he's less than pleased. My ninja-like escape. Uh-oh.

As I unlock the door, he bursts into the store.

"What the fuck, Tess?"

"Well, good morning to you too," I say calmly as I lock the door and make my way to the work room. He grunts at my reply but follows me nonetheless. Before I manage to slide behind the table to keep some distance between us, he grabs me by my shoulder and turns me to face him.

"What happened to you last night? I woke up this morning and you were gone. I called you, like, fifteen times, left messages … and nothing. I haven't heard a single word back from you."

"First of all, fifteen times would be borderline stalkerish." I try to make light of the situation, though I'm not sure I'm succeeding from the look of exasperation on his face. "Second of all, I haven't had my phone on since last night." I respond nonchalantly and go back to working on the cake, as if everything is a-okay. That will be an interesting set of messages to listen to later.

"Fine, it wasn't fifteen, but it was several. It's just, you made me so damn worried. I had no idea where you were, why you left, if you were okay." He seems genuinely concerned.

"Well, I'm fine. So no need to worry." I smile innocently, hoping to ease the tension he's created.

"No need to worry?" He lets out an exasperated sigh. "Fuck, Tess, I went by your place, buzzed your apartment for five minutes before realizing you weren't coming down. This was the only other place I knew," he continues, as if trying to justify why he barged in here like a crazy person. 'Cause right now, he really is acting kind of crazy. Maybe he's just being protective, though. He pulls me by my hand and looks at me with a mix of anger and concern. "You can't just leave like that."

"Why not?" I retort. "Why does it even matter? We just had sex. You didn't actually expect me to stay the night, did you?"

His look changes as if something just registered with him. "*Actually*, I did."

Oh. Well, completely misread that one.

"But, I just thought ... I mean, it's not something people normally do after a one-night hookup, is it?"

"But I asked you to stay. Why didn't you?"

"Because it made no sense, that's why. I mean, you're leaving in a week. Staying the night would ... complicate things. It would mean something, when it doesn't mean anything. It can't..." I trail off as I try to convince myself.

"Tess, maybe I want complicated. I want it to mean something. I want to give us a try. Don't you?" His voice is gentle, almost pleading.

His answer surprises me, but it shouldn't. Luke has been honest about his intentions since he arrived. I've been too pragmatic, too set in a I'm-happy-being-on-my-own frame of mind before I spent time with him. I take a minute to respond because my mind is racing trying to figure out what I want to say.

"I do ... and I don't. I mean, I don't know..." It's like I'm afraid to trust my instincts. And his. "I just... I don't do this well."
"This?" He asks, confused.
"This ... us. Whatever *this* is," I say, almost as confused.
"I would call *this* giving chemistry a chance to develop into something more." He sounds so convincing.
"How can you be so sure that it will?"
"I told you already. Unlike you, I don't need to think this through. I know what my instincts are telling me. I don't need any lists. *You*, Tess, are the one I want." He's not making this easy on me.
"I just ... I can't let myself get hurt again. I just can't." I look down, avoiding his eyes, not letting him see the way he's affecting me. My voice is a shaky mess.
"You can't or you don't want to?" I shrug as if uncertain.
"Tessa," Luke says softly. I don't dare look up. "Look at me." He pulls at my chin, forcing my eyes to meet his. "I'm not like *him*. Trust me."
I know he's not – he's nothing like Jason. I trust Luke. I just don't think I'm ready to trust myself.
"Tessa, say something. Anything. Just don't give me the silent treatment. Say that last night wasn't just fun and games for you. Say that it meant something more."
That's exactly the problem. It felt like it was more. Why am I making this more difficult than it needs to be? Why can't I just let my brain take a vacation somewhere warm and sunny so it can relax and let my feelings take over decision-making instead?
I need to pull away from him so I have space to think. I break from his hold and walk back to the table. I childishly stare at the ingredients – the icing sugar, the food coloring, the butter. It's simple. I know exactly what to do to make them flourish. But this, with Luke – I have no idea what to do, what to say. So I'm stuck there. Staring. Thinking. Overthinking.
"Last night was..." I hesitate and take a deep sigh. *Wonderful, passionate, romantic* – those are all the words that would describe last night, but instead I choose to whisper, "Fine," as I turn to look at him.

"Fine?" he sounds frustrated. Hmm. I'm guessing it's not quite the answer he was after. "Do I need to remind you what 'fine' felt like last night?"

I shrug. "Maybe?"

I may have just pushed his last button.

"Was it fine when I took these off?" He pulls my black lace panties out of his pocket.

Well, at least I found my underwear. I was actually worried that I'd never get them back. They're one of the few lacy pairs I own. Kind of expensive, too. But I digress.

He takes a step closer, but I have a feeling he won't just pass them along without asking for something in return. No, I'm pretty sure he's going to make me work for them.

"And when I made you desperate for me?"

Another step closer. I suck in a nervous breath and feel myself blush.

"Was it fine when you screamed my name as you climaxed around my cock?"

That was, in fact, more than fine.

The subtle anger combined with frustration are turning Luke into an irresistible predator. With one more step he is so close that our lips are nearly touching. He holds my gaze with a look that says he's in control, and that look is so damn sexy. The hairs on my arms stand up from the rush I feel from him being so close to me. I'm trapped between him and the table, with nowhere to run. I'm squeezed so tight against him that I can feel his hard-on push against my belly. Certain body parts of mine are getting so excited in response that I've forgotten what this conversation was all about. Something about whether things were fine last night, I think. Yes, that's what it was.

I'm about to open my mouth and say, "It was more than fine," but as I do, he places his fingers gently on my lips, preventing me from speaking.

"Shhh," he says softly, but the greediness in his eyes remains. "I fucking want you, Tess. I wanted you the first time I saw you. I wanted you that night at the movies. I've wanted you ever since I landed after what seemed to be the longest fucking flight I ever took. I wanted you last night, and I want you again. I can't seem to get enough of you. So don't give up on me now."

I've wanted him since the first time I ran into him too, and, despite myself, definitely since his magic fingers did a number on me. My lady parts more than want him again. I don't think I'm ready to give up. That much I'm willing to admit to myself, but I can't seem to say it out loud. It would make this too real.

He holds my gaze, then pulls me closer and mumbles grouchily, "Christ, woman. What do I need to do to convince you?"

I sense his frustration has reached its peak. This is different. Not so nice-guy Luke right now. Not so soft and gentle. Desperate, maybe. Desperate enough that he kisses me so hard that I'm nearly breathless. My mouth responds, kissing him back like I don't ever want to miss his kiss again. Because I missed it. I missed *him*. My body is betraying my resolve.

Our kissing becomes frenzied. Mmm, I love this side of Luke. He's not taking it easy on me. He brings my dress up, then yanks down my comfy cotton boy shorts. I was not expecting to have them taken off by anyone but me when I dressed this morning. Thankfully he's not interested in my underwear. He turns me around and bends me over the table, drawing his hand down my spine all the way to my bottom.

He leans into me, his mouth nearly touching my ear. I feel his fiery breath on me as he commands in a low, rough voice, "Tell me you want me."

"I do," I whisper.

"Good," he mumbles as caresses my behind, like he's admiring my ass. At the corner of my eye, I'm pretty sure I see a spatula move off the table – no, it *definitely* moves, and then … he spanks me. He *actually* spanks me. With a spatula.

"That's for leaving last night," he growls. "For being stubborn."

My reaction is some kind of a whimper-moan because god, that felt different, yet incredible. I feel a slight burn from where the spatula connected with my skin, but the tingling feeling that travels the short distance to my very wet and worked-up pussy is beyond arousing.

"Again," I whisper, and surprise even myself. "Spank me, Luke."

I'm asking to be spanked. With a spatula. *What has gotten into me?*

He caresses the tender spot and then he does as I please. I shiver because my nerve endings feel like they've succumbed to torture. I wonder if I'm going insane, because I want more of it.

"You're driving me mad, woman," Luke growls, like this is the most fucking fantastic thing he's ever done, then buries his cock into me so deep, so hard, that I breathe, "God, Luke," in response and don't make it past two words.

He holds my hips, my legs spread wide, as he pushes into me, hastily at first, then gently. I can feel every inch of his thick, long cock. My body mirrors his moves, my hips pushing against him in rhythm. He's claiming me, and I feel like I need him even deeper, beyond what is physically possible. He's cupping my breasts, squeezing, kneading. My orgasm is so close, I close my eyes in an effort to hold onto this high for longer, to hold onto Luke.

"God, I am so lost in you," he groans. Those words, that simple revelation, sound so sincere. My heart swells at the realization that he's genuinely infatuated with me, perhaps just as much as I am with him. Perhaps more. My body responds, and the only feeling I register is pure pleasure as I moan his name and come undone.

He may be lost in me, but in this moment I am just as completely lost in him. How am I feeling like this? It's too soon, but it's not something I can continue to downplay.

I tuck that thought away and instead focus on Luke and the way he finds his release. He crashes down against my back, burying his face in my hair, breathing heavily.

And I'm smiling. No, I'm beaming. "That was more than fine," I whisper when my breathing finally returns to normal.

He tugs at my chin and turns my face to the side so that I can see the sly grin spread across his face, validating my comment. But then his expression shifts. I notice the change in the way his eyes search mine. He whispers, "Don't fucking leave me again, Tess. Not without saying good-bye."

I know he can't possibly just be referring to me leaving him last night. I know he can't bear to be broken again the way he must have been when his mom left. I know how scarred that must have left his heart. And I also know how much I hate not hearing good-bye too. Dad never had a chance to say it. Jason never cared to.

I know that good-bye will come sooner than we're willing to accept right now. I'm not so sure I'll be ready to say it when the time comes. My heart may not be able to handle it.

What am I getting myself into? The thought I tucked away is back and apparently needs further analysis. Whatever this is that Luke and I have feels so good and so right, yet it's so terrifying and unpredictable at the same time. What if Luke is The One? God, I'm starting to sound like Clara. But what if he is? After all, I do feel this connection with him – I'm drawn to him like icing to a cupcake. Without him, I'm just a plain, boring muffin. Not nearly as sweet. Not nearly as exciting.

And if I don't completely embrace the connection, the possibilities, will I forever regret not giving us a chance? Will I wonder what could have been? Committing to wherever this may lead could break me again, but for some reason, I feel like it's the right thing to do.

"I won't," I whisper, but hate myself the second I say it. Why did I say it with such certainty, when I'm not completely sure if I'll actually be able to follow through? The last thing I want to do is lie to Luke, especially since I know how difficult saying good-bye will be. Leaving without a word will be much easier. When the time comes, I may be too much of a coward to say it to him face to face.

Chapter 15

When we're done doing what it is we just did – in the work room of the bakery, I might add – I turn to Luke and we stand together, breathing each other in, our bodies molded. He wraps his arms around my waist, holding me tight, before bringing his hand to my face, brushing my lips with his thumb. He looks at me with soft adoration and boyish infatuation, and I revel in the moment. But a few seconds later, that look is replaced by a strange one, like something just registered with him.

"Oh god, Tess, I'm so sorry. I got carried away."

That he did. No complaints, though. That was *so* hot.

"I think we both did."

"No, that's not what I meant. I … we … we didn't *use* anything."

Oh. *Oh.* Oh god, he's right. And here I promised myself I'd never be irresponsible again. I try to process what this may mean as thoughts of Luke and other women cross my mind. Even though I know it's been a while for him, I don't know the details of his history, and from the intel I've got so far, I'd probably be foolish not to question his record. And vice versa.

"I'm perfectly clean since that drunken mistake I told you about. Trust me, I had to make sure," I say with a grimace. "And on the pill. You?"

"Ditto," he says. "To the making sure, I mean. Not to the pill. That would be, well, odd." He laughs with obvious relief and a little bit of mischief. I'm relieved too. And surprisingly, it doesn't bother me that it happened the way it did. I'm kind of turned on by the skin-on-skin contact.

"No need to apologize. Really. That was... Hmm, how should I put it?" I'm struggling to find the best way to describe it. "*Definitely* feel free to do that again."

"If you misbehave again, I just may. In all seriousness, though..."

"Yeah?" I ask expectantly.

"What you said earlier, Tessa, about me leaving in a week and what that would mean for us." He looks at me, searching for a reaction, recognizing the unease in my eyes at the mere mention of him leaving. "Let's not think about next Monday, okay? Let's just focus on one day at a time. I really would like it if we could spend some time together over the next few days. I want to show you what it would be like being with me." His voice pleads with me, his eyes hopeful.

"You make it sound so simple." I sigh.

"That's because it is. It should be. Don't overthink it, don't complicate it. Just say you will."

"Okay, I will," I whisper, leaning my forehead against his, rubbing his nose affectionately with mine.

"That's better." He grins as if I've promised the world, then kisses me, holding my cheeks in the palms of his hands. It feels so intimate, so lovely, so connected. I kiss him back, my kiss filled with emotion, with the hope that he understands I trust him to not break my heart.

"I've got a busy day today, wrapping up a few things at the office here that have carried over from last week, and then I'm having dinner with my dad later on tonight. But tomorrow, can we spend some time together? Just the two of us? Maybe even the whole day?" A day with Luke sounds wonderful. "Do you think you can make it work?" he asks expectantly.

"I think that can be arranged. After all, I'm the boss." I chuckle. "Since I've been working non-stop due to a very important wedding this weekend, I should be able to take a day off. Especially if I have no more *interruptions* today."

"Can't guarantee that, but I'll try."

"TESSA, SOMEONE'S HERE TO SEE YOU," ROSE CALLS AFTER me while I'm in the stock room checking our inventory.

A familiar voice follows. "I said I couldn't guarantee. Sorry. You like Chinese?"

I turn around, and of course I should have known. Luke grins as he walks over and plants a kiss on my mouth.

"I do."

"I needed a break from the office. I needed to see you again," he admits, and I feel giddy because he's taken time from his busy day to see me.

"I'm glad you're here. And thanks for lunch. Oh, I'm sorry, Rose." I realize that she's still standing in the doorway, a crazy grin plastered on her face. "I assume you guys have met?" She nods. "Do you mind if I take a short break?"

"Not at all. Let me take over. You go and enjoy your *lunch*," Rose says with a wink. She could not possibly be any more obvious. Rose is a great friend, but she's also a bit of a smart ass.

Luke and I eat and talk about nothing and everything. He tells me about the things he's working on and some of the potential acquisitions they're looking at. He talks about the business trips he plans on taking to explore those possibilities. He's passionate about his career and how the travel allows him to combine work with pleasure. I wonder if he'll ever consider giving it up and moving back to Chicago. Though I know I shouldn't because his answer will likely be disappointing, I ask anyway.

"Would you ever consider moving back? To Chicago, I mean?" I hold my breath as I anticipate his answer.

He takes a minute to process. I assume it's probably not something he's had to contemplate, at least not for a while. He holds my gaze, and something on his face changes, like he's looking for a certain reaction and hoping he'll see it. "If the right opportunity presents itself. If there's a good enough reason … I would."

Oh.

I hope I'm not reading too much into his answer, but I can't help but wonder if I would be a good enough reason for him. There's no way I'm asking. Knowing and not knowing his answer are equally terrifying options, so this will have to do for now.

"So you're seeing your dad today?" I ask, intrigued to find out more about their relationship and take my mind off all the questions that are swirling in my head. I'll have to make a list of those later.

"Yeah, I haven't seen him since I got here. It's been a while since I last saw him." I can sense a hint of guilt in his voice.

"Do you guys talk often?"

"Not often enough," he says, sounding somewhat disappointed. With himself, maybe?

"How come?" I realize I may be prodding, but I can't help myself. I want to know more about Luke, more about everything that defines him. I know his mom left – though that's about all I know at this point – but I don't really know what his relationship has been like with his dad since.

"To be honest, I don't know." He hesitates, which is unlike him; he's normally so forward. "After Mom left, I probably didn't handle everything the way I should have. I said some pretty shitty things to my dad when she didn't come back." Remorse is evident in his voice and his eyes. This obviously isn't something he wants to be reminded of, and here I am, dragging it out of him anyway.

"You were too young to know any better. I'm sure your reactions were not unreasonable given the circumstances," I say, trying to comfort him.

"I just wish I didn't say some of the stuff I said. He's always been there for me, and I was a difficult teen, blaming him instead of my mom."

"We always manage to hurt those closest to us. It's the easiest way to handle emotions that are spiraling out of control."

"Yeah, no kidding."

"Have you ever talked to him about it?"

"We've talked, in not so many words."

"I'm sure if you just do, if you talk to him about it, you'd see that he probably forgave you a long time ago. He probably never blamed you for anything to begin with. He must have known how difficult a time it was for you, how much it would have affected how you behaved."

"I just– I don't want to bring up the ghosts of the past. We're past that now, and our relationship is a thousand times better than it has been in years," he clarifies.

"That makes sense, I guess." I know I shouldn't push this any further. So I just leave it at that. It's between him and his dad. Since I don't know all the details, I'm not the best person to be passing judgment. "So where are we off to tomorrow?" I ask, hoping to deflect our discussion.

"It's a surprise." He winks playfully.

"You won't tell me?" He shakes his head. "Will you give me a clue, please? I need to at least have an idea. I don't deal well with surprises."

He laughs. "Just wear something comfortable. That's all. Oh, and a skimpy bikini." He grins mischievously. "I'll pick you up at nine."

A bikini. I already like where this is going.

We finish our impromptu lunch, and before he leaves he kisses me so fiercely that my mind momentarily spins out of control. I let out a raspy moan, and when I finally find my voice, I whisper, "Normally I'd recommend you have dessert, but I think you should take a rain check instead. I might let you cash it in later. Well, soon later." I smile.

"You got it, cupcake."

KNOCK KNOCK KNOCK.

I hear the banging, but I'm unable to place it.

Knock knock knock. Again. *What is that damn noise?* I turn my night light on and realize the noise I was hearing in my dream is coming from my door. I look at the clock. Who the fuck is knocking at my door at eleven thirty?

Knock knock.

"I'm coming, I'm coming," I say groggily, almost angry about being woken up. I really, really love my sleep. Wearing only my white cami top and a pair of pink boy-short panties, I manage my way to the door in a daze and take a look through the peephole.

It's him. Delicious as always. In an instant, my heart begins to beat at a pace I usually only feel when running. Or those times when I run into Luke. Which seems to happen a lot. What is he doing here? I run my fingers through my hair, hoping the sleepy mess will turn out to be half decent as I open the door and face him.

"Hey," Luke says in a husky voice as his eyes scan my outfit. Or lack thereof.

"Hi," I manage barely audibly, my voice still sleepy, though my breath catches at the sight of the magnificence in front of me. His dark gray tie is loosened around his neck and the top buttons of his light gray dress shirt are undone. He's got a day's worth of scruff and his eyes are beaming. "What are you doing here?"

"I needed to see you."

"How did you get into the building?"

"I convinced the doorman that it was an emergency," Luke says with a playful wink.

"An emergency?" I ask confused and concerned at the same time, and still a bit asleep. "Is everything okay?"

"Everything is more than okay, especially now." He grins, a look of mischief on his face. "It turns out the dessert I had tonight just didn't do it for me. I'm still hungry for something sweet, so I'm here to claim my rain check."

Oh. The rain check. I'm suddenly completely awake, charged with the energy that radiates off him and gets sucked into every pore of my body.

He takes a step toward me, closing the door behind him. "Very, very hungry," he continues as he pulls me toward him and wraps his hands around my waist. A soft moan escapes me when I feel his erection. "And it couldn't wait until tomorrow morning. So yeah, definitely an emergency," he continues.

"There's only one thing I can think of that tastes sweet enough." He doesn't elaborate. Instead, he plants a kiss on my lips. A very hungry kiss. The restaurant dessert must have really sucked. But I'm not complaining.

Our tongues tangle, taste, explore. The way he kisses me nearly makes me mad; I'm frantic with need. Luke reaches for my breasts and pinches my nipples through my camisole. They're so tender and harden instantly at his touch. All I can think of is how much I love it when he does that … and wow, definitely *that* … and … *God, I want him so bad.*

Without taking his mouth off of mine, he starts to pull my panties down, and I wiggle them the rest of the way off. I unbuckle his belt and work on bringing down his pants. When we're both naked from the waist down, he doesn't hesitate a minute. Instead, he pulls me up by my bottom and slams me against the door. It's aggressive and so fucking arousing. I've only ever read about this and always questioned if it was in fact possible, but damn, it's *so* happening. Right now. In *my* apartment.

"God, I love feeling you against me," Luke whispers in his roughed-up voice, breaking the mouth-to-mouth action. Then he reaches for his cock and finds his way into me. I can't help but moan; that feeling of connection between us is pure ecstasy. We find our rhythm, and I'm going on a pretty good assumption here that he's enjoying this dessert a lot more than the one at the restaurant.

"So fucking sweet," Luke whispers, thrusting with each word. I lean my head against the door, and he licks and sucks down my exposed neck, marking his territory with his mouth. My breasts are swollen from the hunger he's awoken in me. I moan, chasing the orgasm that's building, the orgasm that's now on the verge of breaking me. He's relentless – in and out, in and out – and really, quite strong. This is so hot. *How does he even…?* I don't finish my thought because the thought itself, combined with the latest thrust, brings me to a point of frenzy. And while I'm still in post-orgasmic bliss, he pushes a couple more times and then he's there with me. Drowning. Gasping for air.

We hold onto each other like that for a few seconds, or minutes. I'm just guessing, because I'm in no way capable of telling time right now.

"Well, that was unexpected." I finally manage to find my voice.

"That definitely hit the spot," Luke chuckles.

I can't help but smile. He kisses me one more time, then eases my legs down.

"I guess I better get going," Luke says as he brings his boxers up and tucks his you-know-what neatly in. I realize I'm staring, unabashedly. His you-know-what brings me joy. Lots of it.

I also realize I don't like the feeling of him leaving me. That's troubling.

"I don't..." *Hmm.* I catch myself before I say it. If I tell him I don't want him to leave, that means I'll be inviting him to stay. I'm not ready for that yet. So I settle for a pouty look instead.

"That look's going to get you into trouble," he warns. He pulls on my bottom lip with his teeth and then places a gentle kiss on my forehead.

"I like getting into trouble with you."

He grins and looks at me like he's torn. I wonder what he's thinking. I wonder if he's thinking about how he likes to get into trouble with me too. I wonder if he wants to ask if it'd be okay for him to stay. But instead, he just says, "I'll see you tomorrow morning, okay?"

"Okay." I nod and let go of his hand unwillingly. His fingers linger on mine, letting go just as hesitantly. I open the door and usher him outside. The thought of having him stay the night enters my mind for a split second again, but I know it's not the right time. I mean, considering we just did it, I'd technically be inviting him to stay the night and sleep with me, cuddle, all that fuzzy stuff. That would be weird. It's way too early to even consider, yet letting him go doesn't feel right either.

He smiles warmly, then says, "Sleep tight, cupcake," and takes off. I watch him walk confidently toward the elevators. He turns to take one last look at me and blows me a kiss. I pretend to catch it, grinning from ear to ear.

How do I become this mushy whenever Luke's around? I'm not a mushy kind of person, I don't think. At least I don't recall ever being this swoony over Jason.

When he's gone, I close the door reluctantly and lean against it, then slide down to sit on the floor. First of all, I'm not sure I can move – my legs are weak, and I still feel a throbbing sensation down there. Second of all, after this unplanned – though, I have to admit, very welcome – interruption, I'm not sure whether I'm going to be able to get back to sleep right away. I'm so wound up I could do cartwheels if I was at all gymnastically inclined, which I'm not

Tessa, you are so fucked. My conscience creeps in. And she's right. I'm fucked, thoroughly, in more ways than one.

I finally find the energy to pull myself off the floor and go straight for the kitchen cupboards. I grab a few chocolate-covered biscuits – I may keep a stash of baked goodies for times of need – and put on the kettle for tea. All that dessert talk and all those calories burned have left me in dire need of some sugar. After I've indulged in the oh-to-die-for delight, I crawl into bed and go off to sleep almost at once, contrary to my presumption. Happily, blissfully exhausted.

Chapter 16

"Good morning, cupcake." Luke's infectious smile greets me as I open the door. It's nine in the morning and he's here just as promised. He's sporting a casual look – a dark baseball cap that casts a shadow over his smoldering eyes, a t-shirt that hints at the firm definition of his chest and arms, and khaki shorts that hang low on his hips, just low enough to make me want to pull them down all the way. Yummy.

"Morning, stranger. Long time no see."

He leans in to kiss me, and I savor Luke's lips, those same lips I haven't been able to wait to kiss again since I got up this morning. We stay at the door making out like teenagers who can't get enough of each other.

"Mmm, I've missed you since last night," Luke whispers.

"I've kind of missed you too."

"Just kind of?"

"Fine. I've missed you too."

Luke smiles in response, and as he steps back, his eyes travel from my lips down the rest of my body. "Fuck, Tess. Is that what you're planning on wearing the entire day?"

"What?" I ask with feigned innocence. "You said wear something comfortable."

I point to my washed-out jean shorts and simple pink tank, which I'm wearing over top of my somewhat skimpy bikini. I have my hair pulled into a ponytail and am wearing very little makeup, au naturel–style.

"I know what I asked for," Luke says. "I just didn't think 'comfortable' would turn out to be this fucking sexy." He pulls on the strap around my neck. "I can't even imagine what's hiding underneath."

"If you're lucky enough, you just may get a glimpse." I love being playful with him.

"I better. But how am I supposed to manage this *situation* in the meantime?" He points to his crotch, where his "situation" seems ready to tear a hole in his shorts. Tempting.

"Hmm. I guess you've got yourself in quite a pickle. We may have to do something about that," I tease as I reach down and rub my palm against his irresistible problem. He makes a hissing sound and I … I'd better restrain myself. Although there are not too many things I'd rather be doing right now than dealing with his situation. "Of course, that will depend on how the day goes and whether you behave," I taunt as I pull my palm away, giggling at Luke's pouty look.

"We'll see about that. You just may be the one begging for it by the end of the day," he challenges.

"You'd be so lucky." There's no way I'll be the one begging. I am the epitome of self-control.

"Oh, I'm pretty sure I'll get lucky today. Just a matter of time."

Cocky. But I'm pretty sure he's right.

LUKE HASN'T GIVEN ME MANY CLUES AS TO WHAT WE'LL be doing today, but when we pull into a marina, I have a pretty good idea of what he's planned for us today.

"Are we going sailing?"

"You got it."

"I've never been sailing before."

"Never?" He seems pleased, like it's his chance to show me something new, make it our adventure.

I shake my head. "I've lived here my entire life, but it's just something I've never had a chance to try, though I've always wanted to," I clarify. I have no clue what sailing involves and if

I'll know what to do. Then a thought occurs. "Do you sail?" I ask a bit nervously. Maybe it should be obvious, since this is what he chose for our date today, but if I'm going to be stuck alone with him in the middle of the lake, I kind of want to be sure.

"As often as I can. My dad taught me. It's safe to say you've got nothing to worry about," Luke replies as we make our way down the dock.

"That's reassuring."

He grins smugly. "Whenever I'm back in town, I make it a point to go sailing. It's just something I really enjoy." He squeezes my hand tightly, like he's letting me know how much having me here means to him, just as he stops in front of a sailboat.

"That's a nice boat." It's pristine-white, simple, and not overly big, yet large enough for several people to hang out on. "Is it yours?"

"No, it's my dad's."

"How long has he had it?"

"For a while," Luke says as he deposits the backpack and a cooler he's brought with him in the boat. "Since Mom left."

"Oh, I see." I didn't expect that as an answer, and I don't want this to turn serious, so I go with a casual, "Anything I can help with?" as we settle in.

"I think I can teach you a thing or two." He winks, then explains a few key things. It seems simple yet complicated; I wouldn't dare do it without his lead.

As he prepares the boat for sailing, I try to help as best as I can, but I'm kind of distracted because it's hot – I mean, *I'm* hot from watching Luke move around the boat, his strong arms and broad shoulders displayed for my viewing pleasure. I can't help but ogle him and drift off for a minute as I imagine all the parts of his body I have yet to explore. Damn, he's sexy.

"I wanna fuck you today." Luke's voice brings me back from my trance.

Did he just...? "I'm sorry, what did you say?"

"The wind is working in our favor today." Oh, of course. *That's* what he said. I swear I've got heat stroke from all the ogling. I need a drink of water.

"It should be smooth sailing. We're heading up the shore, so make yourself comfortable and enjoy the ride."

"I'm sure I will." Especially given the, um, view.

Sailing really is wonderful; liberating, energizing even. It's an escape from the crowded and hectic city that I know and love. From the distance, downtown Chicago looks somehow pristine and quiet. There's just the right amount of wind, which makes it feel as if we're gliding on the water. The sun's rays are reflecting off the lake, and the sky is ocean blue, with barely a cloud.

Luke's definitely in his element: poised, confident, happy. He twirls my ponytail, all the while gazing at me with that purposeful look, like he knows something I have yet to discover. Though the tingling I feel all over has me questioning if I've discovered something I've been afraid of finding. I remind myself to take a mental picture of Luke right in this moment, because it's a moment I should treasure. And then Luke pulls out his phone and takes a few pictures of the two of us wrapped in each other – a tangible treasure to add to our collection.

AFTER SAILING FOR A WHILE, WE DOCK NEAR A BEACH and spread a blanket on the sand. We manage to get through lunch without any unplanned distractions. I'm lying – Luke has been plenty distracting in swim shorts and nothing else, just brawn and skin that I've barely been able to keep my hands off the entire time we've been eating and talking.

Though I made sure to hold up my end of the bargain and distract him just as well, with my not-so-subtle skimpy-bikini display and such. I think I've got him all wound up and ready to beg. I know it's coming. I can feel it. The way he's looking at me, the way he's probably thinking how much he'd like for the bikini to disappear, the way he'd like to taste what's underneath. Oh yeah, I've got him.

"Are you ready?" Luke asks. *Here we go.*

"Ready for what?" I play it coolly. I'm *so* ready.

"Come on." He pulls me up and drags me toward the water.

"Oh no no no NO!" I shriek, realizing what he's about to do. Not even in the slightest what I thought he had in mind. "The water will be freezing!" It may be July, but I know the lake is not nearly the temperature my body welcomes. As far as I'm concerned, it might as well be January.

He just laughs and keeps dragging me with him. I try to fight him off, pushing against his chest, desperately trying to break away, which I do, albeit ungracefully, and then start running, all the while laughing with him. But before I make it even a few feet, he grabs my hand and tries pulling me back toward him. I pull in the opposite direction and manage to get free, except the motion propels me forward, my feet stumble, and I fall. How familiar. At least the sand is soft. Luke lands on top of me and tickles my tummy, making me giggle uncontrollably.

"Stop it! Stop, please," I plead through laughter. "You've got me."

The tickling stops suddenly, his eyes lock with mine, and after a moment's thought, he says, "I may have you pinned, but you've got me trapped, Tess. I don't think I could escape you, ever."

How can a girl not get all wrapped up in a guy when he says things like that? I'm a lost cause, it appears – I'm really starting to believe his words, and I don't think I could escape him either.

"Never," I whisper, almost convinced by my own reply.

"Never," he breathes, still gazing at me.

Then his lips tangle with mine and I forget what I may have just promised. Instead, my brain decides to take a short vacay, leaving my heart to control my thoughts and emotions for a change. I realize that the heart somehow makes everything more exhilarating than the brain does, especially when the heart is overwhelmed by Luke's sexy moves.

Exhilarating move number one: Luke's hand travels up my body, from my hips toward one of my breasts. My skin tingles from his touch. My nipples take notice.

Exhilarating move number two: His other hand connects with my palm as he brings it above my head, pinning it down. My body blends with his. My breath hitches.

Exhilarating move number three: Luke pushes my legs apart with his knee, and I feel his thickness nestled just where I want him. I pant, desperate for more than the current offering. Luke's response, a groan from the back of his throat, only makes me crave him more.

The few beachgoers that are nearby are probably witnessing what one could almost describe as sex on the beach. Not quite full-throttle action, but it's as close as we can get without the full exposure. If I were a passerby, I'd probably take another route altogether. Or maybe I'd just cough for effect – it seemed to work when we got carried away during our first kiss at the park. Or I'd have us arrested for public indecency. *Oh. My. God.* What are we doing?

Frankly, though, I'm not really in a state to process this realization with any kind of weight, so I am most thankful for Luke and his uncanny ability to maintain control, because I am a complete mess.

And completely unaware of what his sneaky self is about to do next. When he pulls me up by my hands, grabs me by my waist, and lifts me over his shoulder, I realize almost instantly I've been played. *Damn it!*

He hauls me toward the lake, splashing us as we get deeper and deeper. The cool water is enough to bring me out of the la-la-land I was lost in. I fight him with all my womanly strength, my legs kicking against his stomach, my fists punching his lower back – I'm like a kung-fu master. In reality, my attempt at escaping this predicament is kind of pathetic. I can't stop laughing, so I'm barely in control of my motions.

"Don't you dare," I snort-scream, but it's of no use. I sense the dreaded fate that awaits me.

Before I know it, Luke dumps me into the water. I shriek and take a few seconds to orient myself, figure out my arm from my leg, my leg from my arm. When all the parts appear to be in their rightful places, I surface as gracefully as one can having just been tossed into the water like a beach ball. When I do come up, I'm smiling; beaming, in fact. That was so much fun. I'm startled by my reaction, because I don't normally enjoy surprises, yet I love how unpredictable Luke is. He's laughing so hard his whole body is shaking.

I run my fingers down my hair to drain it. "Was that just some evil plan of yours to get me wet?"

"Possibly." He smirks. "I like you wet." Suddenly I feel warmer. "I know of a few other ways to do just that." *A lot* warmer.

"Nuh-uh. No more movie-worthy make-out sessions." I don't think I could handle any more without risking arrest.

"Movie-worthy?"

"Hmm, did I say that?"

"You did." His lips are pressed in a tight line, but the corner of his mouth twitches like he's completely amused by me.

"You know, like those ridiculously hot kissing scenes in chick flicks." I can't believe I'm trying to explain this right now.

He reaches over to move a wet strand of hair behind my ear. "God, you're adorable," he says, and I'm that same swooning girly-girl I was when I first ran into him. I'm also very, very distracted by the trickles of water running down his naked chest. Drip. Drop. I'm suddenly thirsty and more than willing to risk spending a night in jail.

"But if kissing is off limits, there's only one thing left to do," he continues. *What could he possibly be–?* I don't get a chance to finish my thought because he actually splashes me.

"Oh, you're in so much trouble." A splashing war commences, and I'm laughing like I haven't laughed in a long time, loving the playfulness that Luke brings out in me. Absolutely loving it.

AFTER THE WATER ADVENTURE, WE MAKE OUR WAY BACK to the beach and crash down on the blanket. Luke's on his back and I'm resting on my side, absorbed with Mr. Delicious. Even though I've seen Luke a lot over the last few days, I can't get enough of his masculine, edgy beauty, of his flawless body. I'm making small circles on his chest with my fingers and he's playing with the wet strands of my hair.

"Tessa, I know this will sound crazy, and I'm not sure how I've gotten to this point so quickly, but when I'm not around you it sucks."

Umm, is he serious? Sure, I'm infatuated and more than captivated by Luke, but am I at the same point as he is? Not quite. Though I have a feeling I'm getting there faster than I ever thought I would again. Yet the image of a ticking clock flashes in my mind, taunting me. Five more days and he'll be gone. *Don't go there*, I remind myself.

He smiles softly. Before I'm able to think much more about what his words mean, Luke continues. "I can't bring myself to think about losing you, Tess."

"You won't." I react on impulse. It's like my brain doesn't want to consider the probability. I've done it again – provided false assurance. I question whether I'm truly being honest or just worried about hurting him.

But Luke's gaze is serious. There's affection there, and fear. "When my mom left," he says, "it messed with my head. I was thirteen, and I know that was such a long time ago, but at the time it really hurt."

I knew there was more to his feelings after he brushed them off so indifferently during our first date, and even more so after our talk over lunch yesterday. And I'm already feeling sorry for the thirteen-year-old Luke before he even gets to explaining this further.

"My dad used to remind me that if you love something enough and it's meant to be, it will come back. So I thought eventually she would, but she didn't. I couldn't understand why she didn't love me the way I loved her. I mean, she's my mom. And what I couldn't understand even more was how my dad was just able to let her go and not fight for her. Why he wouldn't have gone after her. He just shut down; never expressed any anger, never talked about it. He just kept it all in, hoping she'd come back to him. He was so loyal to her, yet she exploited that loyalty by running off with some investment banker and moving away. I remember being so angry with her, yet I couldn't help but wonder if the reason she took off had anything to do with me."

"I'm sure that wasn't the case." I try to rationalize his comment. There must have been another reason. Parents don't just do that, do they?

"I realized that several years later, but by then the damage was done. I never could quite figure out, though, how she could have been so selfish. She cared about herself more than she cared about me, more than she cared about my dad. I would never want to put anyone in the situation she put me in. I would never want to disappoint someone like that." It's like he's trying to tell me he would never do that to me, even though he's leaving in a few days. "And I'd never want to put myself into a situation where I would feel again how I felt when she left."

That's a lot to absorb, but I have an urge to comfort him. "Thank you for sharing this with me, because I know it's not an easy thing to talk about. I mean, I know how difficult that experience must have been for you." He's shared a part of a very personal history with me, so I feel like I should tell him at least a bit about mine. "I lost my dad too, only under very different circumstances. And I was much older. I was in my early twenties when I found him lying lifeless in his office. He'd suffered a heart attack, I found out later, and it was devastating. I felt so hopeless, so scared and lost. I called 911 and realized there was nothing else I could do to bring him back. It hurt so much to lose him and to realize that I would never see him again, never hug him or say good-bye. And that he never had a chance to say good-bye either. It hurt for a long time."

"I'm so sorry to hear that, Tess," Luke whispers, and he kisses my forehead. "I'm also sorry for hurting you. It was never my intention."

"Hurting me?"

"That night, after the movie, I was a total ass. I knew it and hated myself for it I hated the fact that I left without talking to you again after. I was pretty sure that you would despise me for what I did, and I did nothing to fix it. And I couldn't quite figure out why it bothered me so much. I cared about how you'd feel after, even though I barely knew you."

"Don't worry about it. We're past it now. I'm fine. I'm more than fine." Sure, it was something I lost sleep over and wanted to inflict sweet revenge on him for, but that was before I got to know him better.

He shakes his head, then continues. "I wondered countless times what would have happened had I not left for London. When things worked out between Marcus and Clara, I knew there was another chance – a chance to get to know you, for you to get to know me, for me to apologize. I just … I wanted to make it right this time around."

"You are making it right."

"Maybe so. But I had no idea where you stood when I saw you Friday night. You really threw me for a loop." He chuckles.

"That was kind of the intent." I smile. My Evil, Kick-Ass Plan may not have worked out as intended, but I like this alternate ending – or, I hope, beginning.

"When you left me on that rooftop, I thought to myself, Luke, you fucking deserve it. I couldn't stop thinking about you Friday night. I could barely sleep." If he only knew how little sleep I got that night too. "When I woke up Saturday, I knew I wasn't ready to let you go without at least trying to get you back. I have this weird feeling that you could be my forever."

He looks at me with adoration and lust and something more, something I can't quite decipher. His eyes have this intensity about them, and I get lost in them for a minute, like I've done too many times before. *His forever?*

"You probably think it's crazy, but all I'm asking of you is to take a chance with me, take the leap."

He's right – I do think it's crazy. I know it's only been a few days; I know I've been back and forth on this a lot, but for some just-as-crazy reason, I also feel like I'm ready for that leap. I'm ready to jump all the way. I'm almost certain he'll be there to catch me.

"I will."

I say it, but words are just words. Actions matter. Rather than explaining myself further, I show him that I will try to keep an open mind and an open heart. I kiss him until I feel him surrender to my mouth. He returns my kiss with the tenderness and affection mixed with passion that is all Luke, that perfect combination that always has me feeling weak in my knees. I stroke his cheek and he does the same. I mess with his hair and he runs his fingers through mine. We mirror each other's movements as if he is my reflection and I am his. Like we're pieces of one. No one else exists. Just us.

When I pull away, I look at him and hope he can read in my eyes what I'm feeling, more than I can say with words. I nuzzle my nose against his, then bring my lips down to his chest and kiss him right where his heart is. I know it's been years since his mom left, and though I realize he's past it now and probably has been for several years, it must have left an impact. I can only imagine that deep down he probably fears he may experience that disappointment again. I want to show him I get him and that I'll do whatever I can to help him believe in happily-ever-after again.

But will I believe it too? Up until now, I didn't even think it was possible.

I'd like to think that I'll never run again, but I'm reminded that my actions are perhaps promising more than my own heart can handle. I haven't been in a committed relationship since Jason, and I'm not sure if I'll be able to fully commit this time around, even though I'd like to think I will.

I bailed on Luke once already and promised him I'd never do it again. If I'm going to hold myself to that promise, it will require the strength of both my heart and my mind. If that's the case, I need to start acting like it now. I need to show him I do want to give us a try. Enough with the indecision, enough with wavering. *Put it down on paper once and for all, Tessa.*

"It sucks a little less now." Luke smiles softly.

"Whew. What a relief," I tease, hoping to lighten the mood. "I was worried we may need to consider another form of intervention."

He laughs, then wraps his arms around me, and my cheek nuzzles his chest. He squeezes me so tight that he nearly takes all the air out of my lungs. Then he kisses me tenderly on my forehead. We lay entangled with each other, taking in the beauty of the moment, forgetting for a while about all that lies ahead in just a few short days.

Chapter 17

Here's the thing: Last night, after our encounter, I was certain asking Luke to stay the night would have been too rash. But after today and the revelations at the beach, I've come full circle. *This* is what I want. And there's no reason to wait. In fact, time is our worst enemy.

So when we're at my apartment building and I ask him, "Do you want to come in?" I think he's taken aback. But from the spark in his eyes, I also think he's positively giddy. And probably beyond horny. We've spent a whole day together. We did a lot of teasing and touching on the boat, at the beach, and in the water, but we haven't had a chance to do anything else about it. We've been so close for hours, yet not nearly close enough. I can't be certain how he interprets my question, but I'm definitely certain what I mean by it and what my intentions are.

I want him. I want to feel his skin on mine; I want to feel his lips on me; I want to feel him in me. I want us to have naughty, naughty sex in my bed and stay tangled together the entire night. And this time I'm not running. No middle-of-the-night sneaking out. I really have no choice, actually – running out of my own apartment would be kind of, well, odd.

"I think you know the answer." Luke smirks. Oh, I do.

Unlike Clara's loft, every single thing I own in my apartment has its place. Logically organized, clean, purposeful.

Creative elegance with modern décor, yet somehow still cozy. I like that things have their place; I've really enjoyed meticulously putting it all together so that it looks like a picture from a magazine.

"Well, now that I'm finally past the doorway, I have to say your place is pretty spectacular," Luke comments, taking it all in.

"You like it?"

"Are you kidding me? This is just like out of a magazine."

Maybe he *is* able to read my mind.

"It's not too showy?" I ask, although by now I should know that Luke says it like it is.

"It's perfectly you."

I kind of want to grab him and kiss the breath out of him, but I don't want to come across as completely uncontrollable. "Let's get dinner ready," I suggest, even though all I can think about is how much I'd rather just have Luke instead. "I don't know about you, but I'm starving."

"Why don't I take care of dinner, you take care of dessert?" he suggests.

"That sounds like a great idea." Or a really terrible idea, because the second he suggests dessert, I can't think of anything but how much I enjoyed his rain-check visit last night. I'd rather just have dessert. And by dessert, I mean Luke.

Self-control, Tess.

Luke prepares vegetables for a stir-fry while I work on cupcakes, of course. He sneaks in glances, kisses, tickles, and caresses whenever he gets a chance. And I do the same, even though displays of affection are not normally my thing. But I can't help it. Luke is making my lady parts very aware of his presence.

He puts the pot of water on for the noodles just as I get the cupcakes in the oven. Next task: strawberry icing.

Luke is hovering over me, waiting for the water to boil while I add the ingredients for the icing to the mixer. He's being helpful and it's sweet, but from the feeling of his erection against my behind, I think he's got his mind on something more than just dinner.

"Luke?" I ask when the pink icing is just about right.

"Tess?" he whispers against my ear, so that I feel his breath on my skin. I think he's doing it on purpose. I *like* that he's doing it on purpose. I also think he knows how he affects me and is testing my composure.

But I'm not begging. Nope. Though I'm becoming really quite impatient. I don't know how much longer I'll be able to control my craving.

Then an idea comes to mind. Maybe I'll get to try the dessert before dinner is served after all.

"Would you like to taste some?" I ask as I dip my finger into the icing. I turn and wiggle my finger in front of Luke's lips. He tries to go after it, but rather than letting him lick it, I bring the finger to my mouth instead. I suck the icing, then lick my finger like I'd rather be licking something else. I know its driving him crazy; I see his eyes darken and feel him twitch just below my belly button in response.

"Fuck, Tess, you're too tempting for words," he growls. "I don't think I can wait for the cupcakes. I need a taste. *Please.*"

Who's begging now?

He grabs my hand and dips my finger into the icing again. He brings it to his mouth, sucking slowly, purposefully. My breath hitches and I feel goose bumps on my arms the second his tongue encircles my finger. I am so aroused by the thought of what his tongue could do to me, all over me. I may have imagined that a few times.

One kiss leads to another, and then we forget all about the cupcakes in the oven and instead think of only the icing. And sex. Naughty icing sex. At least that's what I'm thinking about.

"I want to spread this all over you, then lick it off."

Oh, good god. That's definitely what he's thinking about. Glad we're on the same page.

Luke grabs the bowl as we stumble to my bedroom. I'm not sure who's more impatient, him or me, but by the time we get to my bed, we've left a trail of clothes crumbs on the floor behind.

He lays me gently on the bed, and I am spread for his decorating enjoyment as he towers above me. I'm practically salivating at the sight. Just thinking about what he's going to do is taking over every comprehensible thought in my mind and is turning it to pure mush. I'm so high on anticipation, I can barely think straight.

Luke dips his finger in the bowl of icing and brings it to my mouth, offering a taste. *Gladly.* I lick and suck on it, teasing the tip with my tongue. He stills and groans, and I can't help but giggle. Not because his reaction is funny – quite the opposite. It's sexy and arousing, and I feel like sucking a lot more than his finger. But I also know what I'm doing to him is torture.

"Is that funny?"

I nod.

He grins mischievously like he's ready to retaliate. In a really, really good way. This time, he takes the spatula from the bowl and trails it down from my collarbone to my breasts. He spreads icing on each of my nipples, and when he's done decorating, he smiles wickedly, as if proud of his work. Then he brings his mouth to one breast, and his tongue does all sorts of wicked things to it while his hand cups the other, kneading it. What he's doing to me is nothing short of erotic, yet so sweet. And not funny at all. With every taste he takes, my body trembles; with every suck, I beg for more. It's definitely torture. The most delightful kind.

"Still funny?"

I shake my head and mouth a barely audible, "No."

"Good. Because what I plan on doing to you next is not funny at all."

He dips the spatula again and trails it down my abdomen. His lips follow the path, kissing, licking, making my skin tingle. When the spatula finally reaches my throbbing clit, the icing feels cool. But the light spanking that follows brings the heat right back. Once. Twice. *Holy shit.*

"Ah," I cry out, squirming. I think I may have orgasmed a little just now. The connection of his mouth that follows nearly wrecks me. His lips devour me, his tongue teases me. "God, Luke," I whisper, and I run my fingers through his hair, lost in the sensations melting my brain.

"So sweet," he growls in between the licks and sucks, his voice raspy, his eyes crazed with desire.

"Please don't stop."

"I'm not nearly done with you," he breathes. "I want to feel you when you break apart for me." He shifts up so that he hovers above me and brings his cock between my trembling legs. He teases me with it, stroking up and down my pussy, and I moan, writhing against the tip, anticipating the moment that is imminent. When he thrusts deep inside me, I cry out. He's so hard it's almost painful. But the pleasure that follows is beyond heavenly. His strokes are intense and fast, like he's delirious with the need to have me, like all control has left him. I'm nearly breathless and equally wild with need. And just when I think he's about to come apart, he finds the control that he's been chasing. He takes a moment to steady his breath. The way he's looking at me, with eyes full of such intense emotion, is paralyzing.

"What are you doing to me?" he whispers, like he's completely lost. What is he doing to me? To my heart?

He doesn't wait for an answer – I think he may be too afraid of what I'll say. And I'm too afraid to voice it. Instead, his mouth finds mine and drowns all reason. It's passion and lust and sweet affection as our eyes close and our bodies continue where we left off. But this time, the motion is slow, his strokes purposeful. I wrap my legs around his waist and tighten around him, feeling every inch of his length. I can't help but lose myself completely in him, in us, in the way we fit.

"God, this feels so good," I moan, urging him to go deeper.

"You feel better than good, Tess."

Somewhere in the background I hear what I assume is the oven beeping, indicating the cupcakes are ready, but I'm not in any state to process it. Any other time I would jump up and get the cupcakes. Then again, any other time I would not be in the middle of being devoured by the sexy stranger I've fantasized about for months. Right now I'm focused on nothing but him, logic forgotten. Pure pleasure, sweet oblivion, and a mind-blowing orgasm that leaves me utterly spent and limp – those are the only things my mind's able to process.

Luke finds his release moments after I do and crashes down on me. His body feels relaxed, and his breath warms my skin.

The oven timer beeps again and startles me from the sugar rush I've just been subjected to. "Shit, cupcakes!" I shout, then push him off of me as I scurry off the bed and toward the kitchen. I hear Luke laughing behind me, and I can't help but laugh too.

When the cupcakes are out of the oven, I feel like I can breathe again. They appear to be edible, despite being slightly overdone. They'd never make it past the garbage bin at Lovely Cakes. The water that Luke had on the stove for the noodles has nearly evaporated. As I shut it off, I startle because Luke grabs me from behind and nuzzles his nose in my hair.

"Jesus, you scared me!"

He just laughs and teases, "Are you trying to burn down the place?"

"That was not my intent."

"Then what was your intent?"

"To have naughty icing sex with you." I turn around to place a kiss on his lips.

"That's exactly what I had in mind."

"And now I think we both need a shower. I'm sticky in places I'm not normally after making a batch of icing," I admit.

"A shower sounds real good right about now."

I agree. After all, I'm sure Luke will be of great assistance. "Then follow me, stranger," I say as I break away from him.

"Don't mind if I do. The view is magnificent."

And the shower with Luke turns out to be even more so.

AFTER THE SHOWER, WE FINISH WHAT WE STARTED earlier. We almost inhale the stir-fry once it's ready, desperately needing to replenish the calories we just burned. When we're done, we decide to watch a movie, armed with cupcakes and yes, tea. Tonight's choice – caramel-apple-almond with a hint of cinnamon. Sweet. Spicy. Warm.

"I feel like I'm at a fancy high tea back in London." Luke smirks, amused by both my offer of tea and by the porcelain cups I chose to serve it in. "Where did these come from?"

"They were my Nan's," I clarify, trying to sound cool, even though I may just be a tad overexcited to be using the cups. I've only ever pulled these out for special occasions. Which has been – never. Until tonight. "My mom inherited them and passed them onto me when I opened Lovely Cakes. I've never met my nan, so it's kind of nice to have something of hers. A family heirloom."

"They're quite unique. And the tea is wonderful, as are the cupcakes. And you." He says this as he holds my gaze in such a way that I may feel the need to drop the tea-talking business and engage instead in naughty business again. But I keep my composure. For now.

"You're welcome." I smile as I take a bite of the cupcake.

When our calories are most definitely at full count (yay!), Luke and I snuggle up on the sofa. His arm is wrapped around my back and his fingers are stroking the sensitive skin just above my tailbone. My fingers find their way underneath his t-shirt and copy his movements. It's so intimate to have him all to myself, in my own apartment, in my personal space. I catch myself thinking about how much I prefer snuggling with him compared to just snuggling with the sofa-pillows on my own. Interesting observation.

But movie watching with Luke appears to be problematic for me. Whenever I'm around him, I find it difficult to focus on anything but the way his fingers feel on my skin, the way his heart beats underneath my ear, the way his breathing intensifies only minutes into the movie, quite possibly because having me so close has the same effect on him as it does on me. My fingers get greedy and trail lower and lower down that sweet V of his. And find that Mr. Callahan is ready for action. A throaty breath escapes Luke as he turns away from the screen. When I look up, his eyes are searching mine, questioning my intent.

"I think someone may be ready for another round," I say, stating the obvious.

"I think you're right."

"You know, this really is not fair."

"What's not fair?"

"I have yet to sit through this movie uninterrupted," I pout. I don't actually care about the movie so much. I might have seen it on the big screen several months ago with Luke by my side. Or at least attempted to see it.

Luke flashes me his crooked grin. "I think you've got all the action you need right here, cupcake."

"That I do." I smile as his hand reaches for the nape of my neck and he brings my lips toward his. He's so close that every breath of his becomes mine. Then he kisses me in that signature sweet yet demanding kiss of his. The one I crave every time I'm near him just as much as when we're apart. The kiss that speaks volumes, that holds all his emotions in it and can last for hours.

The kiss that becomes heated so quickly that we can barely contain ourselves again, our tongues hungry to taste and feel. Our clothes are off in a matter of seconds, and I'm on top of him, straddling him, taking in his thick length. The moment he enters me, I gasp softly, because having him in me like this is so damn stimulating. He's deeper than I've felt him before and as I rock back and forth I feel him everywhere. He cups my bare breasts, and then those magic fingers of his knead them like they're meant to be played with. My nipples harden and beg him to bring his mouth closer, to suck, to twirl, to bite – and he does just that. He's nearly making me lose my mind.

I moan, desperate for more. Sugar may take me to a high, but Luke takes me beyond, to a place where only sweet ecstasy exists. And I want to stay there for hours upon hours. I lean my head back and revel in the way he's making me feel. The chemistry we have is undeniable, pure, intense.

"God, you're so perfect." Luke's roughed-up voice echoes through me, and I bring my head back to look down at him.

Our eyes connect, and I swear I can see in them beyond what his expression is telling me – that he's completely smitten with me. I close my eyes because what I think I'm seeing petrifies me. But the moment I do, Luke whispers, "Look at me, Tess. I want to see you. I *need* you to see."

So I do. Movie forgotten, we focus on each other and on the way we move. The friction we create is so pleasurable I don't ever want it to end. My mind is devoid of any coherent thoughts other than the feelings that register in my heart and tease my brain. And while the heroes are saving the world in the background, Luke is saving my heart, opening it up to the possibility of more. Of finding that one person who makes my world whole again, and needing that person more than I ever thought I would. As scary as it feels, I somehow feel perfectly content.

"That was ... Fuck, Tess." Luke swallows deep once we've both reached our climaxes. "That was..."

"Yeah," I concur as I try to catch my breath.

He lifts me off the couch and carries me to my bedroom. I'm wrapped in him and don't protest, not one bit. And he doesn't let me out of his hold, not even for a second. His arms stay wrapped around me until he places me on the bed, and his eyes stay locked on mine as we lie facing each other.

"I really, really like you, Tess," Luke whispers sleepily as he kisses me. His breathing levels off, and I assume he's dozed off to sleep.

I gather the courage to reply, "I really like you too. More than cupcakes." I'm not sure if he's heard me, but the way he squeezes me in response, the way a subtle grin appears on his face while his eyes are still closed, means he must have. I am more than okay with that. Really, I am.

I stay up staring at him for a few minutes – at the flawless lines of his face, his jaw, his nose, taking in every pore, every freckle. I take in his content and level breathing as he falls deeper into sleep, and I can't help but think about how quickly my resolve changed when it came to having Luke stay the night. Here I am, after only a few short days, embracing the very cuddly being next to me. In my own bed.

This bed that will now forever be ruined by Luke's presence. It will never feel quite the same once he's gone. Even though I clearly realize that, I decide to hold onto the here and now and push the not-so-distant future into, well, the future. Instead, I tangle myself as tightly as I can with Luke, and sweet sleep comes to me as if I am the most carefree person in the world. If only for tonight.

Chapter 18

I hear my phone ring through my slumber. I move unwillingly, my limbs still numb from the night's sleep. I manage to untangle my arm from the hold Luke has on me – he's such a cuddle monster – and reach over to pick up the phone.

"Hello," I say quietly, hoping not to wake him. I look at the clock – it's just past seven.

"Hey, sweetie," my mom says in her too-perky morning voice. It took her a while to get that voice back after Dad died.

"Hi, Mom," I respond, waking right up. "Is everything okay?" First, I'm genuinely worried, but second, I'm hoping this isn't going to be one of her long-winded, I-hope-you're-doing-well-being-twenty-six-and-still-single kind of calls. Those have been happening way too often since Clara got engaged.

"I hope so," she replies almost hesitantly.

Ugh. It's the second, I just know it. Here it goes.

"Honey, I know it hasn't been easy on you since your dad died, since Jason left," she says in her nurturing voice, her British accent still noticeable after all these years, "and I just wanted to make sure you were okay. You know, with Clara's wedding a few days away." As always, she dives right into it. Typical Mom.

"Gee, Mom, I had no idea Clara was getting married," is what I feel like saying, but instead go with a less-snooty, "I'm fine, Mom," reassuring her just like I always do.

The thing is, she never used to be so vigilant. Not that I remember. She was always a free-spirited, easygoing, never-a-worry-in-her-heart kind of mom. Until my dad died. It took her at least a couple of years to get her sense of self back. When she did, it was like she funneled all those emotions into becoming a worry-wart, and I've been her primary target. Because – single.

"You say that all the time, Tessa. But I can't imagine how you can be doing well given your *younger* sister's getting married and you're nowhere close to having someone special in your life, let alone a relationship, sweetie."

I should just hang up. I can feel the irritation starting to build. She's concerned, I know, but in my mind it sounds more like she's criticizing. I close my eyes, try to find my happy place, and hold the line.

Of course, little does she know that, as we are speaking, I'm tangled in the messy yet comforting embrace of a man I thought existed only in romance novels. And that man is becoming more and more special by the minute. If she only knew I was running on a sugar high, my sweetener of choice being Luke, perhaps she wouldn't be calling at this ungodly hour.

"And you can say you don't need anyone to make you happy, Tessa," she continues, "but trust me when I say this." I know what's coming next because she's said it too many times before. "You need someone in your life to feel like you're whole. I know, because I miss my half every single day." Her voice trembles just like it does every time she starts to talk about Dad.

Up until now, I've always downplayed the two-halves-make-a-whole argument, even though I know how much my dad and mom loved each other. But over these past few days, I've started to realize that maybe I wasn't really whole before I met Luke. Maybe there was always something missing, and I was just never able to pinpoint what it was. Still, I get a tad bit annoyed at having to listen to her go on about her favorite subject over and over.

"Mom, please don't worry," I reassure her again, hoping to keep exasperation out of my voice. "I really am fine. Who knows, I may find my Prince Charming sooner rather than later," I say, then cringe at the thought of Luke overhearing me in his sleep. That would be embarrassing. But, thankfully, he doesn't even flinch. His hand is protectively resting on my naked chest and his legs are entwined with mine. I catch myself staring at him, at his face, at the way his lips are parted, the way his nose crinkles ever so slightly with each breath, and suddenly I feel sentimental. Before I even consider it fully, "Maybe he's already found me and I just don't know it yet," escapes me in a breathless, adoring voice.

"Oh, Tessa, you don't have to make up stuff to make me worry less about you."

And the sentiment I felt a moment ago is gone. *Make up stuff? Argh!* She can be so irritating. Of course she's going to think I'm making stuff up. Why would me finding my Prince Charming not be a likely possibility?

As I consider that, I remind myself the reason she thinks that way is because I basically swore off the opposite sex after Jason. Perhaps her assumption is not unreasonable after all.

"I just really wish you would give your heart a try. You need to open it to the possibilities that are out there, honey. You've always been a strong, independent woman, but it would be nice to have someone soften you up."

I've heard it all before; I'm pretty sure I'll hear it again. I just need to end this call so I don't have to listen to her any longer and so I don't say something I may regret later.

"Fine, I'll try."

"You will?" she asks, and I hear the suspicion in her voice. She must misinterpret my curt answer for something else – a possibility. "Tessa Maria Conte, is there something you're not telling me?"

Damn it. I forgot how intuitive she can be. Now she's onto me. I was really hoping to figure out this whole thing with Luke before I have to make it more public. Of course, I don't have much time to do that. The rehearsal dinner is tonight, and the moment she sees us, she'll probably know that we're more than just fellow members of the wedding party. Even if I try,

Luke will likely make it impossible for me to appear single, knowing how forward and uninhibited he is.

"No, Mom, there isn't. I just said I'll try," I say matter-of-factly, hoping to convince her.

"Fine, honey, but remember what I said, okay?"

"I will."

"Okay, sweetie. See you tonight. Love ya."

"Love you too, Mom." Of course I do, even after conversations like these. I know she's only got the best intentions. Still, they can be suffocating sometimes.

I take a deep breath and resolve to go back to my happy place now that the phone call is over. I snuggle up against the warm body next to me, inhaling the scent that makes me tingle all over. It's funny how, even though I've gotten used to sleeping on my own, right now I can't seem to get enough of the soft–hardness that is Luke. Every time we're this close, I feel nothing but cared for, safe in his embrace. I sigh contentedly as I close my eyes to catch a few more minutes of rest. But just as I do that, a raspy, flirty voice says, "So, Prince Charming, huh?"

Oh god. He heard me.

I cringe and wonder how much he heard while I try to figure out a response.

"Well," I feel like something's stuck in my throat, "figuratively speaking."

"I think I can be a whole lot more than charming."

"Oh yeah? How so?" I challenge. I have a feeling being compared to a prince is not something Luke considers flattering.

His reply starts with a kiss, a raw, passionate kiss, as my sweet, loving Prince Charming turns into this primal creature, his eyes dark and lusty.

I struggle to decide which Luke I like better – the charming prince or the tiger on the prowl. It really is a toss-up. I'm smitten with both of them equally. My prince goes on to worship every inch of me like I am his princess. And then devours me as only a tiger would.

"I'LL SEE YOU LATER, OKAY?" LUKE PLACES A LINGERING kiss on my mouth before heading out for the day. He's meeting up with Marcus for breakfast and then has a few meetings to attend before we see each other again at the rehearsal dinner tonight.

I close the door behind him and lean against it. I haven't felt this elated, this hopeful, in a very long time. Maybe never.

Since the whole mess that Jason made of my already fragile heart, I haven't really dated seriously again. Going down that emotional black hole wasn't what I would call a pleasant experience; not one I wanted to put myself through again, at least. I guess I just didn't open myself to the possibility of finding someone with whom I could connect – not only physically, but emotionally too. Not until Luke stumbled into my life.

I've never met anyone who makes me feel the way he does. But beyond the physical attraction, beyond the chemistry that binds us, there's so much more I like about him. I feel like I'm finally ready to open my nearly healed heart to the possibility of more. To the possibility of love. And that excites me ... and scares me. So I'm more than grateful that I've got lots to keep me busy today. There's less likelihood that my meandering thoughts will take me down a path of emotional self-destruction.

I head to Lovely Cakes to work on Clara and Marcus's wedding cake, among other orders. I'm sure Rose has everything under control, but then again, I like to double check it actually is. My hunch turns out to be correct – things are peachy.

As a matter of fact, I'm on such a high the entire day that I manage to accomplish almost everything I'd planned before heading home to get ready for the rehearsal. The cake is just about done – only a few finishing touches left, which I plan to wrap up tomorrow morning. What an awesome, kick-ass, productive day.

On my way home, I listen to music with what I can only imagine is a crazy perma-grin stuck to my face. This whatever-it-is Luke and I have feels right. I am so lost in my world, in my head, that I'm oblivious and barely notice my phone ringing as I reach my building.

"Hi, Tessa."

"Hey, Marcus!" I say cheerfully as I make my way up the elevator. "How are things?"

"Good, good ... you know, D-day is almost here." He laughs nervously, noticeable unease in his voice. "How are things with you?" he asks, but I wish he would cut right to the chase and spare me the small talk. He doesn't normally call unless it's something important. Since he and Clara have been dating, he's called to talk to me directly only a few times, one of which was to tell me he was planning on marrying my sister and another to ask if I would make their wedding cake. So yeah, this is slightly unnerving.

"Same here, D-day is almost here. The cake will be ready, though. Don't worry." I chuckle, trying to make things light.

"I'm sure it will, I'm sure it will." He pauses, and a few seconds of awkward silence fill the air. "Anyways, Tessa, I wanted to talk to you."

"What about?" I ask, but then it occurs to me almost at the exact time as I ask him the question. *Oh. My. God.* Is he having second thoughts about it all, about Clara? Please don't let it be about that. Clara would be devastated, absolutely heartbroken, given her previous relationship disasters. And this time it may just break her for good. Now I'm totally dreading what he'll say next.

"I'm not sure how to say this, or whether I should say anything at all, but I feel like I need to warn you."

Warn me? I'm confused by his words and fumble with my keys as I try to unlock the door to my apartment.

"Tessa, seems like you and Luke have a thing going on," he continues. *Oh shit.* Of course this is about me and Luke. That would be more logical. I'm so relieved it has nothing to do with the wedding and with Clara. How could I have even thought that would be the case? They love each other so much.

But I'm not sure I want to hear what comes next. In fact, selfishly, I might have preferred to hear that Marcus is experiencing cold feet.

"Mm-hmm." I try to sound unaffected, uttering no words so that I can hide the worry in my voice. I wonder how much

Luke has shared with Marcus about us. I'm not sure if guys talk much about stuff like this. I wonder if Clara said something.

"Tessa, you know Luke's like a brother to me. I've known him for a long time. And I love the guy to death, so I feel awful for even bringing this up. But you're going to be my sister-in-law, so I feel like I need to let you know."

I think I may need to sit down for this. "I'm all ears," I say confidently, yet underneath the surface, I brace myself. I have an eerie feeling this conversation won't warm my heart.

"Women seem to fall for Luke so easily. I don't know what it is, but there's just something about him. But Luke's not one to commit. He's never been in a serious relationship for as long as I've known him."

I'm very quickly seeing where this conversation is headed, and I'm thankful for the comfort of my loveseat, as well as the pillow I'm clutching in the hope that the action itself will help me get through the rest of the call.

"Not one that's lasted more than a few weeks," Marcus clarifies. "I can probably count on one hand the girls he's even considered to be more than a one-night stand. And they only turned out to be a *several*-night's stand, after all. It's just how he's always been, the lifestyle he's lived. Once the novelty wears off, he seems to lose interest. I can't help but think that, with you being here and him being in London, this is just another pursuit that will end the way they all have."

I open my mouth in response, but nothing comes out. I want to tell Marcus that he's wrong, that what Luke and I have is different – *will be* different in the long run. I've spent time with Luke and feel like I know him. I remember all he's shared with me – his sincerity, his feelings for me. But Marcus's words have rendered me speechless. An awkward silence fills the line again. In light of my non-response, Marcus continues.

"I don't know, maybe he's fallen for you. Maybe for you he's willing to change. But I just want you to be careful. I don't want to see you get hurt, okay? I know how difficult that would be for you," he concludes, his voice laced with concern.

Obviously Clara must have told him about me and my past relationships. Well, relation*ship*.

What Marcus has shared is the last thing I need to hear from him, especially because he knows Luke much better than I do. It's not like what he's said is anything new, though. Luke said so himself – the relationships he's had in the past have never been serious. Things never worked out, for one reason or another, I remember him saying. But Marcus's words resonate with me because they're an unwelcome reminder. I seemed to have neatly tucked in the obvious for the time being and, perhaps blindly, went on the assumption that this time things would in fact work out, that Luke would feel differently about me.

The questions I haven't really wanted to consider since my ninja-like escape are bubbling up. *How did I ever think we would work? What will happen when this week is over and Luke's gone back to London? Why would he want a relationship with me when he hasn't considered one with anyone else before? Why would I?*

The related answers are coming to the surface at lightning speed. *Long distance won't work – this was doomed from the start. You'll fall into that emotional black hole again, so don't make it any more difficult on yourself than it has to be. Of course he's only in this for a few days, a convenient novelty. What relationship?* Cue the scoff.

Even though I'm sitting down, my legs suddenly feel weak, my stomach unsettled. My heart is trying to keep pace with my tumultuous emotions. It's as if I hear my brain shouting, *"Abort! Abort!"* but my heart sneaks in and whispers, *"Give it a chance, Tessa."* Ugh! I need time to re-think this.

I have a sudden urge to make a list. A new one. One that will confirm I haven't fallen for Luke, even though I hoped that maybe he would have been it for me.

"Tessa? Are you still there?" I hear Marcus through the clashing emotions that are crowding my brain. I completely forgot he was still on the line.

"Yes, I'm here," I respond, my throat coarse and dry.

"Are you okay?"

I cough, trying to get rid of the lump in my throat. "Yeah, I'm ... I'm fine. It's not like it's anything serious," I say hurriedly, convincing myself that it isn't. It can't be. My heart may be telling me one thing, but my mind knows differently. And I always listen to my mind. The heart can be too emotional. Foolish, even. Whatever it is that Luke and I have can't be serious after only a few days. Things don't just develop out of the blue. People don't just fall for each other so quickly. Do they?

Think logic. Right. Logic tells me that what Luke and I have must be just physical attraction mistaken for something more profound. The honeymoon phase. A cake batter without the ingredients to make it flourish. After the lust cools off, we'll be left feeling, well, cold. After all, we'd never be able to spend enough time together to find out whether this would develop into anything more anyways, so it can't be that serious.

"Are you sure you're fine?"

"Yeah, yeah. Don't worry. I'm glad you said something. Thanks for the heads up," I reply convincingly. At least I think I sound convincing, but the teeny-tiny voice that's been hibernating in my head for a couple of days starts wiggling out from underneath all those comforting blankets. I tucked it in, I placed those blankets there. The denial felt incredibly cozy, but it was just a temporary lapse of judgment. I'm suddenly shivering, but I realize I'd rather be cold. It's something I've gotten used to. I don't deal well with unpredictable changes in temperature – or feelings, for that matter.

"Okay, then. I just wasn't sure if it was my place to say something to begin with," Marcus continues, sincerity evident in his voice. "I don't want to make things worse, you know?"

"Of course I do. I know you're just looking out for me."

"Yes, that's all this is, Tessa. And if I'm wrong – I mean, I *hope* I'm wrong – please don't hold it against me, okay?"

"You know I would never do that." I couldn't. I know he only has the best intentions in mind. "I'll see you soon." I need to end this call.

"For sure."

I don't even think I press the end button. I stare at the phone in a state of shock, like I've just woken up after a very confusing yet vivid dream. Though what Marcus said clearly wasn't a dream. In fact, he didn't need to say anything at all. I should have known better.

I can't help but curse myself for being in this predicament. A realization hits me: I know I've nearly fallen and gotten in further than I intended to. I made promises to Luke that I shouldn't have. I let the attraction, the lust, fog my judgment. But the vivid picture Marcus painted, which should have been clear from the start, means only one thing.

I need to break things off. I need to break them off now, before I do any more damage to either one of us. Before Luke wrecks me completely and I'm back to the same place I've successfully avoided visiting for the last three years. I can't afford to go back there. No, this stops here. I know just what I have to do next; after all, I've done it before. *Break. Detach. Run.*

Chapter 19

Can't wait to see you, Luke texts an hour before the rehearsal.

Sorry. Gonna be late. Work emergency, I reply.

There is no work emergency. Did I mention I hate being late? Especially to the rehearsal of the vows of my sister's wedding in which I am the maid of honor. But tonight I don't want to get there any sooner than I have to. I don't want to have to talk to Luke before the rehearsal. I couldn't bear to face him and pretend that we're okay. Because we aren't, right? I mean, we definitely won't be in a few days anyways, so what's the point?

Is everything ok?

Luke's perceptive, as usual.

Cake problems.

I'm sure you've got everything under control.

I'd better. God, I feel like such a loser for making this up. How did I let myself get to this point?

I call Clara and explain my "work emergency." I tell her too that it has to do with her wedding cake, even though I told Marcus earlier that everything will be ready. I should have come up with something more solid. I am such a bad liar. And a horrible human being. Clara's not pleased, but she wants to make sure the cake is perfect, so she says she understands. At least she's bought it for the time being. But she warns me to get to the rehearsal as soon as possible. I hate lying to her, but the last thing I want to do is get into a conversation with her about Luke. *That* I don't want to talk about.

I get to the church just as Liz, my cousin and the last of the bridesmaids, is starting her practice walk down the aisle.

"Thank god you've made it," Clara sighs.

I smile and whisper, "Everything's taken care of." Of course she thinks I'm referring to the cake and getting to the rehearsal like I promised, but I'm thinking of something completely different. Something I've spent the last couple of hours planning. And I've figured it all out. I've definitely got it under control. *I do,* I think convincingly.

As I begin my practice walk down the aisle, I don't dare look up, but I can sense Luke's eyes on me, like they're pleading for a reaction. I'm looking down at my crimson toenails, hesitant to meet his gaze, worried that he'll see right through me, right down to my heart. But the pull he's got on me is too strong, the urge to give in and see his face is too tempting. Our eyes meet, and Luke smiles as if seeing me just completely made his day. His smile nearly knocks the air out of my lungs. He mouths a silent, "Hey." I'm so proficient at reading his lips. *God, I love his lips.*

I smile in response, then force it back and look away. For the rest of the rehearsal, I focus on Clara and Marcus and my maid-of-honor responsibilities, avoiding any further eye contact with Luke. I'm such a chicken.

Once the rehearsal is done, I take a moment to tell Luke I'll ride with Clara and Marcus and meet him at the restaurant. When he tries to kiss me, I try to avoid direct mouth-to-mouth, so instead, more than a little awkwardly, he kisses my cheek and I pull clumsily out of his grasp. Holding my resolve when he's so near, when his lips are mere inches from mine, is an absolute necessity. Otherwise, my plan – my The Writing's on the Wall Plan – will backfire. I absolutely cannot let that happen this time around.

"I gotta go. I'll see you shortly," I say, and hurry over to Marcus's car before they leave the church.

"You're not riding with Luke?" Clara asks suspiciously.

"No, I thought it would be better to ride with you guys. That way we can discuss any last minute details," I lie. *Again.* Horrible, horrible person.

"Oh. Okay. I guess it can't hurt," she agrees.

I avoid Luke when we get to the restaurant and find my assigned seat next to Clara. I notice the questioning look he's channeling my way, but I don't dare show anything on my face other than what I hope is a radiant smile.

On the inside, though, I am anything but radiant. I'm tormented by what I know tonight will bring, but I need to end this, end *us*, before it's too late. After all, all lovely things come to an end eventually. No need to prolong the inevitable.

Once the dinner – which, by the way, is otherwise wonderful – and all the customary pleasantries are done, I excuse myself and head to the ladies' room. I need a break from the façade I've been displaying; it's getting heavy. I splash some water on my face, then dry it off, making sure I don't mess up my makeup. I stare at myself in the mirror and see hints of the old Tessa – jaded, impassive. Luke's brought out a new Tessa, a cheerful and passionate person, and I'm not sure I want to go back to being my old self.

There's no other way. I'm better off on my own. I gather enough courage to head out.

"What's going on, Tess?" Luke's voice startles me as I exit the washroom, and I gasp. I wonder how long he's been waiting for me, but knowing Luke, I wouldn't be surprised if he's been at the door since I left the table. I was hoping not to get into this until we could be on our own. The last thing I want to do is make a scene, though there's enough separation between us and the room for anyone to really notice.

"What do you mean?" I feel awful for being so evasive with him, especially when I clearly know what he's referring to.

"You seem distant tonight," Luke says softly. "What's wrong?" He's too good at reading my body language.

"Nothing's wrong," I lie, and I look down at my fingernails, which I am not-surprisingly picking at. "Just feeling a little tired." The biggest cop-out ever.

He takes my hand and laces his fingers through mine, then brings them to his lips for a gentle kiss. The connection pierces right through me. His lips create a spark the moment they touch my skin and send a current of what might as well be sugar-coated electrons because I instantly crave more than just Luke's kiss.

"Tessa, be honest with me. That's one thing you can do, after all the time we've spent together over the last few days. Talk to me. You've barely said a word the entire night."

He's right. I do need to talk to him. I force myself to think past what my body is begging for and focus on what I need to do next – The Writing's on the Wall Plan, Step One: Break it off. I figure I'll just say what needs to be said, what I practiced before the rehearsal, and we'll go back to the dining room once it's all out in the open. Okay, maybe *I'll* go back. Luke may need a few minutes when we're through.

"Luke, these past few days have been ... I can't even begin to explain the way you affect me. You've somehow managed to make me feel hopeful again. I've never quite felt how I feel when I'm with you. But I can't ... I don't think we should continue seeing each other."

"You can't? Or you don't want to?"

"Both." I look at him, hoping he can see how difficult this is for me. I don't *want* to be doing this, but I *have* to.

"Damn it, Tess, don't do this. Not again. I've heard you say this once already. You don't mean it."

I sense annoyance in his voice. He's doubting me. Of course he is. I would be too, given the see-saw of feelings I've displayed over this past week. But there's no turning back. Luke won't trust me again anyways, so I might as well finish what I started.

"I mean it." At least I've convinced myself that I do. "It's just ... this won't work."

"Of course it won't if you're not willing to try."

"I did try."

"You tried? For all of a few days," he scoffs as he runs his fingers through his hair. I'd really like to run my fingers through his hair too. *No!* No distractions from said hair, no matter how messy or playful or similar.

"It was a mistake. I shouldn't have led you on." I'm pleased with my composure.

"Led *me* on? We're both in this together. If you give up on us right now, I don't know if I'll be able to take you back again. I'm serious, Tess. This will be it."

He looks and sounds serious. Interestingly, it's with mixed feelings I process his statement. It feels as if a sharp object has sliced my heart, and what I can only interpret as anxiety takes hold for a brief moment, but I shrug it off. I need to be logical about this. I *won't* need him to take me back.

"Are you sure that's what you want? We've started something here. Just give me – give *us* – a chance to see this through. Please." The frustration from moments ago has now been replaced with soft vulnerability. It's sweet and sexy and appealing. No, no – it's not. I can't think of him this way.

"I can't," I say simply, because this is what's best for both of us.

"Tessa, please, when something feels so right, how can you just let it go?"

I don't respond. It *does* feel right. Just a few hours ago I was practically ready to sing about it, I felt so happy.

"Please, don't break us. Not like this."

I know he'll only be able to hold onto his composure for a little while longer before anger is the only emotion left. I know, because I've felt it before.

"I have to, if I'm going to survive you." My voice quivers, and my eyes pool with tears on the verge of breaking. I close my eyes, hoping to collect myself and hold back the tears. I almost manage – I hold back all but one of them, which slowly rolls down my cheek. I open my eyes, confident that I've averted the full-on downpour, but I don't dare look at him. Instead, I find myself picking at my fingernails again.

Luke cups my face, then gently wipes away the tear. This simple, affectionate gesture has a profound effect on me. I look up and meet his gaze, and the soft desire I see in his eyes nearly makes me forget about my plan. He doesn't wait another second before he kisses me. Deep and hard, like he won't let me go. Like he's going to take what has freely been his for the last few days and no one's going to stop him. Like the kiss will convince me to take back all that I just said.

I almost do. The taste of his mouth, the scent of his skin, the feeling of his body against me, the touch of his fingers ... It takes all of my determination to control the urge. *Maybe just one last time, just one more taste.* So I give in, if only for a minute. I kiss him back just as intensely, holding onto this one last connection before I force him out of my life. Before my resolve wavers, I find the strength to pull away and move on to Step Two: Detach. Let go of the emotions. Let go of Luke.

"Don't." I place my fingers on his lips, stopping him from any further attempts, even though I crave the connection the moment it's broken. "Just ... good-bye," I whisper as I step back.

I promised I would never leave without saying it, so I keep my promise. Even though it's heartbreaking saying it and even more heartbreaking seeing his reaction – a stunned, hopeless gaze, like it's finally sunk in.

I turn away and don't dare look back. This is it.

Step Three: Run.

I expect to hear him call my name, I expect him to come after me, but he doesn't. Not this time. Perhaps he's realized it would be futile to fight for something that's doomed to fail.

I'm certainly taking the easy way out. Or at least I think I am. According to my carefully planned-out plan, this is the hardest step. It can't get any worse than this, because we're done. We're over. What a relief.

Except that I also feel deflated and sad. It's not surprising, given what just transpired. I'm sure it will fade over time, though. I'm positive, because I've lived through it.

When I get back to the table, Clara reads right through my everything-is-peachy expression and asks, "Are you okay?"

"Yeah. Why?" Am I really that transparent?

"You were gone for a while. And Luke followed right after you left. But he hasn't come back with you." And why does she have to be so damn intuitive?

"He must have gotten sidetracked." I try to sound unaffected, hoping to deflect her question. That seems to do the trick because she doesn't probe further.

"Are you ready to get going, then?"

"Yeah. Definitely." I'm all smiles as I finish my glass of wine. I so need it right now. Or maybe a shot of something stronger or, better yet, sugar. I have a sudden urge to raid my own bakery. But composure prevails. The façade is back – happy, confident Tessa, who's hoping the confusing, gloomy thoughts that are crowding her brain won't show on the surface.

I grab Clara's arm as we make our way out of the restaurant and to the club with the bridesmaids for a girls' night out, a mini-bachelorette party. We had an official one a month ago, and Marcus had his bachelor party several weeks ago too, because Clara didn't want to have them too close to the wedding. She wanted to make sure there were no last-minute hiccups. I think she must have seen the *Hangover* movies too many times.

The guys are heading out on their own tonight as well, but I don't really want to think about what Luke might end up doing after I left things the way I did. I really hope he's not going to jump the first opportunity who presents herself just because he's pissed at me. I'm being irrational – he wouldn't do that. *You broke things off*, I'm reminded by the tiny voice that tries to reason with me. Like I need the reminder.

Once we get to the club, we head straight to the dance floor. I'm hopeful the deafening music and the distance from Luke will make me feel lighter, freer somehow. More confident about the decision I made. But dancing doesn't help as much as I thought it would. I can't seem to let go like I normally do. Drinks don't seem to help either. There are plenty of guys here, but all I can think about is the one guy I just forced out of my life. I tell Clara I need to get some fresh air and that I'll be back in a few minutes. She looks concerned, but I tell her it's just the drinks and the heat and the crowd that are getting to me. *If only...*

I walk out to the patio and take a calming breath, but even the air outside feels stifling. I'm so confused. I search my brain for the sense of relief I should be feeling. After all, I just avoided potential heartbreak. I should be ecstatic. But the eerie feeling can't seem to disappear.

"Tessa?" A familiar voice startles me. I search through my bucket of memories, trying to place it. *It cannot possibly be.* I turn around and am faced with the last person on the planet I want to see at this moment.

"Jason?" I ask as if uncertain, although I'm fully aware it's him. I haven't seen him in ages, but I recognize him easily. He seems older and broader, and his hair is longer, but he still looks attractive.

I brace myself for an onslaught of anger, resentment, infatuation, lust, forgiveness, need ... but I don't feel a thing. Nothing. As if I never knew him. He's just a good-looking guy who appears to know my name.

I'm relieved. Time really does make a difference. I don't doubt for a second that I am over him. I'm just not over the scars he's left on my heart.

"I thought I caught a glimpse of you on the dance floor." He seems shocked that it is in fact me.

"Turns out you were right."

"How are you?" he asks timidly, probably wondering if I even want to talk to him after the way he left things between us.

I've thought of what I would say to Jason if I ever ran into him, but now that I'm actually face to face with him, everything I ever wanted to say seems pointless, a waste of breath. He's not worth it. He doesn't deserve a second of my attention.

"Good. Things are good. Real good," I reply, and I smile confidently. Never mind that just a little while ago I forced a certain someone out of my life because I have commitment issues that span three years and I have no one but this jerk to thank. "How about you?" I'm being polite, because that's what mature people do in situations like this, right?

"Things are great, yeah…" He trails off, and I wonder if he's being honest with me or if he's pretending, just the way I am. But he's never been good at saying what he really means, so his less-than-expressive response doesn't surprise me one bit.

An uncomfortable silence finds its way around us, the kind I absolutely despise. *Awkward.* I pick at my nails nervously as the space around us becomes suffocating. How did it ever feel anything but? I have that impulse to ask a question just to break the quiet.

"So I see you're back?"

"Yeah, I've been back for almost a year."

I'm surprised by his answer. I can't believe he's been back that long. And I can't help but wonder where things would have been right now if we'd run into each other sooner.

"Oh, wow, I had no idea. How come?" I'm not even sure I really care to know the answer.

"Things just didn't work out," he says, not giving much away.

"I'm sorry to hear that." *Not at all.* Karma's a bitch.

"What have you been up to?" he asks.

"A little bit of this. A little bit of that. I did manage to open up my own bakery, actually." I smile, but it's bittersweet. I'm happy to inform him that I did in fact go after that dream of mine, but it reminds me of all the times I told him about it, the countless hours I spent planning, the fact that he didn't bother to stick around and dream with me.

"I'm glad to hear that." I can sense he wants to ask a question but is hesitant. "You wanna grab a drink or something?"

"Sorry, I can't." *Not after the way you left things.*

"Oh." He sounds disappointed. Good. "Are you seeing someone?" He surprises me with his bold question, because being frank is so not like him, and I can't help but falter.

Yes, I was. But I was too afraid to keep him.

"Umm, yes ... yeah, definitely." So convincing. I lie and tell the truth at the same time. I wonder if he can see right through me. "How about you?"

The last thing I want Jason the Jerk to know is that he left scars that are still with me, smothering me, preventing me from finding my happily-ever-after. *Argh!* I was wrong. Anger is one emotion I still feel toward him.

"Not really. No one special anyways," he admits.

At least he's being honest. Not that I really care to know, though. Okay, maybe I do care a little. But only because I'm hoping he's as miserable as I was when he first left me. I'm hoping he's scarred from his experience overseas, even though I have no clue why he returned. But I'd like to think getting dumped by a pretty brunette is what caused him to come back.

"Well, it was nice seeing you," I say, and I'm ready to scurry off. It's liberating knowing his life doesn't seem to be much further along than mine. No wedding ring, no kids, no special someone in his life.

"You know–" He holds onto my arm to stop me from moving past him. "I really am sorry about how I left things with us. I know it was forever ago, but I want you to know that I made a mistake. I thought better things would come my way. I was wrong. I do still think about you. And wonder."

Wow. Okay. Did I just hear him right?

But I'm not letting him get to me this time around.

"Well, I don't," I say with conviction, as I pull out of his grasp, making my way past him, leaving him stunned. Taking control. Freeing myself of the scars that have pained my heart for three years too long.

Chapter 20

I know what heartbreak feels like. Jason made sure of that. I've seen it happen with Clara, and with Mom, too, after Dad died. One thing's for sure: It's not pretty. In fact, it can be paralyzing. Yesterday, I was convinced that I'd made the right decision – letting go of Luke was the smart thing to do. Thought out thoroughly, courtesy of my plan. I put emotions aside and used my brain, just like I normally do and just like my dad taught me. And logic has served me well in the past.

But after the chance meeting with Jason last night, I'm no longer sure. In fact, I'm even more confused. Something that I've been holding onto for the last three years seems to have simply vanished. What's more, I think I've realized that I wasted time mourning over Jason when I really didn't care about him as much as I thought I did. I'm wondering if my fear of commitment, of taking a chance on love again, was never quite as significant as I let myself believe, given how easy it was to face Jason last night and not feel a thing. Maybe it was never fear after all. Which makes me wonder: If my fear was irrational, was letting Luke go a mistake?

No, I'm not going to think about that. What's done is done, even though I'm starting to realize that the heart should play a part in the decision-making process. I certainly wouldn't have opened Lovely Cakes without it. It couldn't have been just my brain convincing me to do so. My heart definitely had a lot to do with that decision. There were risks and rewards, and the reward of having my own business has been far greater than the risk I knew existed and still exists. I love doing what I do. So why in the mother-fucking cupcake did I choose to ignore what my heart was trying to tell me this time around?

I'm too tired to run this morning, but I force myself anyways so that I can clear my head. When I'm done, though, I'm no closer to figuring out what I'm feeling. Normally I'd make a list, but I'm starting to think it won't do me any good. List or no list, I may just need some time to get past this nauseous feeling in my stomach. It will fade eventually. I hope.

After I shower, I make my way to Lovely Cakes, ready to spend the day working so that I don't have to spend another minute thinking about the decision I made last night or the things I said to Luke. Or the hurt I must have caused him. *Again.* Or the hurt that I undeniably caused myself, even though I'm fighting incredibly hard to not admit it. *Nothing can possibly be hurting if I didn't fall in the first place*, I remind myself. *I didn't fall; no, I didn't fall; I didn't fall for Luke*, I repeat until I'm sure I've convinced myself.

When I get in, I decide to sort through mail before I immerse myself in everything else. I'm thrilled to see a thank-you card from one of my clients and a picture of her adorable son celebrating his first birthday. He's covered from ear to ear and forehead to chin in icing, and his eyes sparkle with the innocent happiness that you only see in a one-year-old, someone who is truly, undeniably happy. I smile because his eyes remind me of Luke's and the way they glistened with warmth and joy every time he saw me.

My brain may not have quite figured it out until now, but I know in this particular moment that when a little boy's eyes remind me of Luke, I really am deeper in than I thought.

What have I done?

This plan to spend the day at work isn't going quite the way I imagined, considering the first thing I think of is Luke's eyes. *I will not cry*, I repeat to myself for the umpteenth time.

I pin the card to the board and take a step back, admiring the happiness the thank-you cards express. When I'm done reminding myself that pure, true happiness does in fact exist – just maybe not in my life – I go into the work room to put the finishing touches on Clara's wedding cake. The one thing left to do is to add the crystal rosebud brooches. They are absolutely breathtaking, just like Clara will be on her wedding day. That I am sure of.

But the thank-you cards are messing with my head. I can't stop myself from taking another look at them. My eyes well up at the sight of my wall of happiness. Those same thank-you's that have made me smile every time I've looked at them are now just a reminder of how pathetic my life actually is.

And that's when I kind of lose it. Not in a bat-shit-crazy way, because that would be too melodramatic, but emotionally. All the pent-up feelings and my stupid decisions and indecisions grab me by my throat.

In fact, I'm so bitter that I seriously contemplate grabbing Clara's cake and throwing it. Thankfully, the tiny voice of reason reminds me that *that* would not go over so well tomorrow. So instead I grab an icing-covered spatula and, in defiance of my normally poised and self-controlled existence, throw it at the wall. *Stupid, stupid Tessa!*

The red icing splatters all over as I drop to my knees, weak, defeated. Just like that, anger gives way to sadness. It starts off with a sob and within seconds turns into a waterfall.

I've spent the last three years living through other people's happiness. I have helped head-over-heels-in-love couples get married, celebrate their anniversaries, celebrate their kids' birthdays, celebrate life ... and all I got to do was watch. I've watched them smile when they first saw their cake design, I've seen their excitement build as their wedding day neared, and I've appreciated their awe when they finally saw the real thing. They were all just so damn happy.

I was almost there too, but now any possibility of having my own happily-ever-after with Luke has been ruined. Not because of anyone else, but because of me. I have squashed those exhilarating, blissful feelings with the heaviness of my own rigid determination. It hurts knowing there's a chance I won't be able to get past this. It's such a sad fucking existence.

The tears continue rolling down, and I can't bring myself to get back up. My hands are covered in red icing – a bloody mess. My makeup's probably smeared all over my face, my eyes feel puffy from the tears, and my nose is runny. I gasp for air but am unable to catch a breath.

"Tessa?" Rose's voice pulls me from my inner monologue. She must have just come into the bakery, only to find me in this mess on the floor. "Come here," she says as she envelops me in her arms, holding me, letting me cry it out. "It's going to be okay. Just breathe," she says in a comforting voice.

Well, this is kind of awkward. I'm crying in front of my employee. Because that's what all bosses do, right? If there were any lines left between us, they've definitely been erased. Rose and I are officially in the friend zone.

She's probably dying to know the reason for my emotional breakdown, but she doesn't ask like she normally would. She just holds me until I finally manage to calm down and pull myself up.

"Go home for the day," she orders, helping me get up. "You need time to figure things out. I'll call you a cab, okay?"

I nod. "Rose," I find my voice, "please don't mention anything to Clara, okay? I don't want to trouble her with this, not the day before her wedding." I have a feeling Rose would have asked Clara to come to my rescue, and that is the last thing I want her to deal with right now. She has more important things to focus on.

Rose nods in agreement.

"Thanks," I say, wiping at the remnants of my tears. "The cake?" I suddenly remember it and worry about getting it finished, even though it's nearly ready.

"I've got it," she assures me. "Don't worry, I'll have everything done as planned. We've talked about it enough, and I've seen your drawings. I know exactly what's left to do. It will be just like you imagined."

"Okay," I say, my voice still shaky. "You're the best."

On the cab ride home, I can't help but analyze what just transpired. I haven't cried like this in years but, surprisingly, I feel better having let the tears out. Maybe I should have done it sooner. I might have realized that being guided by emotions is okay. It's what life is about. It's about ups and downs, happiness and sadness, and summers and winters. It's being able to recognize that life goes on, even if you have to leap over hurdles and stumble along the way. Jason made me stumble, but I'm picking myself up, I'm letting myself feel again. And even though it's border-line terrifying, I welcome the hopefulness, the fear, and everything in between.

ONCE THE CAB DROPS ME OFF AT MY APARTMENT, I CRAWL into bed and inhale the lingering traces of Luke's scent in the sheets. Just yesterday morning he was here. Right beside me. I have a sudden urge to wrap myself up in my covers so I feel like I'm being cuddled. I miss being wrapped up in someone else. Someone like Luke, specifically.

I startle when I hear a knock at the door. I must have drifted off to sleep. A long one, it appears. It's been more than two hours since I got home.

"Honey, open up." I hear another knock.

Great. What could *she* possibly be doing here? *Not a good time, Mom.*

"I'm coming, I'm coming." I make my way groggily to the door, but I'm feeling more rested, more composed. Probably a good thing, since I'm about to come face to face with ever-vigilant-over-my-heart Mom.

When I open the door, she swooshes in, giving me a tight hug, barely letting me breathe. Her hug is comforting. Sometimes it's just what a girl needs.

"Oh Tessa, honey, are you okay?"

I look up at her with puffy eyes, on the brink of crying again. I can't speak because the lump in my throat is too big. Instead, I nod, but without the reassurance I would like to give her. I guess the composure I thought I had woken up with is still wavering.

She takes my face in her hands and says, "You'll be fine. I know you will."

I nod again.

"Let me make you some of my special homemade tea to make everything better." She smiles and I smile back. I absolutely love her tea blend. I have no idea what she puts in there, but I do know it always makes me feel better. Mother-daughter boy-trouble talks are always more fruitful over a warm drink.

"I'd love some, thanks. Maybe a couple of cookies too."

She nods and I make my way to the sofa. The same sofa Luke and I snuggled on. Now I'm just snuggling the pillow. It's soft, but not nearly as cozy and warm and ... hard. Nope, not hard *at all*. Really, it's quite depressing.

"How did you know to come?" I ask as she whirls around the kitchen.

"Rose called and told me about the morning you had. Don't worry, I haven't said a thing to Clara." It's like she can read my mind; I was just about to ask. I'm sure Rose gave her very clear instructions. "Tell me more, sweetie."

"I'm such a mess, Mom. I have no idea what to do," I say with a shaky voice as I take a sip of the tea.

"Just tell me whatever's on your mind. Sometimes just being able to talk things through helps."

She's right. At this point I have nothing to lose. I tell her the story of Luke and me, and how wonderful the last few days have been with him. How frightened I was to let him in, and how, once I did, I was even more frightened to let him stay. And how I panicked and needed that sense of control more than I'd ever needed it before, to keep my heart from shattering once again. Except it did and I realized it too late. My mom, of all people, knows how difficult it is to lose the person you care about.

"Sweetie, I know Daddy always told you to think with your head, not your heart, and I know that it's stuck with you even more since he's been gone and since Jason left. But you should know by now that you can't control everything that life throws your way. There was no warning when I lost your father–" She pauses and takes a sip, collecting her thoughts. Even years after my dad passed away, it's still so difficult for her to talk about his death.

"Sometimes the head can be more confusing than the heart," she continues. "I never told you this before, but your dad wasn't always so set on having his head rule his decisions."

I look up at her expectantly, more than a little confused. My dad was as set on his ability to control his emotions, his sense of self, as any person I know. Except for maybe me.

"Tessa, before we had you, your dad was more easygoing, something I always loved about him. He'd do things on a whim and enjoy the consequences, good or bad. One of those consequences was, well, you."

Huh. That's an interesting little piece of information that I get to find out at twenty-six. I must give her a questioning look, because she reassures me as she continues.

"And it *was* a good thing. You were our pride and joy. But after we had you, your dad changed somehow. He wanted to be there for you, he wanted to make sure you were well taken care of. He made it a point to raise you to be a level-headed, strong woman, able to fend for yourself. And you've been that woman. All these years, and especially since he's been gone. You've always been so self-sufficient."

I have been. Definitely something that has served me well in life. "He did a pretty good job." I smile.

She smiles back and pauses, like she's trying to think of just how to frame the rest of the story, and then asks, "Sweetie, did I ever tell you how your dad and I met?"

My dad told us the story several times. His face would brighten up and he'd get this giddy look about him. "Yeah, you did. You met him at a coffee shop, when you came to visit with your aunt and uncle."

Her expression is reminiscent, and her eyes sparkle. "Yes, that's how we met in Chicago. But I don't think you've heard the whole story."

"Oh?"

"It was a summer when I came to visit Auntie Amelia and Uncle George. I was just eighteen. It was the first time I'd ever left home, and I was traveling all on my own. I was beyond excited. Heathrow was very busy – the crowds, the hustle. It was a bit overwhelming, I must admit. And while I managed to get to the gate to board the flight, I was so focused on keeping my purse, my passport, and my tickets on me that I left my carry-on behind when I lined up to board the plane. It was then that I first met your dad. He called after me and brought me my carry-on. And god, he was so handsome, with his dark hair and those deep brown eyes, I could only stutter to thank him. As fate would have it, when I was finally in my seat and ecstatic that I'd made it that far, guess who sat next to me?"

"Hmm, Dad?"

She nods. "Yes, it was your dad. It was at that moment I felt a little spark. Like something had led me to that point in my life, to that exact flight, to that assigned seat, only to meet him. He was on his way from Italy to the States, hoping to make a life for himself. He was so young back then, full of hopes and dreams and aspirations. Nothing was going to stop him."

That's how I'll always remember him – ambitious, determined, someone who always followed through – and how I've always wanted to be. Yet, I'm realizing, with Luke I failed to follow through on my promise.

"We talked the entire plane ride over, even with his broken English. He was quite charming. When we finally arrived in Chicago, we parted ways before we were able to exchange phone numbers. It was kind of bittersweet, I must admit. He stayed in my thoughts for days after. A week later I was at a coffee shop, and just as I was leaving your dad was on his way in. I ran straight into him and spilled my coffee all over his shirt. We couldn't believe that another chance encounter had led us to finding each other again. If I had left a few minutes earlier or he'd come in a few minutes later, who knows – you may never have been born."

She cups my cheek and smiles, and all I feel is pure love and affection. I lean into the palm of her hand and can't help but smile with her.

"This time he didn't let me go without getting my number," she continues after a moment. "We met up later that evening, and the day after, and pretty much spent the entire summer together – crazy, young love – until it all too quickly came to an end. I was leaving; he was staying in Chicago. But your dad never gave up on us. We managed to stay in touch over the next year, although it wasn't as easy as it is today. The phone calls are cheaper, there are video chats and texting – all sorts of ways to stay connected."

Is she trying to tell me something, or has she just taken a course on how to become a tech-savvy mom?

"What happened?" I ask, since this is not where their story ended. After all, I was one of their "consequences."

"I never thought I would be back, but when your grandparents died in a car crash the next summer, Aunt Amelia and Uncle George invited me and Auntie Maddie to stay with them. Losing my parents was devastating. But if I hadn't lost them, I'm not sure I'd ever have made it back to your dad. I wasn't as strong of a believer in chance as he was. He always knew in his heart that I was the one for him and that he was the one for me. That we were right for each other. He told me so many times. And he never doubted that we would be together again." She wipes away a tear that has rolled down her cheek.

Well that's a story if I ever heard one. As I'm processing the details, I can't help but compare my relationship with Luke to that of my mom and dad. So many similarities, but also some noticeable differences. *One* noticeable difference.

"But I don't *love* Luke. I mean, I can't possibly. Not when I've only known him for a few days. How can I be sure that this is it? That Luke and I are meant to be? That we're made to fall in love?"

"The thing is, honey, you don't know. You may not love him – yet. And maybe you're not meant to be together. But you will never find out if you don't try. You owe it to yourself, to him –

to both of you – to give it a chance. For once, forget reason, forget logic, and just go with what's in your heart. Life has a funny way of working out. And when it does, it's pure bliss."

Hearing my parents' story has effectively shattered what I thought I knew and what I've lived by. What made me the person I am today. I need to process what my mom has said and figure out if my heart is ready for this leap of faith.

I spend the day thinking, writing out lists and plans, then scratching things off, crumpling the paper, tossing it in the trash. I take another nap, think, eat, check in with Rose, and attempt writing more. With the same outcomes. The trash can is kind of overflowing. I check in with Clara to make sure she's doing fine with the wedding a day away. Then think some more. It's exhausting.

By the end of the day, I still haven't collected enough courage to acknowledge what my heart has been telling me all along – that I have fallen for Luke. Though there is one thing I'm starting to realize. Feelings like these need no lists, no plans. No, these types of feelings just happen naturally, it appears.

Chapter 21

The wedding day has finally arrived. I wake up feeling excited and petrified all at the same time. I have no doubt Clara and Marcus are meant to be together. That's the exciting part. My not-so-little-anymore sister is getting married to a guy who means the world to her, and she means the world to him. What scares me is the sickening feeling that I may have made a huge mistake and let the one guy go who could potentially have meant the world to me.

I was sure that I would wake up and everything would just magically make sense. No such luck. The talk with my mom yesterday was helpful, but also confusing. I have thought of every possible scenario, of all the pros and cons. Would Luke move back? Would I ever be able to leave Chicago? Yes, I've actually considered it. Crazy, I know. Would long-distance work for the time being? Would it all be worth it?

Of course, none of the above questions are even relevant given there's nothing to consider. I'm the one who broke things off with Luke. I'm almost certain even if I tried to convince him to take me back, he wouldn't. *If you give up on us right now, I don't know if I'll be able to take you back again. I'm serious, Tess. This will be it.* Luke's words echo in my head. And he certainly hasn't made the effort this time around. He's probably given up on me. If I were him, I would seriously doubt my trust, my commitment, and my emotional strength. If I were him, I would find me terribly disappointing. I abandoned him even though I knew that was the one thing he was trying to protect himself against ever since he was abandoned by his mom.

I also know there's no point in dwelling on this any more than I already have. I spent pretty much all of yesterday doing just that. I'm moving on. The controlling, rational Tessa can kiss my ass. I'll just have to see how things play out. Maybe if I do I'll have that moment of clarity, when everything just comes together. Or maybe I'm delusional in thinking that's even a remote possibility. I have a feeling it may be the latter.

I drag myself out of bed and head straight for the bathroom. *Jesus!* I nearly jump in shock as I see myself in the mirror. My hair is a tangled mess, my face still looks exhausted from the emotional rollercoaster I went through yesterday, and my body's tired from the restless sleep. A complete overhaul – that's what I'll need if I'm ever going to show myself in public again.

Once in the shower, I close my eyes, welcoming the warmth of the water, and just stand there, letting it run down my body. This is nice. This is just what I needed. This is so– *Ugh!* Fucking Luke! He's all I see, even with my eyes closed. The memories of our short-lived "relationship" appear like movie stills in the digital archive of my brain, one after the other. I'm overwhelmed by them, and I'm almost certain I'll hold onto them forever, even if I make a conscious effort to forget. It's like they're a part of me, *he's* a part of me, and I can't seem to be able to let go of him.

Shake it off, Tessa!

Channeling my inner Swifty appears to be futile. Just when I think my mind can't possibly handle any more of Luke, my senses take it to another level. As I rub the soap over my skin, I feel the softness of his touch where his fingers trailed down my arms just a couple of days ago, in this very shower. I sense the warmth of his breath against my neck, as if he's right here with me. I can almost feel his kisses trail down my skin, teasing, tasting every inch of my body. I ache deep down, aroused by the mere thought of him inside me. My nipples harden at that same thought and I am utterly lost in the illusion of Luke. I want nothing more than to have him right here with me.

How could you be so stupid, Tessa? I don't know. I need to set things right. I need to let him know how I really feel, or I'll forever be miserable and alone. Old, gray-haired, stuffing my mouth with cupcakes to fill my empty heart. I shudder at the disturbing image. I love cupcakes, but I don't love them *that* much.

I need to fix this; no more moping. I need a new plan. I need to think big. This one I'll refer to as Mission: Impossible. I know how ridiculous it sounds, but it's accurate, and I'm resolute. I know as soon as I see Luke today that I will want nothing else but to be with him, and I also know there may be no way in hell he'll even consider being with me. But I have to try. I have to convince him, just like he's convinced me, that we are meant to be.

As I step out of the shower, a new Tessa emerges. I have control of not only what's in my head, but also what's in my heart. I have control over the feelings that I finally let resurface. This time, I don't care if I get hurt. I will be an emotional wreck if I don't try. It's as if everything that used to scare me now makes me that much more determined. I'm ready to let my heart heal and begin to love again. That thought alone is so freeing, so emotionally uplifting.

I've definitely fallen for Luke. I know it's not love, but whatever it is, it feels incredible. I can't let any doubt of whether he feels the same cloud my thoughts right now. *That* I have to shut out for the moment. I have to win him back, and there is not an ounce of me that doesn't feel seriously giddy at the thought of spending more time with him. If only for two more days. I know just what I have to do. And I really, really hope this time my plan doesn't backfire. Third time's a charm, right?

I spend a few minutes writing out the list. I want to share it with Luke so that I can tell him exactly how I feel. I can't risk missing any important details. I read and re-read it and smile because – let's face it – I'm awesome at making lists.

When I'm happy with how it's turned out, I grab the bag I packed last night and leave my apartment. Clara and Marcus are having their wedding at the Ritz, and the wedding party is staying at the hotel courtesy of Marcus and his connections. I know for a fact Luke has been staying there since the night of the rehearsal dinner. I need to call Marcus and find out what room Luke is staying in. Having connections like these can be extremely valuable when one is attempting to complete Mission: Impossible.

Next, I head to Lovely Cakes to pick up the wedding cake so I can deliver it to the Ritz before I meet up with the girls for our hair, makeup, and all-around pampering – much-needed therapy considering my current state.

Rose did an amazing job putting the finishing touches on the cake. I knew I could count on her. It really did turn out just the way I envisioned – elegant, luxurious, and one-of-a-kind romantic. The five layers alternate between red velvet and chocolate cake, each filled with buttercream. Dark chocolate edible ribbons tie the white fondant layers together so the look is clean yet grand. Lush crimson sugar roses with crystal rosebud brooches nestled in them are scattered over the layers. The cake is spectacular, and I am positive Clara and Marcus will love it.

After I load it carefully into the bakery van, I pick up a little something else that I hope will help me accomplish my plan. I'm on a mission – not only to get the cake delivered in one piece, but also to make sure my heart stays intact.

When I get to the Ritz, I set the cake up in the ballroom, arranging dark-red rose petals around it. I smile in satisfaction at how beautiful it looks and give myself a mental high-five for bringing it all to life. Then I take a deep breath, knowing that even though one mission's been accomplished as planned, there is another one still waiting. And the one several floors up will definitely not be as easy.

I find my way to Luke's floor, my knees shaky, my heart racing. In my mind, all I can imagine is Luke opening the door, wrapping his arms around me, holding me tight, and never wanting to let me go. He tells me he's missed me and then kisses the hell out of me. *All of me.* And then we live happily ever after. Or something like that.

But after the way I left things between us on Thursday night, I have a hunch the vision in my head is probably not the reality that awaits. The thought of that is nearly paralyzing, but I choose to ignore it.

When I'm finally at his door, armed and ready with a small box in one hand and my list in the other, I take a moment to gather my courage and then knock. And wait – rather impatiently. This is it; he'll answer any moment, I can feel it. Just a few more seconds... *Damn it!* No response. Perhaps he didn't hear me knock?

My fear of not being able to get to him like I'd planned intensifies. With the adrenaline pumping, I knock louder, then look around to make sure no hotel staff are around before shouting, "Housekeeping!"

Pathetic. Apparently that's what happens when heart trumps reason.

"Coming." I hear Luke's deep, sexy voice from afar. "Be right there."

You can do this, Tessa, my subconscious cheers me on, even though my composure may be faltering, unlike moments ago when I was in my element, arranging the cake. This is different, but I've totally got this. As Luke opens the door, I'm ready to read him my list: all the reasons I need to be with him, and all the reasons he needs to be with me. I may be his cupcake, but he's my icing. We belong together.

Except that there's one little problem. My voice, which was so ready to speak up, stalls. My jaw drops and I freeze. The only things that seem to be functioning are my stupid, stupid hormones.

What I'm faced with is this: wet, messy hair. Naked sculpted chest. Chiseled abs. Trickles of water running down said chest and abs. White towel hanging low, revealing the V-shaped area that leads to the ever-so-tantalizing Mr. Callaghan. My mouth waters with the need to have him, to feel his wet skin on me, to taste those lips that tempt me. God, he is a sight to behold.

"Hi." I somehow manage to collect my scattered brain cells. Putting two letters together is barely a step forward, but I'll take it.

"Hey," Luke says coldly. If he's affected at all, his eyes don't give him away, nor do his words. No "cupcake," no "Tess" – none of the endearments I got used to over the few days we spent together. My heart shivers knowing it has a steep and icy uphill climb.

We stand there, unmoving, as if separated by an imaginary wall.

"Umm, can I come in?" I ask, trying to break the tension between us. He doesn't say anything; instead, he ushers me into his hotel room.

I step in and shut the door behind me. The eerie silence between us fills the room. My palms are sweating and my heart's beating a million miles a minute. I have an urge to pick at my nails, a sure sign that I'm nervous, but my hands are kind of full.

Thankfully, the courage I gathered to come here in the first place comes back just when I need it the most. I don't hesitate a second longer. With Luke standing right in front of me, staring at me with the most unreadable look, I step closer until he's within my reach. Before he has a chance to back up or say something that will shatter every last bit of hope in my heart, I simply hug him. I need to somehow feel the connection. I need to have him feel it too. Because I know it's there.

I lean my face against his damp chest and hold on as tight as I can. *God, how I've missed him.* He hesitates for a moment, but then his arms wrap around me, his face sinks into my hair, and I feel him take a sated breath. A small victory, but one that makes me think the climb ahead may be slightly less steep.

"I'm so, so sorry," I whisper against his chest, trying to hold back the tears that have pooled in my eyes.

I fumble with the list in my hand. Everything I need to say is written so eloquently. I have an urge to start reciting it all, but I think better of it. I scrunch it up behind his back and decide to say instead what I'm feeling in this moment.

"I messed up. I seriously did. It's just that … you, and I, and … us…"

Ugh! Bad idea. I can't seem to spell it all out like I was so certain I would only a moment ago.

Follow your heart – say what you feel, not what you wrote. Right.

I look up and search Luke's eyes, hoping they'll give me some indication that he's at least willing to consider what I have to say. And I think I see it. A glimmer of hope that my attempt may not be futile. That he's giving me the silent okay to continue.

"Things are just happening so fast between us and I'm … I'm *feeling* again, more than I've ever felt. And I'm so scared, Luke. I'm scared that I'll be left heartbroken again and that I'll never hear back from you. I'm scared to take the leap, but god, I really, really want to. I don't want to give up on you and on the possibility of us. I hope you aren't ready to give up on me, on us, either."

He doesn't respond right away. It's like he's holding himself back from acting impulsively. It's not like Luke. The silence is unnerving.

"Please say something. Please." Now I'm the one begging.

He grunts like he's exasperated. "You can be real frustrating, you know?"

Okay. Maybe not quite what I was hoping for. "I know." I go for an innocent smile, hoping to ease the tension. But he doesn't smile back.

"How can you be so sure this time? I mean, two days ago you had it all figured out. 'It was a mistake,' were your exact words. You said good-bye. You either feel it or you don't. There's no in-between." I search his eyes, but his blank expression frightens me. How will I convince him to trust me again? How can he, when I've betrayed that trust and done the one thing I promised him I wouldn't? I've disappointed him. I left. Just like a certain someone in his life.

"The only mistake I made was to say good-bye. I convinced myself it was the logical thing to do, but sometimes logic is flawed. Sometimes, what the heart feels is all that matters. My heart has fallen for you, even though I never thought it would fall for anyone again. I tried, but I don't think I can make it *un*fall. I feel all sorts of crazy things for you, and even though I can't quite place what these emotions are, I know now that I can't just brush them off either. Because I think you could be my forever too." I hope these words are enough to convince him. I hope he remembers sharing similar words with me at the beach. I may not have been ready to acknowledge it back then, but I'm ready now. "I know how difficult it must be for you to trust me again, but please, Luke, please do trust me. I don't ... I don't want to lose you."

My voice breaks, even though I'm trying to hold myself together. I don't want him to doubt my emotional strength. But a single tear betrays me yet again. I feel it slide down my cheek. As I reach up to wipe it away, Luke grasps my fingers and stops me. He brings his finger to my cheek and trails it down the path the tear has left. The affection in his touch, the tender look in those beautiful hazels of his, is almost too much to bear.

"I don't ever want to be the one to cause you tears, Tessa. I trust you. But I really need *you* to trust *me*. I'm just not sure that you do, even after everything you said." His expression is a mix of conflicting emotions: a hint of a smile, a touch of gravity, a glimmer of hope, a flash of doubt. He takes a deep breath, and something in his look changes, becomes softer.

"I do trust you," I try to convince him. "Just ... please be with me again. Let me prove to you that I want this."

"I'm not sure that I can. Not just yet." He's calm. Aloof. And I'm neither.

"But ... but when?" I ask anxiously. He's only here for another couple of days. I can't let him leave before I know where we stand. If we stand anywhere, that is; if there is an "us" to even consider.

"I just... I need more time."

I don't like this answer. Not one bit. "Like, a couple of hours?"

He almost smiles. Almost. I see a hint of it in the corner of his mouth.

"No, Tess." That hint of a smile disappears. "You should just go."

Punctured. Deflated. Empty. That's what my heart feels like, because this is it: the end of the future that never was and never will be. Not at all the way I hoped our encounter would play out.

Luke breaks the hold he has on me and takes a step back. I'm not sure what to do. Do I leave? Do I stay? Do I hope that the ground will miraculously open up and swallow me whole? There's one thing I know for certain. Love stories suck. Honestly, they are so deceiving. I'm never subjecting myself to reading another romance again – real life doesn't always end with a happily-ever-after. No more Channing Tatum movie nights either. I'm going to start reading paranormal books. I'm watching every gruesome horror movie that exists. Because right now, *this* feels like my worst nightmare.

"I guess I should get going then." There's nothing else left to say. Aborting the mission is the only logical conclusion.

"It's best if you do."

"Okay. But don't take too long." He looks at me, confused. "To decide," I clarify.

He actually smiles. A glimmer of hope after all, even if it's short lived.

I make my way to the door, and Luke follows behind, his steps measured. As I open the door, I back right into him. I swear I sense him inhale, like he's breathing me in. I gasp, because I feel him, feel all of him around me. I close my eyes, anticipating that he'll pull me in, wrap his arms around me, stop me from moving any farther, but he doesn't. The moment vanishes, and the silence is all that's left. I step through the door, leaving him behind.

"Good-bye," he breathes.

But I can't say it back. "Not for me," I whisper, though I'm not sure if he's heard me.

He closes the door and I try to move, but my legs are stuck. This did not just happen, did it? I'm in denial. It must have been an alternate reality. *Wishful thinking...*

I lean back against the door and sigh. I need a minute to absorb this before I move on. I can't possibly meet up with the girls right now. The only thing that can make this whole mess in my heart somewhat more bearable is sugar. Luckily, the box I brought with me contains just what I need: a cupcake.

It was meant for Luke. I was going to offer it to him, he would gladly accept it and take me back, and then we'd make out and have naughty icing sex. Obviously my imagination can get the best of me sometimes. Instead, it's just me and the cupcake. It's all that's left. Crazy Cupcake Lady – that's what they'll call me.

I pull it out, anticipating its sweetness, missing the sweetness of the guy on the other side of the door, and take a bite. More like a giant mouthful, actually. Just as I do, the door opens and I stumble backwards, landing in Luke's arms.

"Jesus, Tess. What are you still doing here?"

Ugh! I just needed a minute to myself. I needed to drown my sadness in the heavenly taste of sugar. I did not anticipate him leaving his room so soon. This is so embarrassing.

"I'm … I'm having a cupcake." I state the obvious as I struggle to swallow the cake and lick the mustache of icing and cake crumbs off my face. I'm sure I look and sound pathetic, but whatever. I don't even care anymore.

"That I can see." Of course he can. It's all over my face. Again.

Then it registers. He's still only got a towel wrapped around him. He wasn't leaving. Was he…? No, there's no way. He couldn't have been going after me. Could he?

Luke inhales and murmurs, "Mmm, strawberry chocolate. My favorite."

I'm taken aback. But those words are familiar. His fingers trace the outline of my lips and have the same impact they always do – I'm captivated and feeling flushed and tingly all over. Then he brings his lips to mine and kisses the icing off, bite by bite by bite, and I melt into him, little by little by little.

"Only minutes, cupcake," he breathes between kisses. "That's all I needed."

His words click as I close my eyes and drown in the sweetness of his lips. I'm equal parts frustrated and ecstatic. The first, because he made me leave, because he toyed with my heart, but I guess I deserved it after everything I put him through. I'm ecstatic at the same time because he's not giving up on us. He came after me. Perhaps I'll stick to love stories after all.

"Luke..." My words are a whisper because I still can't believe he's back in my life. If I say it too loud, I worry I'll wake up from a dream, and the moment my eyes open, he'll be gone. But when I do look at him and realize he's still, in fact, here, I ask, "Does this mean we get to start over again?" because I need his reassurance that this is our beginning.

"No," he says, dead serious, and my heart literally stops. I think I'm going to faint. He can't keep doing this to me. "I'd rather start where we left off." *Oh, thank god.* My heartbeat returns and I can breathe again.

I close the door behind us, and my fingers travel down his damp torso toward that sexy V that leads to my personal la-la land. I hook my fingers in his towel and whisper, "Oops," as I pull it off him. When it lands on the floor, I can't help but smile, and he smiles back knowingly. My fingers travel to his erection, and when I touch him, when I take him in the palm of my hand, he lets out a groan that tells me whatever ounce of control he's been holding onto until now is about to disappear.

"Fuck, Tessa ... I thought I'd lost you." His voice is a mix of relief and need. Then his mouth's on me again as he lifts me up and carries me to his bed. We're both too desperate for each other to take things slow and easy right now. I know just how deprived I will be of moments like this when he's gone, and all I can think about is how much I don't want anything else but him over the next two days.

"I thought I'd lost you too," I moan, but I don't want to talk. Sure, I'd like him to know all that's gone through my head these last couple of days. I want to let him know that he won't ever lose me again. But words are just words, so instead I lose myself completely in him. I show him how much I've missed him and how much I don't ever want to let him go. I show him how much I trust him, how much I believe in us.

Chapter 22

Clara looks absolutely stunning in her wedding gown as she's ready to walk down the aisle. She radiates beauty, elegance, and confidence. The figure-defining, strapless mermaid dress with a sweetheart neckline shows off her toned physique and shapely curves.

I remember the day we went shopping for her dress. It was just the three of us girls: Mom, Clara, and me. We planned to visit some of the best bridal boutiques in town. I figured it would take us a few days and countless hours until we found that perfect fit, that special one. That's how long it would have likely taken me. I could see myself pinning down three or four styles that I liked and thought would look good on me before even heading out to shop, and then searching, searching, searching.

But not Clara. She didn't need to plan. She had absolutely no idea what kind of look she was going for – she was just going to decide on the spot. When we got to the first bridal boutique, the sales associate brought out a few dresses for her to try on, and dress number two was it. Clara knew it the instant she saw herself in it. No hesitation, no doubt. That's just typical Clara. Diving in head first, no matter what the consequences may be.

I love how she can make everything seem so simple and enjoyable. Even significant life events such as picking out a wedding dress. We got to spend the rest of the weekend looking for bridesmaid dresses instead. After some deliberation (mainly on my part) over a few promising looks, we finally decided on a strapless black dress, cut just above the knee, with a sexy slit up one leg and a sweetheart neckline to match Clara's.

"I can't wait to see the look on Marcus's face when he sees me walking down the aisle!" Clara says, beaming. Then the look on her face changes. "I just wish Dad were here to give me away." Her lip quivers and I'm almost certain tears are imminent, even though she's been holding it together amazingly well so far.

Maid of the honor to the rescue. We can't afford any last-minute meltdowns. "He'll be here with you in spirit, and you know he couldn't be happier for you. Marcus, on the other hand, will want to get you out of that dress the second he sees you."

She grins, her eyes glistening with unshed tears and utter joy. "You're right about Dad and *definitely* right about Marcus. Let's get this party started!" Aaand she's back.

After a flawless tear-jerker of a ceremony, stunning pictures at the park, and an absolutely delicious dinner, it's the time for the speeches. While dessert and coffee are being served, Ian has the room roaring with laughter with his dead-accurate impression of Marcus and his not-quite-family-friendly advice for the couple. Not surprisingly, I suppose, the spotlight suits him. Not surprisingly, the spotlight scares the sprinkles out of me. When it's my turn, I apologize in advance for lulling everyone to sleep with both my speech and the sugar coma from the dessert, and everyone laughs, making me feel slightly more relaxed as I begin.

"Clara, even though you'll always be my little sister, I have to admit I've always looked up to you. I've always admired your spirit and bright personality. You're wonderful and I love you, and I hope you know how proud I am of you and the choices you've made, including your choice today." I smile at Marcus to give him a silent affirmation. "I know Dad would be proud too."

Clara's eyes are filled with tears, but her smile is radiant somehow. It's a mix of emotions, but what stands out the most is how happy she is, and that means the world to me. Seeing her like this makes me more emotional than I'd normally let on. I clear my throat, hoping to get through the rest of the speech without my voice trembling too much.

"The events of the days leading up to the wedding have taught me a lot. I've realized that sometimes we have to let go of the past. Sometimes we can't control the what-ifs. Life is about the now. The moments. It's cherishing the experiences we've had and embracing the experiences that are to come. Experiencing life together with that special someone, no matter how short or long that life may be, is what it's all about. Marcus and Clara are a perfect example of what it's like when you find that special someone. A reminder to the rest of us that having is so much more exhilarating, holding is so much more comforting, and loving and having someone love you back is a feeling unlike any other. Love grabs your heart and stays with you forever." I search for Luke's eyes and give him a meaningful look, which he returns with an affectionate smile.

"Please join me in raising your glasses to Clara and Marcus, the two people who were meant to have and to hold and to love each other. From this day forward. For the rest of their lives. Cheers!"

This earns me applause and a few cheers from the wedding guests – apparently my speech isn't a complete flop after all – and I'm relieved that this part of the night is done. I walk over to give Clara and Marcus a heartfelt hug, but underneath it all I can't help but feel the rapid beating of my own heart.

I know I'm not yet *in love*, but I also know that I'm feeling more than I've felt in a while. Having Luke in my life is definitely more exhilarating, having him hold me so much more comforting then being on my own, and loving ... God, giving myself a chance on love when I never thought I would again is pure, sweet bliss. I can't change the past, and I realize I can't control the future either. It's all about the now.

JUST AS EVERYONE'S GETTING READY TO JOIN THE HAPPY couple on the dance floor, I make my way to the bar, needing a refill to settle the nerves that seem to be creeping up on me. I don't know how many times I've imagined Clara's wedding over the last few weeks and pictured myself sitting alone while the happy couples twirled around in front of me. I realize that this unwelcome vision was very close to becoming a reality, had I not found the courage to recognize what my heart's been telling me all along, and had Luke not found it in his heart to take me back this morning. I certainly didn't think that I would be here, at Clara's wedding, completely smitten with my delicious, sexy stranger, and that he would be as equally smitten with me.

That being said, I'm starting to wonder where my stranger has disappeared to. I haven't seen him since Clara and Marcus had their first dance as a married couple. Fine, maybe it's only been several minutes. Seems longer, for some reason. I'm not being clingy; it's just that I know our minutes are literally numbered, so I want to make sure we spend as many of them together as possible.

"Beautiful wedding." An unfamiliar yet affectionate voice startles me. I nod in agreement as I take my glass of wine from the bartender.

"Beautiful wedding cake," the voice continues, and I realize his comment is directed specifically at me. He knows I made the cake. I wonder who it could be. I turn toward the voice, smiling appreciatively.

"Thank you."

When I see my companion, I catch a glimpse of his curious eyes and feel my knees buckle. The resemblance is uncanny. My expression must give me away, because the handsome stranger with graying hair chuckles at my apparent discomfort.

"I can see why he's so smitten with you." I blush at his words, and I'm suddenly unable to respond. *How familiar.* After a short pause, the stranger continues, "You know, he knew you'd come back. Without a doubt." His voice is comforting, appreciative. "Thank you for making him believe again."

The man smiles and all I can do is nod, because I'm still in a state of shock. As I take a sip of my wine, I notice his eyes catch a glimpse of someone behind me, and his mouth widens in an adoring grin.

My body shivers at the familiar presence. Luke's scent is intoxicating. I breathe him in as he wraps his arms around me. His chin finds comfort on my bare shoulder, which he kisses softly. My skin tingles beneath his lips. It's crazy, I know, but I've missed this feeling.

"I see introductions are in order." Luke breaks the silence. "Tessa, this is Carl Callaghan, my dad." Luke's dad extends his hand for a shake. "Dad, this is Tessa Conte, my girlfriend."

Girlfriend? I'm having a minor freak-out from hearing that word roll off his tongue so easily. But I love hearing it. It confirms what we are and where we left things off this morning.

Still caught off guard by his introduction, I extend a shaky hand to Luke's dad. I know there's been tension between the two of them over the years, and I'm not entirely sure where they currently stand, but at this moment, that tension is not at all apparent. Perhaps things are better between them now than they used to be.

"Nice to meet you, Tessa." Carl's sincerity is evident in his voice.

"Nice to meet you too, Dr. Callaghan."

"Carl is fine."

"He hasn't said anything incriminating about me, has he?" Luke teases. "Should I run for the hills?"

No, please don't run. Stay. Forever.

"No, nothing at all," I confirm.

"Well, I'd better leave you to it," Carl says. "Tessa, it was a pleasure, and I do hope we see each other again."

"Likewise."

He walks away with the same confident stride I've seen in Luke.

"So," Luke says as his arms cage me against the bar. My breath hitches at his sudden invasion of my personal space. But I'm more than okay with it. I've missed having him this close to me, so I welcome this intrusion.

"So," I mimic, my gaze holding his as I wrap my arms around him.

"So, you sure you're ready?"

I play along, although I sense there's a double meaning in there somewhere. "Ready for what?"

"For extremely awesome dance moves, courtesy of your delicious, sexy stranger." He grins a crooked grin that is so sexy I can't help but want to kiss him in that moment. But I laugh instead – he's also adorable.

Then his look changes and he breathes, "For us."

"More than you know." I don't wait a second longer. I kiss him just the way he always kisses me. It's tender, yet heated and intense. I kiss him so he's nearly out of breath and I'm nearly panting.

"Whoa. Forget the dancing. I'd rather just have you instead, right here, right now."

"Probably not advisable, stranger, though I'd be more than happy to find a more fitting place."

"Lead the way, cupcake."

I lead us to the dance floor instead. After all, if we went away, we'd probably never make it back, and of course that would require several rounds of explanation. Luke pouts like a sad puppy, and I'm nearly ready to reshuffle my priorities for the night. But reason prevails.

"The puppy thing you've got going on is cute, but it's not going to get you any treats right now."

"How about just a quick visit upstairs?"

I shake my head, yet can't help but smile at his persistence.

"Hmm." His eyes glisten with mischief and a cocky smirk replaces his pout. "Well, don't say I didn't warn you."

I wonder what he's got up his sleeve, but very quickly realize what I've gotten myself into by being defiant. Being on the dance floor doesn't bring the heat down – it makes it worse. His extremely awesome dance moves are, well, not exactly awesome. They're extremely stimulating. The way he purposefully touches me, the way his chest connects with mine, and the way he presses his cock against me are beyond arousing. I'm like a torch, burning all over. The cake cutting, the bouquet and garter toss – none of it can come fast enough. I desperately need those breaks if I'm going to last the night without pulling Luke into a dark corner and having him in a sinfully sweet way. I am that turned on by him right now.

Of course, I'm the lucky one who catches the bouquet. It lands in my lap after it bounces amongst the few high-strung, can't-wait-to-be-next single women in the room. It's kind of comical, because I'm not even close to being the next one. I can't help but smile over the fact that I got the coveted bouquet, yet I'm not certain that till-death-do-us-part will ever happen for me. But as I inhale the scent of the flowers, I catch Luke's smile and find myself more hopeful than ever before.

WHEN THE NIGHT FINALLY (FINALLY!) COMES TO AN END, Luke and I make our way to his hotel room almost faster than our legs can carry us. Luke's patience isn't going to endure another second. And frankly neither is mine. I giggle at his persistent and welcome attempts to grope me in the elevator, but my giggles are silenced by his lips almost instantly. They're on my mouth, on my neck, behind my ear, while he pins me against the elevator wall, in the hallway, against his door. It's like he's afraid I'll disappear if he doesn't keep his mouth on me. He's hungry for me, every bit of me, just as I am for him, especially since our mini-break – due to my not-so-mini freak-out – left us feeling desperately needy. This morning's quickie didn't quite do the job. In fact, it left us wanting more. A lot more.

We can't seem to close the door fast enough. "I've been deprived of you and your body for far too long," he says with urgency as he unzips my dress, although the look in his eyes tells me he's willing to tear it off of me with his teeth if I am not out of it by the time he blinks. I work extra hard to make sure the dress is not torn to shreds, and both it and my bra are on the floor in seconds.

"It's only been since this morning." I laugh, loving the feel of his hands all over me. It's like he's making sure I'm in fact here with him and not just some sort of illusion.

"As I said." He takes a moment to trail his fingers down my cheek before they land on my lips. He rubs my bottom lip, then whispers, "Too fucking long." And then his lips are on me again, and he's tasting, biting, discovering like my mouth holds a world of exotic flavors.

"God, Tess, I love the way you taste. I love the way you feel."

Luke trails his fingers down my neck and all the way to my bare breasts. He cups them in his palms and pinches my nipples. They pucker and need his tongue. He knows it, too, as he brings his mouth to one nipple and sucks with such skill that all I can do is moan at the pleasure. I grip his hardness below, teasing him just the way he's teasing me. Luke lets out a deep groan and growls, "I need to fuck you, Tess. Now." Simple and straightforward. I *love* my Luke.

I don't even get a chance to dwell on that last thought. He kisses me with so much conviction my head forgets what thinking is. "More, more, more" repeats in my mind like I've just had a bite of something delicious and now all I want is an extra serving. Or several. I'm lost in the sensations that seem to take over my existence whenever Luke is in my personal space and doing a whole lot of personal kinds of things to me. Yes please!

The bed is too far away, it seems, because we don't quite make it there. Instead, I find myself pinned against the wall and quite enjoying the serving. And when the first course is done, we move to the bed and feast on each other until we're both satisfied. A five-star menu.

Chapter 23

I have no idea what time of day it is as I open my heavy eyelids from the slumber I succumbed to after yesterday's exhilarating activities. And I'm not just talking about the wedding. No, last night … God, last night was intense. My limbs still feel like Jell-O, and my body is sore from several servings of Luke. I can't help but grin when I think of how yesterday unfolded, how the night ended, and how this morning has begun. I've woken up tangled in my sexy stranger, who's holding me tight like he's afraid I'm going to repeat my escape from a few nights ago. *Not this time.*

"Hey you," Luke murmurs in his throaty morning voice. He sounds so sexy, raw, exposed. I feel like I could orgasm just listening to him first thing in the morning. His eyes have this soft, adoring, yet needy look in them. And he's naked. *Naked!*

"Hey," I whisper back. He reaches for my cheek and caresses it gently, then outlines my nose and lips. His focus is entirely on me and nothing else. Now *I* feel exposed – it feels as though he can read every thought that flutters in and out of my mind. "How long have you been up?" I ask, because I'm jealous of the time he spent looking at me, wishing I'd had the time to reciprocate while he was asleep.

"A while. Long enough to take in every single detail of your face so I can remember it all when I'm gone tomorrow."

It's words like these that make me a swooning girly-girl over Luke. But I don't want to think about tomorrow. I don't really want to talk about it either. It's too depressing, and not how I want to remember my last day with Luke. I have a better idea. Several, actually. And they don't involve a lot of conversation. Mainly gasps and moans and unintelligible sounds.

"No. Nuh-uh." I wiggle my index finger in his face and he tries to bite it. "We're just going to forget that little fact and not talk about it, okay?"

"What fact?" He's teasing as he continues his futile attempts going after my finger. Failing at that, he grabs me by my wrists and rolls on top of me so that I'm quite cozily pinned underneath him. He's hard. Everywhere. Muscles toned, abs chiseled. Cock erect.

"Not talking about it." I'm actually not even sure what we're not talking about anymore. I'm very, very distracted. "So what's the plan for the rest of the day, Mr. Callaghan?"

"Today's about you and me, this bed, and nothing else." I love it when we think alike. "Okay, maybe not just the bed – *that* is negotiable."

"I'm pretty good at negotiating. As a matter of fact, I can be very persuasive."

Luke's eyebrows rise. "Yeah? Anything in particular you'd like to persuade me to do?"

"I can think of a few things."

"Try me." He smiles, and I nearly catch fire from the way his eyes focus on me and on my lips.

I don't think I need to persuade him much for what I'm going to ask for next, what I can't help but want, even though it was only a few hours ago that I was on the receiving end of it all. But first, I'm in desperate need of a bio break and could probably use some mouthwash. Otherwise, I'll be completely self-conscious.

"I will. In just a moment." I try to scoot out from underneath him, and just when I think I'm in the clear, he grabs me and tosses me back on top of him. I laugh and try to fight him off. Pillows are my best friend as I smack one in his face, then another, but he barely flinches. He just tosses them to the ground and I'm left defenceless again. Then I remember his ticklish spot, just below his ear – my only chance at not peeing myself. I lean in and go for his mouth, then his cheek, then trail my kisses lower, down his neck and up to where his weak spot is. But instead of a kiss, I blow a raspberry, twice, then add tickles for good measure. Luke completely looses it, laughing wholeheartedly, begging me to stop. Which I do, but only because I've managed to escape.

"You're in so much trouble, cupcake," he calls after me while trying to catch his breath.

"I don't mind," I reply as I make my way to the bathroom. "I think we've established that I like getting into trouble with you."

A few minutes later, just as I finish brushing my teeth, I'm startled by the unexpected warmth that sneaks up on me from behind and the unexpected hardness that pushes between my butt cheeks. I smile as I meet Luke's eyes in the mirror. He kisses my bare shoulder and draws a line down my spine with the tips of his fingers, then wraps his arms around my waist. I lean into him, and his body molds against mine.

"If I recall, you were saying something about persuading me." Luke grins as he rests his chin on my shoulder.

"I most definitely was." And I'm so, so ready to do just that. I take Luke's hand and move it down between my thighs. "Touch me here," I whisper.

He leans in closer, so that his breath tickles the skin just below my ear, and murmurs, "Gladly."

I watch him, I watch what his fingers are doing to me, and I'm beyond saving. I'm drowning in pleasure, making incoherent sounds. And the way he's watching me, his eyes full of mad desire, the way he can see how lost I am in him, makes me need him that much more. My body's arousal is climbing. I moan because I need him. I tremble because I crave him.

He turns me so that I'm facing him, his fingers continuing their motions inside me. Then his lips are on my mouth, his tongue searching urgently. He draws out every little whimper, every little sigh from me. My hands find his hair and tangle in the morning mess as I writhe against his fingers. I'm obviously very persuasive. Or perhaps he is. In either case, I wouldn't be opposed to this being my morning every morning.

"Fuck, Tess. You're so sexy."

I close my eyes and revel in the sensations that are nearly ready to tear me apart. And when I do, when I completely break and I'm weak in my knees, I wrap my arms around Luke's neck and am whisked away, back to bed. Unlike last night, when patience wasn't a consideration, Luke enters me unhurriedly and pleasures me with sweet torture, all the while kissing my lips, my neck, my nipples. What follows are muffled noises and the sounds of two bodies together creating infinite, undefined patterns. I'm wrapped around him, I'm wrapped *in* him, and it feels almost too personal. It's more than lust, even though I can't pinpoint exactly what this in-between feeling is. I'm not even sure there's a name for it. But I love every second of it. Even more than cupcakes.

I LIE ON LUKE'S CHEST, LISTENING TO THE CALMING BEAT of his heart, while he plays with the tangled strands of my hair. I love the comfort and safety his embrace gives me. I love the closeness that I feel whenever our bodies are near, just like they are now. I'm tracing my fingers on his abdomen, up and down his happy trail, lost in my thoughts.

I do wonder one thing now that my brain is back to thinking, considering the slow start it had this morning – it was rather preoccupied by lust. I'm not sure if I should ask, but I know that if I don't, it will just mess with my head. Luke's always so honest with me, so there's no reason why he won't be this time. I prop myself up on his chest so that I'm facing him and can read his expressions when he answers me.

"Why didn't you come after me?" I ask anxiously. "It's the one thing you've always held against your dad – that he didn't fight for her." I stop there because even though I didn't say much, I'm afraid I've gone too far.

Luke thinks about it for a moment. "When you left Thursday night, I was so frustrated with myself for letting you go, for not being able to make you stay. But I was just as angry with you for not being stronger, for not believing in us." He looks at me as if he's hoping I'll understand where he's coming from, and I do. I know exactly what he's referring to, and it pains me to know I've put him through that again. "Trust me, if I'd acted on impulse only, I would have come after you and fucked the hell out of you, just like I did at the bakery."

"That was fun," I tease, though the look he's channeling toward me says he's trying to have a serious conversation. After all, I did ask a serious question. "I'm sorry. Please continue."

"I needed time to think about what you said, to clear my mind and figure out what to do next. I went sailing with my dad on Friday. We talked, more candidly than we ever have. I needed to ask questions I should have years ago. I needed answers."

"I'm glad you did. I hope you got the answers you were looking for." I smile, and he kisses my forehead softly – a lovely feeling.

"I did. After spending the day thinking of all the possible ways to get you back, I finally understood why my dad never went after my mom. He really did believe that if they were meant to be, she would come back to him. If he reached out to her, begged her to come back, and she did, he'd never know if it was because she wanted to, or if it was only because she felt sorry for him. He would never know if she really loved him the way he loved her. He wouldn't have been able to trust her again. And I realized just how much strength and determination it took for him to stay away all those years."

"That must have been so hard for him." I can't help but feel for his dad, for how it must have affected him.

He nods, then continues. "I didn't want that with you. I needed to know you were stronger than you let yourself believe. I honestly believed you could be. And deep down, I knew you felt it, felt the connection we have. I just had to, for once, let my mind, not my heart, lead the way. If I wanted you unconditionally, I knew I had to let you think it through and find your heart again all on your own. And if you did, you'd come back to me because you were willing to give us a try." His eyes are captivating, and they don't let go of mine. "I knew you'd find your way back to me. I had to believe you would. I just hoped you'd figure it out sooner rather than later. We were kind of running short on time." Luke chuckles, and I love how he can make even serious conversations like these feel somehow lighter.

His words remind me of how close I was to losing him. If I hadn't come back to him, he really wasn't going to come after me this time. He was going to let me go. And that scares me.

"I think my heart found its way back to you long before I was able to admit it. It just took my mind a little while to catch up," I say with the sweetest smile I can manage.

Yet here we are, counting the hours until we're going to lose each other again. At least temporarily this time, I hope. I'm dreading every minute that passes and brings us that much closer to the inevitable. Luke will be gone tomorrow. That much I know. What I don't know is how I'll function with him being miles away, without being able to see him for weeks or months. How will we make this work? Are we crazy to try? *Out of all the guys, Tessa, this is the one you set your heart on?* I know. The irony is not lost on me.

"I feel like I owe you an explanation," I continue. "I want to make sure that you understand why it's been so difficult for me to let myself feel again." I've given him snapshots and glimpses before, but I never quite put the pieces together.

"You don't need to explain. I'm just glad you're here."

"No, I want to. You're always so honest, and I want to make sure I am too." He looks at me expectantly. "When my dad died, and later, when Jason left, it hurt. It hurt a lot. The only way I thought I could avoid feeling that way again was to avoid getting emotionally attached. That was the only way I thought I was going to be able to get over the loss and the hurt, the fear, over the anger. I've spent the last few years burying my emotions and not letting them escape. And over these last few days, I've struggled with letting my guard down and then picking it back up again. And then Marcus called, and it was the impetus for what ended up happening. I panicked and I–"

"Marcus called you?"

Uh-oh. I probably shouldn't have said that. The last thing I want to do is get Marcus in trouble. His intentions were pure.

"Yeah. But he didn't say anything that I didn't know already. He just, you know, warned me about you and, well, the relationships you've had in the past ... or lack thereof. He was just looking out for me, given my previous situation. I know I shouldn't be, after everything you've said and done, but I'm still so scared that you won't come back and I'll have to deal with that again. I can't let it happen. I want to make this, whatever it is we have, work."

"Tess, I'm afraid you're stuck with me – at least for another twenty four hours or so." He laughs, but then his tone changes. "Seriously, though, I'm not letting you go. I know the fact that I've never been in a serious relationship scares you. But that's only because I've never found someone I wanted to be with that way. With you, it feels different somehow. I can't pinpoint why exactly because I like *everything* about you."

I nod because I feel the same way. "I like everything about you too, even the fact you don't ever make lists."

He chuckles. "We'll make this work. We'll figure it out along the way. You know that, right?"

"I know. But you'll still be gone in less than twenty-four hours. That sucks." I pout. "It's like missing a key ingredient when you're baking a cake. It just falls apart. I don't want to fall apart when you're gone. That would suck even more."

His eyes are full of amusement when he says, "God, I'll miss you, cupcake."

"I'll miss you too, stranger." Then he's kissing me, and I nearly forget about his looming departure. He's got this way about him that makes everything seem easier, even when it's anything but.

"Tess, I'll desperately need to see you again, and soon. Will you come?" Luke asks almost timidly, so unlike the Luke I've come to know over the last few days.

"Come? I think I've already done that this morning. More than once, actually," I tease, though I know exactly what he's asking me.

"Come to London," he clarifies. "Travel Europe with me. Just like we talked about."

I remember our discussion at dinner during our first date. There's nothing more I'd like than to do just that. Well, except for actually come. Definitely more chances of that happening if I'm with Luke in Europe than by myself in Chicago.

"I'd like that." I can't help it, but my brain automatically begins crafting a new plan: The European Adventures of Luke and Tessa. Sounds like a novel, or maybe a movie. In any case, it sounds wonderful. And also R-rated. So many possibilities. A private capsule on the London Eye, a hidden corner of a vast museum in Paris, skinny-dipping in the waters of the Italian Riviera…

"Tess?"

"Huh?"

Luke is smirking like he's reading my naughty, naughty thoughts. "Where'd you disappear to?"

I smile. "To Europe." I have a feeling that could be a trip of a lifetime.

Chapter 24

Six months later

I read it somewhere – *Cosmo*, most likely – that relationships typically go through milestones: the six-month, three-year, and five-year we-need-to-figure-out-where-this-is-going milestones.

Luke and I have been "together" just short of six months – not that I've been keeping track or anything. I ended up visiting him in late August for three weeks, just like we'd planned, and they were three weeks I'll never forget. We had an amazing time together. In addition to exploring London and visiting my mom's hometown, we spent several days in France and Switzerland. After that, we spent a week in Italy, including a visit to my dad's hometown. There were definitely some R-rated moments on the trip. Lots, in fact.

Luke visited for a week in October while on a work trip to Chicago, then I went to London for a week in late November, surprising him and celebrating Thanksgiving with him. And that has been it.

So Luke and I haven't physically been together for six months – we've actually only seen each other a total of about six weeks. But mentally, we've been head over heels about each other for much longer. So why am I considering all these numbers and thinking about what's next for us?

Luke is supposed to arrive on Christmas Eve. That's exactly five days away, almost to the minute as I look up at the clock in the work room at Lovely Cakes. When the time we have together is so limited and precious, every minute of every day counts. We'll spend another week together over the holidays enjoying family time and each other. The "each other" is the part I'm looking forward to the most. That in itself means this will without a doubt be the best Christmas of my adulthood.

Coincidentally, today is my birthday, and I'm feeling the pressure of turning twenty-seven. I'm still far from being in a seriously committed relationship, given our situation, and I have no idea if it will ever get to be real-real. Normal. Like most couples. As in, "I'll see you in five," rather than, "When do you think we'll be able to see each other again?"

Luke and I are *together*, but mostly I still spend my time alone. With my friends, among family. Grocery shopping, making dinner, watching a movie. Alone. Honestly, it sucks.

To make things worse, Clara is planning a night out for us tonight, hoping to lift my spirits and remind me that just across the Atlantic, a mere 3,945 miles away, I do have a boyfriend. As if that should make me feel ecstatic. I mean, I'm beyond happy when I'm with Luke, but not so much when I have to be alone. The latter has been the case on more occasions than I'd like.

The last time we saw each other, everything was great. Well, sort of. Great until the last couple of days of my visit. I got caught up in overthinking where this is going and I-won't-say-what's-bothering-me kind of behavior. The thing is, Luke has been in this one hundred percent, and so have I. But I can't help but wonder how long we're going to do this back-and-forth and one-week-here, one-week-there thing.

I know I may sound selfish, but I want more. A lot more. I want us to spend every possible moment together, so we have no regrets over the time we didn't. I want to be just like a typical couple, without having to plan the next week-long date and when it may work best for both him and me. It's almost nauseating how much I want to be with him all the time, how much I miss him. It's funny because I used to find Clara and Marcus's displays of affection nauseating. I never thought I would feel that way about a guy, yet that's exactly how I'm feeling.

Even though we both made commitments to each other that we'd make this work, after the last time we spent together I wonder if I want this more than he does. I wonder, because when we saw each other in November, we ended up having our first serious argument.

Not surprisingly, I wasn't quite able to keep what's been bothering me to myself for long, and once we got into it, our argument didn't really provide any clear answers. Luke said he's tried his hardest to give me as much of himself as he could, given our situation. He said that I needed to trust him and that it will all fall into place eventually.

Of course, I was being typical me, wondering what's next, where this is going, and losing faith in him and in our future. It was simply because I was scared that at any moment he would pull a Jason on me. I hate the fact that, even after all this time with Luke, I still have issues with trusting men. I stormed out of his apartment and headed to the airport in a taxi all by myself, only to have him follow me there. We eventually made up (and made out) in front of thousands of random travelers. That said, our phone calls and video chats were not nearly enough after that visit. Mainly because I needed him near. I needed his kiss, his touch, his body, his warmth. I wanted to make sure we were okay; I wanted reassurance that we *would* be okay. I'd be lying if I said that I wasn't completely head-over-heels, madly in love with him. I'd be lying if I said I wasn't counting the seconds until I see him again. Okay, I'm lying, because it's not realistic that I'd spend all this time counting, well, time. But the twenty-fourth can't come fast enough.

Luke called earlier today to wish me a happy birthday, and we talked for a while. Apparently he's got a big birthday surprise for me, and I can't wait to see what it is. I don't want to build my hopes up, but I'm positively giddy just thinking about the possibilities. A weekend getaway, perhaps? A puppy? I've been thinking about getting one ever since I met and fell in love with Elsie, his Lab. A pair of earrings, or maybe a shiny something for my finger? No, don't even – too fucking early to think of anything life-altering like that. But that's what my crazy, infatuated brain thinks about. I suffer from withdrawal, obviously, and I'm clearly in need of a dose of Luke. Probably double. With sugar, please.

Given the current lack of physical Luke in my life, I've been wrapped up instead in my work. I've barely had a chance to text him after we talked today to update him on the latest Christmas plans. My mom's got carried away a little bit this year, I think. I'm pretty sure she's still in shock that I'm actually in a relationship, no matter that it's a long-distance one. She's the happiest I've seen her in a long time. Just knowing that both Clara and I have found our other halves makes her more cheerful. Less worried. More like the mom I knew before Dad passed away.

Because of the holidays, it's been another busy week at Lovely Cakes. Which is a great distraction, I must admit. I have put in countless hours working so that I can, one, take my mind off of Luke and counting the days until I see him again; two, get as much done as possible now so that I can actually spend quality time with him once he's here; and three, stop worrying about where things will land at the end of the week and whether I'll still be looking to get the commitment I've been seeking. Even though I know it's completely unreasonable. That doesn't mean I don't want it.

It's almost seven o'clock in the evening, and the bakery has been officially closed for an hour, but I haven't even had a chance to lock up yet since I'm in the midst of a full-on push to get things done. I swear I'm going to get going just as soon as I finish icing these festive cupcakes.

The store is in full Christmas mode. There's a tree, seasonal music, and lots of Christmassy treats. Outside, it's lightly snowing, giving the gloomy gray snow banks a fresh, winter-wonderland look. Maybe it all just seems prettier to me in my distorted reality – since I was born so close to the holidays, this is my favorite time of the year. Who says no to double presents? Not me.

"All I Want for Christmas Is You" comes on over the speakers, and all I can think about is one very specific present I want: Luke, preferably wrapped up in only me. Naked. Hard. Calling my name. Exploring my body. My heart flutters just thinking of him in bed with me, and I get giddy and a little bit hot. I need to hear his voice again.

As if on cue, my phone buzzes, and I grin happily the second I see his name.

Hey cupcake. I bet it smells delicious.

Of course he knows where I am.

It sure does. You still up?

Can't sleep. Thinking of you. Need you now.

God, I need him too. I don't know if I can do without him for another five days.

Keeping busy so I won't think of you.

How's that going for you?

Honestly? Not so good. You have a way of sneaking in.

In my mind, in my heart, in my soul, I want to add, but that may be a bit over the top. Even if it is nothing but the truth.

You too.

I know he's as over-the-top for me as I am for him. He shows it every time we're together.

BTW, you look sexy in that apron. Life is definitely sweet. Just like you are.

I smile, remembering the first time he visited Lovely Cakes, when I was wearing the same "Life is sweeter with a cupcake!" apron. I know just how much sweeter my life has been since I took Luke up on his offer that day.

Then a thought enters my head. I start to type out the next text, asking him how he knows what I'm wearing, when I hear the chime of the front door. I make my way to the front counter, shouting, "We're clo–" but I can't finish my sentence.

My phone drops to the floor as I let out a squeal. Luke is *here*. Right now. Five days early.

"I finally have a reason," he says, grinning ear to ear.

"A reason?" My voice is a whisper, my heart still racing from this unexpected, but most delicious, sight in front of me.

He takes a step closer. And I am nearly breathless, wondering if I'm hallucinating. Or perhaps I'm just amped up on sugar – I've taste-tested more than a few batches of icing today.

"To stay." His words echo within me, and I remember, as if through a haze, asking him whether he'd ever consider moving back. And his words in response: *If the right opportunity presents itself. If there's a good enough reason ... I would.*

"Stay-stay?" I ask.

"Stay-stay," he says with a soft, adoring kind of smile. "For good."

I can't help but smile back. He is staying. For me. For us. Forever after, I'm certain. And from the look in his captivating eyes and the deep I-missed-you-more-than-you'll-ever-know kiss that follows, I know he's certain too.

Acknowledgments

To Jenny, my editor: I didn't know I could write romantic comedy, until you made me believe I could. I can't tell you how much I appreciate every thought, every edit, and all the comments and feedback you provided. I've learned so much and I cannot thank you enough for that. Without you, this manuscript would never have become a book that I am proud to publish. You're bad-ass awesome!

To Meghan, my publisher: Thank you for all your business expertise and advice along the way. Working together on the cover design was so much fun and we came up with this sassy, original, super retro beauty. (Thanks Ellen!)

To my husband: You're incredible – the most supportive and encouraging husband on the planet (maybe even the universe). I would have never been able to go on this adventure if it wasn't for your patience and your unconditional love. For that, I love you – always and forever.

To my girls: You keep me on my toes and always on the go. You make me smile and laugh every day. Because of you, I can call myself a mom. Because of you, my heart is always full.

Ana, my amazing sister #1: You read my manuscript before anyone else did; then you read it all over again when it was nearly done (and probably a few times in between). You were my number one cheerleader, and your suggestions and comments were invaluable. I'm so thankful that you're a crazy romance junkie and that you were able to play such an important part in this process.

Andrea, you're one of my very best friends. You read my original manuscript and provided such important feedback. Thank you so much for all your help and support.

Thank you to Ksenija, my amazing sister #2; to Tanja – my BFF – you cheer me on even when you're miles away; and to all my friends who played a part in one way or another.

Thanks to my parents for all your help and for always believing in me, no matter what I decide to dream up. Your undeniable support is my blessing. To my mother-in-law: Thanks for all your help and support too.

To my Facebook and Twitter community: Thank you for your likes, shares, tweets, and re-tweets. It's been awesome making friends no matter where in the world they are.

To all the "Sweets": There's an ocean of books out there, and you've chosen to read Sweet Bliss. I hope you loved it as much as I loved writing it. I hope that it has warmed your heart, put a smile on your face, and made you fall in love. And I hope you enjoyed a cupcake or two along the way.

From the bottom of my heart,
Helena

CPSIA information can be obtained at www.ICGtesting.com
Printed in the USA
LVOW06s0522021215

464972LV00004B/168/P